Where the Stars Still Shine

ALSO BY TRISH DOLLER

Something Like Normal

TRISH DOLLER

BLOOMSBURY
NEW YORK LONDON NEW DELHI SYDNEY

First published in the United States of America in September 2013
by Bloomsbury Children's Books
www.bloomsbury.com

For information about permission to reproduce selections from this book, write to Permissions, Bloomsbury Children's Books, 1385 Broadway, New York, New York 10018
Bloomsbury books may be purchased for business or promotional use. For information on bulk purchases please contact Macmillan Corporate and Premium Sales Department at specialmarkets@macmillan.com

Library of Congress Cataloging-in-Publication Data
Doller, Trish.
Where the stars still shine / by Trish Doller.
pages cm
Summary: Abducted at age five, Callie, now seventeen, has spent her life on the run but when her mother is finally arrested and she is returned to her father in small-town Florida, Callie must find a way to leave her past behind, become part of a family again, and learn that love is more than just a possibility.
ISBN 978-1-61963-144-1 (hardcover) • ISBN 978-1-61963-145-8 (e-book)
[1. Parental kidnapping—Fiction. 2. Parent and child—Fiction. 3. Identity—Fiction. 4. Family life—Florida—Fiction. 5. Florida—Fiction.] I. Title.
PZ7.D7055Whe 2013 [Fic]—dc23 2013009609

Book design by Amanda Bartlett
Typeset by Westchester Book Composition
Printed and bound in the U.S.A. by Thomson-Shore Inc., Dexter, Michigan
2 4 6 8 10 9 7 5 3 1

All papers used by Bloomsbury Publishing, Inc., are natural, recyclable products made from wood grown in well-managed forests. The manufacturing processes conform to the environmental regulations of the country of origin.

For Caroline

Forgiveness is the remission of sins.
For it is by this that what has been lost,
and was found, is saved from being lost again.
—SAINT AUGUSTINE

Where the Stars Still Shine

Chapter 1

Yellow light slashes the darkness as Mom sneaks into the apartment again. The muffled creak of the floorboards beneath the shabby carpet gives her away, along with the stale-beer-and-cigarette smell that always follows her home from the Old Dutch. Tonight she is not alone, and the shushing sound she makes as she closes the door is loud enough to wake me, if I wasn't already awake. His features are lost in the darkness, but his shape is bulky and tall, and he adds the sharp scent of leather jacket to the room. Willing myself invisible, I press myself against the cushions of the couch, but when his hands reach for her waist, I realize I already am. Mom's giggle is husky as she pirouettes out of his grasp and leads him into her bedroom.

I can't sleep when she brings men home, so I pull on

my dirty jeans and cram my feet into untied sneakers. The floorboards creak under my feet, too, as I let myself out. A permanent, pungent cloud of curry and grease hangs in the hall courtesy of our right-side neighbors. I've never met them. I've only seen their shoes lined in a neat row outside their front door, and sometimes at night jangling Bollywood music seeps through the thin wall between us.

My breath comes out in filmy white puffs as I push my way out of the building into the November chill. I tuck my hands into the sleeves of my blue thermal, wishing I'd brought my hoodie. Seems like yesterday it was autumn, but tonight winter waits impatiently for its turn. Up on Union Avenue I duck into the empty Super Wash. It's a favorite of mine. Warm, in that steamy, dryer-sheet-scented Laundromat way. Crinkled tabloid magazines. And vending machines that dispense the four basic food groups: salty, sweet, soda, and chocolate.

I burrow my hand into my hip pocket for money to buy a Coke. Among the coins is a blue-painted evil eye bead I've had as long as I can remember. The only thing I have from my life before we left Florida. Someone gave it to me, but no matter how hard I stretch my memory I can never touch on who. I only remember that the bead was one of many, strung on an elastic band. And that the first time she saw me wearing it—after we left,

I mean—Mom tore it off my wrist, scattering the beads and leaving a thin red weal on my skin. I only rescued the one bead. Twelve years I've been hiding it, transferring it from pocket to pocket, place to place. It doesn't work—evil has a way of finding you even when you think you're protected—but I keep the bead anyway. Just in case I'm wrong.

The soda machine is *always* out of the good varieties, leaving me to wonder where they all go. Who drinks them before I have a chance? Do people walking down Union get mad urges that can only be satisfied by the Super Wash vending machine? I hate grape, so I keep my money and inspect the dryers for orphaned laundry and spare change. Every now and then I'll find a single sock or random pair of underwear, but once someone left behind a pale yellow hoodie. Another time, when I was there for official laundry purposes, I found a wallet. I pocketed the six dollars I found inside, cut up the credit cards so no one could use them, and threw the empty wallet down a storm drain.

This time my search turns up nothing. I settle on a green plastic chair with a two-year-old copy of the *National Enquirer*. An hour or two later, I'm trying to recall if my two-year-old horoscope ever came true—definitely no financial windfalls, that's for sure—when a man without laundry comes into the Super Wash. It makes me nervous. Who goes to a Laundromat without laundry? Apart from me, I mean.

He's bulky and tall, and wears a leather jacket like the man my mom brought home. He's older, maybe in his forties, with a nose that's been broken. When he smiles at me I'm reminded of a jack-o'-lantern—a crooked-toothed and slightly sinister kind of handsome—and the urge to run pushes its way under my skin. I put down the magazine, tension curling in my belly.

"You're Ronnie's girl, right?" When he says Mom's name like that, there's no doubt he's the man from the apartment. She hates it when people call her Ronnie. Her name is Veronica. "She said you'd probably"—except he says it *prolly*—"be here."

"What do you want?" I hope my voice sounds more brave than it is.

His gaze slithers down from my face and gets caught on the front of my shirt. My heart rate ratchets up a notch, but not in a good way. I feel naked and I hate the way his eyes touch me. He gives a low whistle. "I thought your mom was a looker, but you—"

The man takes a step toward me, and an old dread sends me sprinting down the aisle of washers to the back door, propped open with a cinder block. I push out into the alley, not looking back. Not stopping.

He shouts something at me, but the only words that

register—following me like my own shadow—are the last two.

"... both crazy."

Both. Crazy. Both. Crazy. Both. Crazy. The words echo in my head with every footfall as I make my way to the apartment. They land in time with every step up the staircase with the peeling paint until I reach our door. I can't help but wonder: Is it true?

My brown tweed suitcase lies open on the couch and I hear the staccato taps of Mom's heels as she crosses from the bathroom to her bedroom. I know what this means.

We're leaving.

Again.

I lean against the door frame, watching as she dumps an armload of toiletries into her plain blue suitcase. We bought our bags at the Salvation Army the day we left Florida. My memories of that time are elusive like smoke, but one that's always vivid is how desperately I wanted the pink Hello Kitty suitcase with a little handle and rolling wheels. She said it was too easily identified. *Memorable*, she said. I didn't understand what she meant, only that there was a finality to her tone that meant I wasn't getting that suitcase. She tried to make up for it by calling the brown case "vintage," but sometimes that's nothing more than a fancy word for "old and ugly."

Beside her bag is a wad of cash in a money clip she didn't have yesterday. My guess is she stole it from the man with the leather jacket.

"So Anthony found you, I see." Mom's eye makeup is smudged and she's got a wild look I've seen before. "Where you been?"

"Nowhere."

"I wish you wouldn't run off to that Laundromat in the middle of the night, Callie." Her tone is soft, but I can hear the anger simmering below the surface, so I avoid mentioning that she already knew where I was. "I worry something bad could happen to you."

Bad things can happen anywhere, even when your mother is asleep in the next room. They already have. But I keep that to myself as well.

"Sorry." And I am. If it wasn't for me, my mom would probably have a different kind of life. A better kind.

"What are you just standing there for?" She gives me the uncertain smile she uses when . . . well, I don't know exactly what she's thinking, but I suspect she wonders what's going on in my head. She flings a wrinkled T-shirt at me. "Go pack."

"Now? Mom, it's the middle of the night."

The cracked-face thrift-store mantel clock in the living room—the one that wakes me up on the half hour all night long—chimes three times, defending my point.

"Don't start." Her smiles fades. "We're leaving in three minutes."

I wonder what set her off this time. It could have been something the man in the leather jacket said. It's as if she hears things at a different frequency, the way a dog picks up sounds the rest of us miss. Or maybe she hears something that isn't really there at all. Either way, when she's ready to go, there is no arguing. There is only leaving.

I don't have many clothes; the ones I'm wearing and a couple of T-shirts, including the one I'm holding. The one that declares me a member of the Waynesville High School track team. I've never been to Waynesville. I've never been to high school. The only thing this T-shirt and I have in common is the running. I throw it in the trash. The next place always has a thrift store filled with T-shirts that will transform me into a soccer player or a Cowboys fan or someone who's attended the Jenkins-Carter family reunion.

My books take up the most space in my suitcase. The binding is starting to come apart on the math textbook I bought for a quarter at a Friends of the Library sale. It was printed in 1959, but I love that it's still relevant, that math is a constant in a world that is not. It worries me that the book might not make it through another move. I pack the dog-eared copy of *The Hitchhiker's Guide to the Galaxy*, the atlas of world history I stole from a bookstore's sidewalk sale, my garage-sale copy of *Walden*, and my favorite novel in the world—a kids' book called *Mandy*, about a little orphan girl who wants more than anything to have a home and a family. I've read it so many times the pages are falling out, but I can't leave it behind. I can't leave any of my books behind. They're the only friends I've ever really had.

"Two minutes," Mom calls from the bedroom.

We're leaving: a sink full of dirty dishes, the old television we found on the curb in front of someone's house, a vinyl couch that stuck to my face when my head slipped off my pillow, and that stupid noisy clock she bought because it reminded her of the one in her grandparents' house when she was a little girl. We're even skipping out a month behind on our month-to-month rent.

We usually live in buildings like this one. Our side of town is usually the rough side, where they don't ask for references or deposits. Where, when you move away in the middle of the night, they shake their heads and cut their losses. Once we squatted in the model home of a development that was never completed. We've lived in a couple of long-term efficiency motels. And another time we "borrowed" a house that belonged to Leo and Dotty Ruskin, an elderly couple who spent their winters in the dry heat of Arizona. I've always wondered if they felt like the Three Bears when they returned. Did they feel violated for a while, locking doors they don't normally lock until they felt safe again? Sometimes I still feel a little guilty about that, but it was nice to sleep in a real guest room. I made the beds and washed all our dishes before we left. I hope that makes up for Mom cleaning out the tin of spare change they kept in their closet.

My curls are tangled and oily as I scrape them into a ponytail. I wish I had time to take a shower. Wish we didn't have to leave. I have no sentimental attachment to this town. No job. No school spirit. No boyfriend unless you count Danny, which I don't because he already has a girlfriend. But I still wish we could stay here—or anywhere. Put down roots. Live. "I don't want to do this."

"You don't have a choice," Mom calls from her bedroom.

I blink, startled that she can read my mind. Then I realize I've said it aloud. Now she's going to be mad at me again.

"You're *my* daughter," she snaps, heading out the front door. "Where I go, you go. And I'm going in one minute."

I tuck spare underwear—which I refuse to buy in thrift stores—into the empty spaces of my suitcase. My blue toothbrush. My journal, so thick with notes, stories, poems, and postcards I've collected over the years that I keep a wide pink rubber band around it to hold in the pages. Most of my life is recorded in this book, starting from when I first learned to write in crooked letters. Most. Because there are some secrets you don't even want to tell yourself.

My minute is up when I hear a beep from the old battleship-gray Toyota Corona that my mother bought from a junkyard with her bartender tips. I zip up my suitcase, blow out a tired breath, and touch my jeans pocket, feeling for the bump of the evil eye bead. The Toyota beeps again, telegraphing Mom's impatience.

The last thing I do is put away my guitar, an old rosewood and spruce Martin with a mahogany neck. Mom bought it in a pawnshop in Omaha. A Christmas present when I was eleven. It wasn't as if I'd never seen a guitar before, but as she flirted with the guy behind the counter, trying to get him to raise his offer on a ring she was selling, I fell in love with the Martin. She didn't get the extra cash she was after, but he threw in the guitar. Mom said maybe I'd be the next Courtney Love. I didn't tell her that on one of the pages in my journal I'd written "I hate Courtney Love" over and over until the page was covered. My feelings aren't so strong about her now as they were back then, but that was before her Hole cassette finally came unraveled. Anyway, my Martin is a war zone of scratches and finish cracks, but the sound is still as rich and resonant as if it were new.

"Ready to go?" she asks, as I get in the car. She tries to light up a smoke, but her hands are shaking. That troubles me in a way I can't identify. I take the cigarette from between her lips, light it, grab a quick drag, and hand it back. She flashes a smile, and for a split second I see the girl she used to be. The girl who held my hand as we walked to the bus stop on the first day of kindergarten. She was impossibly beautiful then, with her platinum pixie hair and bare legs ending in battered Doc Martens. People stared at her, and my heart felt too big for my chest because she was *my* mom. We reached the stop, and she perched on the back of the bus bench while we waited, smoking a cigarette.

"You're gonna do fine at school," she said that day, blowing the smoke up and away from me as she stroked the back of her hand over my cheek. "A girl as smart as you can do anything."

I believed her then, when we lived in a real apartment with houseplants, pictures on the wall, and a tiny balcony that overlooked a river. She worked at a coffeehouse near the park, and when the bell rang at the end of the day, she was always there, leaning against the empty bike rack. Now I don't get complacent because we don't ever stay.

"Where are we going?" I ask, as Mom pulls away from the curb.

She always has a plan. Even when we sneak away at three in the morning, she has our next future mapped out in her head.

"Oh, I was thinking Colorado might be nice," she says, which surprises me. We usually head toward warmer climates when the weather gets colder. "What's the capital of Colorado?"

When I was little, she'd help pass time on long bus rides by quizzing me on the state capitals. I graduated to countries as I got older, but she had trouble remembering all the countries, let alone their capitals. Her fallback has always been the states, even though they've been burned into my memory for years.

I groan. "I don't feel like playing this game right now, Mom."

"Humor me."

"It's Denver. The capital of Colorado is, was, and always will be Denver."

She blows out a puff of smoke that gets sucked through the crack at the top of her window. "Are you sure?"

"I've been sure since I was six."

Mom laughs. "You could learn to ski in Colorado."

I roll my eyes.

"Well, you could," she insists. She reaches over and strokes my cheek with the back of her hand. Her fingers are rough from washing glasses during her bartending shift. "A girl as smart as you can do anything she wants."

I don't say anything. Because if I did, I'd tell her she's wrong. I can't get a library card. I can't window-shop at the mall with friends. I can only wait for the day she gets paranoid because the man at the gas station looked at her funny or she *just knows* the women she passed on the sidewalk were whispering about her. Then we leave. I don't say anything. Because if I did, I'd tell her I don't believe her anymore.

We're headed west on US 34 when blue lights flash from behind, and my heart slides up into my throat. I hold my breath, waiting for the patrol car to shoot past us after its actual target. It can't be us, because Mom always follows the speed limit. She uses turn signals. We wear our seat belts.

"He's probably after someone else," she says.

Except traffic on the highway is thin this time of night, and when my mom pulls over onto the gravel at the side of the highway, the patrol car follows. The inside of the Corona is awash in blue light that illuminates her face. My insides go cold when I see an expression there I've never seen—fear.

"Mom, what did you do?"

"Nothing," she whispers. "I didn't do anything."

The deputy reaches the car and she cranks down the window.

"Something wrong?" She flutters her eyelashes and smiles at the young deputy standing beside the open window. The fluttering pings off him as if he were wearing a flirt-proof vest. She's only thirty-three, but years of smoking and drinking—but mostly the running—have made her old before her time.

"Ma'am." The deputy leans down to her window as a second patrol car pulls in front of the Toyota. This is not good. "I'll need to see your license, registration, and proof of insurance, please."

She puts on a show of searching her purse for the imaginary documents while I gnaw my frayed thumbnail. Her driver's license is long expired, this car is not registered, and there's no way in hell we have car insurance.

"I must have left them in my other purse," she says.

"Do you know why I pulled you over tonight?" the deputy asks. Through the dirt-streaked windshield,

I watch another officer emerge from the second car. He's older and a little heavier than the first deputy.

Mom shakes her head. "No, sir, I don't."

"Your left taillight is out," he says. "And I was going to suggest you get yourself to the nearest auto supply store and get that fixed—"

"Oh, I will," she interrupts. "We'll be waiting in the parking lot the minute they open."

"—but I ran your license and discovered the plate was reported stolen, so I'm going to have to ask you to step out of the car."

The old hinge squeaks as he opens the door, but Mom doesn't move. She just sits there. Stunned. As if it's only now that she realized she is not invincible. That time has caught up with her.

"Ma'am," the officer repeats. "Out of the car, please."

When I was seven and we lived in a tiny town called Kearneysville, I got sick with a really high fever. For three days I wove in and out of consciousness, dizzy and unsure if I was awake or dreaming. That's how this feels.

"There must be some kind of mistake," Mom insists, as the first officer fastens a pair of handcuffs around her wrists and tells her about her right to remain silent. "The plate was on the car when I bought it."

This is probably not true, since her life is a carefully crafted house of cards, constructed of lies and teetering on the brink of collapse at every moment. When they discover the truth, a stolen license plate will be nothing. Because twelve years ago, after she and my father divorced, my mother abducted me. I'm numb as the deputy leads her to his car. Wasn't it only an hour ago that I wished we'd stop running? This is not what I meant.

"Don't tell them anything," Mom says. Her features are distorted through a watery film of tears that turn her into someone I don't recognize. "Keep your mouth shut."

The door beside me opens. My legs shake as I get out of the Toyota, and I grab hold of the door frame to keep from falling down. My world has tilted like the floor of a carnival fun house.

"Is she your mother?" the second deputy asks.

Mom has never had a contingency plan for getting caught, so I don't know what to say that won't throw her under the bus. My eyes fixed on the hole in my left sneaker, I nod. "Yes, sir."

He transfers me to his patrol car. Assures me that I'm not under arrest. Asks my name. My throat is a desert, and my lips are chapped when I lick them. What do I say that won't betray my mom? How do I keep the truth from coming out?

"Callie." I've had so many identities over the years,

plucked from baby-name books, television shows, and fairy tales. Once Mom dared me to name myself after the next intersection, and I spent a month as Loma Linda Charles. A laugh bubbles out of my throat as I think of that, but it's not funny, really. I'm scared. "Callie Quinn."

He closes the door and confers with the first deputy for a few minutes. Then the arresting officer gets into his car and pulls out onto the highway. The blue lights go off, and the car with my mother inside is swallowed up by the darkness.

The second officer returns. On the other side of the cage, he types something into his computer. What it tells him is a mystery he doesn't share; he only offers me a grim smile in the rearview mirror before we drive off into the night, leaving the Corona at the side of the road with my life zipped up in a brown tweed suitcase.

Leaving my guitar behind.

All I have left is an evil eye bead that doesn't work—and me.

Chapter 2

The man standing in the sheriff's office lobby the next day—the one with his hands jammed deep in the pockets of his jeans—is a stranger, but I recognize him the same way I recognize my own face. The brown of his eyes. The slope of his nose. Cheekbones. Jawline. And the way he worries his lower lip is so familiar that I'm not surprised to discover myself doing the same thing. I run my fingers over my chapped lips and wonder if he's as nervous as I am. My father.

He doesn't match up with the picture in my head. Mom usually likes them stocky and pugilistic, with bashed-in noses and thick forearms. Aging men who drink whiskey and drive muscle cars older than her. But in this man I can still see the boy-next-door he used to be.

"All set, hon?" The dispatcher is a woman named

Ancilla, whose puffy grandma hair and bifocals are a strange contrast to her dark-green law-enforcement uniform. But it was Ancilla who sent the deputy to fetch my belongings from the Toyota. She let me sleep in her guest bedroom while she washed my dirty jeans. Fixed me waffles with real butter and maple syrup for breakfast. Took me shopping at Target, where she bought me a red peasant-style top with tiny turquoise flowers embroidered along the neckline. I can't remember the last time I wore something that didn't first belong to someone else. Can't remember ever wearing something so pretty.

Her hand is a comfort on my back as she urges me forward. I want to dig in my heels the way the characters do in cartoons, leaving grooves along the hallway tile. Instead, I take the step.

"Will, um—is my mom okay?"

"She's holding up real fine," she assures me. "And Judge Daniels is a fair man. He'll make sure she gets the help she needs."

The help she needs? *What does that mean?*

Before I can ask, we're through the swinging door and into the lobby, and my father's arms are wrapped around me.

"*Korítsi mou.*" His words are low and deep and choked, and I'm overcome with a déjà vu sensation. I don't understand those words, but I'm sure I have heard them before. "You can't possibly know how much I've missed you."

His cheek rests on top of my head and my face is pressed into the warm, clean smell of his T-shirt, but I'm stiff inside the circle of his embrace because everything about this screams *wrong wrong wrong*. All these years I've believed my father didn't love me, that the only reason he wanted me was so that Mom couldn't have me. I need that to be true because if it's not, it means she didn't just lie to everyone else. She lied to me, too.

"I'm sorry." He pulls away. "I didn't mean to overwhelm you. I mean, you don't even—" He reaches out as if he's going to stroke my cheek, and when I flinch the sadness in his eyes fills the whole room. His hands slide into his pockets. "You don't even know me." He looks up at the ceiling and exhales, and when he looks at me again, his eyes are shiny. "But I'm really, *really* happy to see you."

I have no idea what to say, so I pull my lower lip between my teeth and let the saliva burn.

"May I—?" He reaches for my suitcase and guitar, but I tighten my grip on both and shake my head.

"You take care now, honey." Ancilla comes to my rescue one more time, handing me a business card with her name printed on it. “If you need anything at all, you give me a holler, okay?” I nod and she pats my back. “Have a safe trip home.”

Home.

The word makes my eyes sting, but I don’t want to wipe tears on my new red shirt and I don’t have a tissue. I’m blinking to keep them at bay when my father pulls a crumpled Kleenex from his jeans pocket.

“It’s clean,” he says, and I let him take my guitar for a moment so I can blot my eyes. “Well, mostly. I, um—I’ve been kind of a mess ever since I got the call. I came as fast as I could.”

A hurricane of anger swirls inside me, and I have to fight to keep from hurling my suitcase across the room and screaming until my throat is raw. How could she do this? How could she take me away from someone who talks to me with a voice thick with tears and offers me a ratty tissue when I’m crying? How could she? *How could she?*

A hate so intense I think it could burn me alive flares in my chest, followed by a wave of sorrow that snuffs the hate. Mom has been my entire world for twelve years. I love her.

“So I don’t know what, if anything, your mom has told you about me,” he says, opening the trunk of a silver rental car parked outside the sheriff’s office. I put in my guitar and suitcase. "My name is Greg. You can call me that if it makes you more comfortable." I'm relieved I don't have to call him Dad. "I, um—I'm remarried, and my wife, Phoebe, and I have two little boys, Tucker and Joe."

He flips open his wallet to show me a family portrait. Phoebe is girl-next-door pretty with hair the color of a wheat field. The older of the boys shares her coloring, while the other is a miniature version of Greg. He resembles me, too, which is just . . . weird. Their family is perfect and happy, and I wonder if there is room in the picture for a seventeen-year-old girl. Do I want to be in that picture? Do I have a choice?

"The boys aren't really old enough to understand what's going on," Greg says. "But they're excited to have a big sister."

Even though they're right there, captured in the moment with perpetual smiles and matching shirts, I can't wrap my mind around the concept. I have *brothers*. Greg closes the trunk and smiles at me. He looks so much younger than my mom, even though they must be close in age. His face is unlined and he doesn't have a single strand of gray hair. "Ready?"

I'm not, but I do what I always do when it's time to leave: I get in the car and fasten my seat belt.

He starts the engine, and the little digital letter in

the corner of the rearview mirror says we're heading east. Somehow, though, I don't think Greg has our future mapped out in his head the way Mom did. Mainly because as he drives, he's working his lower lip, too.

We don't talk on the drive to the airport in Chicago, except for when he says to tell him if the heat gets too warm or if I'd prefer a different radio station. Mom always talked—*talks*—she always talks too much, as if the silence makes her lonely. I don't mind the soft musical babble of the radio or listening to the hum of the tires on pavement, and I'm glad Greg isn't flooding me with words I'm not ready to hear. If no one says it out loud, there's still a chance that none of this is real.

"Take the window." Greg gestures toward the far seat in row eight. "You can watch as we take off and land."

He doesn't know if I've ever been on a plane before, so his suggestion makes me feel as if he thinks I was raised by wolves. My cheeks go hot with anger, but his expression seems earnest, and I realize maybe he's being kind. The truth is, I've never been on a plane, and I *do* want to watch as we take off and land.

Sitting beside the window reminds me of Mom. We didn't always have a car. Sometimes we rode the bus, buying as much distance as our money would allow. She always gave me the window seat, putting herself between me and the crazies—like the old lady whose lipstick bled into the cracks around her mouth. She was convinced I was her dead daughter come back to life. When Mom refused to give me to her, the woman screamed until the driver stopped and made her get off the bus. The plane to Tampa is different from the bus. It doesn't smell bad and nearly everyone is smiling. Probably pleased to be escaping the breath of winter that's been at the back of our necks for the past couple of weeks.

"Takeoff is always my favorite part," Greg says, craning his neck to look out the window as Chicago shrinks smaller and smaller. "I guess because the destination—unless you've been there before—is ripe with possibility."

The city disappears beneath a bank of clouds, and I close my eyes to keep from crying again. With every mile I'm farther away from my mom than I have ever been and I am . . . lost. Life with her is wonderful and terrible, but at least I know how to be her daughter. I have no idea how to live in Greg's world.

"I have something for you." He holds out a red leather photo album. I take it and open the front cover. Pasted on the front page is a pink birth announcement card for Callista Catherine Tzorvas.

Running my fingertips over the raised black letters, I speak to him for the first time. "My name is Callista?"

Greg's chuckle dies in his throat when he realizes I'm not joking. "You didn't know?"

I shake my head, and his eyebrows pull together. I watch as a battle wages on his face, wondering if he's thinking the same bad things about Mom as I am. When she stole me, she left behind all the parts she didn't want anymore. Including my real name.

"It's Greek," he says finally. "It means 'the most beautiful one.' And Tzorvas"—the *tz* makes a *ch* sound when he says it—"means you're part of a big crazy Greek family whose noses will be in your business all the time, but who will drop everything if you need them."

I don't want to be angry with my mother all over again, so I push the feeling away and turn the page. There is a snapshot of her holding a newborn me, with Greg beside her. They're teenagers—about as old as I am now—and she's the beautiful grunge girl I remember. Mom is looking down at me and he is looking at her. He *loved* her and she wrecked him.

I exhale as I close the album.

"Sorry," he says. "It's a lot to process, isn't it?"

"Yeah."

"I made it for, um—it's yours, so you can look at it whenever. No rush."

I rest my head against the little oval window, and for a while I just sit, watching the clouds and the miles pass. Through a break I see what I think might be

Tennessee. Mom and I lived there for a few months when I was seven. I remember, because she worked the morning shift at a diner and would sometimes take me to the park to play with other kids. The other moms would circle up to talk—some with babies on their hips—but they never included my mom in their conversations. If she cared, she never showed it. She'd fan herself out on the grass with her portable CD player, chain-smoking cigarettes and singing along with Pearl Jam, her forever favorite band. Tennessee wasn't as good as our first place in North Carolina—where I still went to school—but we were still happy. And Mom hadn't met Frank yet.

"Why did she take me?" I ask.

"She was scared," Greg says. "Our relationship was falling apart, and my parents were pushing me to get full custody so they could take care of you while I went to college. Your mom—she was convinced I wasn't going to let her see you, so she left."

He sounds so sincere that it seems impossible that he's not telling the truth, but in Mom's version of the story, he is the villain.

"Do you think she'll go to prison?"

"Maybe." He pushes his hand through his hair. "Probably." He sighs. "This is not what I wanted for her. Not ever."

The conversation is interrupted by the flight attendant pushing the drink cart. Greg orders Cokes, but I feel guilty that I'm sitting on a plane drinking soda while Mom is in jail. Is she scared? Does she miss me? Does she wonder why I haven't come to see her?

The captain announces that the weather in Tampa is sunny and warm, and that we're scheduled to land on time.

Greg breaks the silence. "Twelve years is a long time. And if you want to know the truth, I'm still pretty pissed off. There's a big part of me that wants to treat your mom the same way she treated me, but I can't do that. It wouldn't be fair to you. So here's the thing . . . I want you to stay. You're my daughter, too, and I want to know you. But if your mom gets out of jail before you turn eighteen and you want to go back, I won't keep you from her."

"Really?" My birthday is in May, only six months away. Half a year. Temporary. And I've got temporary down to an art.

His eyes tell me this is an offer he doesn't want to make, but he nods anyway. "I promise."

Chapter 3

Another airport, an hour drive, and we finally come to a stop in the driveway of a small yellow cottage in a town called Tarpon Springs. A porch swing propped with floral cushions sways slowly in the afternoon breeze. I wonder if I should recognize this place. Have I lived here? Was this our house before Mom took me?

"Phoebe and I bought this place a couple of years ago." Greg answers the question before I can ask it, as he cuts the ignition of the dark-blue compact SUV that was waiting for us in the Tampa airport parking lot. "It was a complete wreck, but we gave it new life. I'm an architect, so that's . . . kind of what I do."

As we walk through the gate of a low white picket fence, the front screen door creaks open and two little boys spill out, launching themselves at their dad. He squats down to their level and lets them bowl him over with hugs. They're laughing and rolling around on the lawn like puppies when Phoebe comes out. She reminds me of one of those perfect moms from the Tennessee park, with her rolled-up denim capris and sparkly flip-flops. She's even prettier than her picture.

"You must be Callie." She tucks a strand of hair behind her ear before she reaches out to shake my hand. Hers isn't rough the way Mom's is; it's smooth and she wears a braided silver ring. "I'm Phoebe. It's so nice to finally meet you."

"I, um—you, too."

Greg untangles himself and stands, brushing bits of grass off his clothes.

"I'm Tucker," the taller of the two boys says. He's the one who resembles Phoebe. "Are you my sister? Because Daddy says you're my sister. Do you want to see my finger? I have a boo-boo."

He extends his hand, and his index finger is wrapped in a bandage with wide-mouthed cartoon monkeys all over it. I'm not used to little kids and unsure of what to say, so I go with, "Cool." He beams at me, then peeks under the bandage to inspect his wound. It's barely a scratch, but to Tucker it's serious business.

Greg ruffles a hand over his son's dark-blond head. "He's three," he says, as if that's all the explanation I need.

"That's Joe." Tucker points to his brother. Joe's fingers are jammed in his mouth and his brown eyes are wary. "He's littler than me. He's not even two."

"Don't take Joe personally," Greg says. "His people motor doesn't warm up as fast as Tucker's, but once it does, he's Velcro Boy."

"Velcro Boy!" Tucker exclaims in a superhero voice, and races circles around us, arms extended as if he's flying. Phoebe catches him up in her arms and gently scolds him—not really scolding at all—that he needs to turn down his volume.

I miss my mom.

Greg notices my distress. "So, who wants to show Callie her new room?"

"Me, me, me!" Tucker's T-shirt rides up as he worms his way out of his mother's grasp. "Pick me, Daddy."

Without waiting for an answer, he catches my hand as if I'm not a complete stranger and pulls me along the side of the house to the backyard. Against the rear fence is an old-fashioned silver Airstream trailer, the kind you hitch to a car to go camping. Tucker races ahead to open the door, then doubles back to me.

"You get to sleep in here." He says it with reverence, as if this trailer is the holy grail of sleep spaces.

Inside, it resembles a mini-apartment with a sink, stove, and refrigerator; a dining table; a built-in couch;

a bathroom with a shower; and even a tiny bedroom. The bed is covered by a purple cotton spread embroidered with flowers and tiny bits of mirror, and decorated with a cluster of throw pillows. Nestled among the pillows is a patchwork owl that gives me the same déjà vu sensation I had at the sheriff's office.

"It's nothing fancy," Greg says, entering the trailer. "The stove doesn't work, and I still need to hook up the propane for hot water and heat, but we only have two bedrooms and . . . I guess I thought you might want a place of your own."

I pick up the owl. Some of the patches are worn so thin you can almost see through them to the stuffing inside.

"You used to carry him everywhere," he says. "You called him—"

"Toot." It's just a tiny flash of a memory, but I remember making sure he was with me every night before I went to sleep. "I thought that's what owls said."

I can see the bitter blurred in the sweet of Greg's smile. All these years I've had very few memories, while he—he's had nothing but.

"Owls say 'hoot,' silly." Tucker cracks up, as if it's the funniest thing he's ever heard, and Phoebe suggests they go in the house to check on dinner. He protests, but she scoops him up and carries him off, leaving Greg and me—and a silent Joe, who regards me with owl-size eyes from the safety of his father's arms—in the trailer.

"So, um—there will be some rules," Greg says. "Not sure what yet, because—well, when you left you were a tiny girl who slept with an owl and called me Daddy. But I'm sure they'll be the typical things. Boys, curfews, and"—he gestures toward a laptop sitting on the small dining table—"stuff about porn."

I nod, dizzy at the idea of having my own computer. I've only ever used the computers at public libraries, usually in moments stolen between card-holding patrons. Most librarians were nice about it, but a few would chase me off, questioning why I wasn't in school. Whenever that happened, I'd hide in the most secluded corner I could find and read. Once in a while, I'd take home a book without checking it out. And if I couldn't return it to its home library, I'd return it to the next library.

"This is only meant to be your bedroom, Callie," Greg says. "The rest of the house is yours, too. Don't feel as if you have to stay out here all the time, okay?"

I nod again, overwhelmed by suddenly having so much when I've gone for so long with so little. Overwhelmed at how my life has been turned upside down.

"We'll probably eat around six," he says, as he carries

Joe out the screen door. He pauses on the step. "You could come join us now, if—"

"I might sleep."

His smile falters a little, as if he expects me to be excited about bonding with his family when I've just lost mine. I'm not ready. "Sure, um—we'll see you at dinner, then."

I lie down on top of the bedspread and rest my head on one of the pillows. The white pillowcase is cool against my cheek and smells faintly of bleach. I feel bad for crying on Phoebe's clean laundry, but I can't stop the tears. I cry until my whole body hurts and then cry until I fall asleep.

The door clicks softly as he comes into my room. I pinch my eyes shut so tight I can feel my lashes against the tops of my cheeks and hope that if he thinks I'm asleep, he'll go away. The edge of the bed sags and the mattress conspires with him, shifting me in his direction. He lifts my Hello Kitty nightgown, his fingers seeking secret places. His breath is tangy from whatever he and Mom were drinking in the kitchen as he whispers, "Doesn't that feel nice?" My own fingers have curiously touched those places and it made me feel tingly, but his fingers are thick and rough-skinned. It doesn't feel nice, but I don't say anything. I hold my breath, taking tiny sips of air, and try not to cry. Because if I cry, he'll cuddle me against him, the tiny hairs under his lip prickling my skin as he kisses my damp cheek, and tell me I'm his special girl. As if someone other than him has made me cry. This time I wait until he's gone before I curl up into my smallest self and sob.

I wake, slick with sweat and tears, wondering where I am. There's no sticky vinyl couch beneath me, no incessant *tick-tick-tick* of the broken clock, and the dust swirling in the fading light coming through the window beside me is not my dust. Not my window.

"Mom?" My voice cracks.

She doesn't answer. Of course she doesn't answer. I'm alone.

Greg said there is no hot water, but I take a cold shower anyway, trying to scrub off the phantom feel of Frank's fingers. He was one of Mom's boyfriends, the one we lived with for almost a year in Oregon. The one who said our special time together needed to be a secret because she would be jealous. She would hate me, he said. The terror of losing her love made the promise for me. And even though I was eight—old enough to understand that special shouldn't feel bad—I let him keep putting his hands on me. Even now I can feel them. And no amount of scrubbing can wash away the shame.

When I finish my shower, I put my clothes back on and cross the small lawn. The sun is fading and light shines out through the windows, making the house appear warm and safe. My nightmare recedes as I let myself in through the back door. The kitchen is fragrant with meat and spices I can't identify. Mom isn't big on cooking, and my skills haven't evolved much beyond macaroni and cheese from a box. Sometimes I'll add a can of tuna and she calls it gourmet.

Tucker and Joe are building with LEGO bricks on the living-room floor, while Greg's laptop is propped open on the coffee table. Curled in the corner of the couch, Phoebe watches the evening news.

I'm not sure what to do. Should I go join them? Announce myself? Make a noise?

Before I have the chance to decide, Greg looks up from his computer screen, his smile as wide as I think a smile can be. "Hey, Callie. Hungry?"

The nightmare has left my stomach queasy. "A little."

"Phoebe made *pastitsio*," he says. "Have you tried it?"

"I don't think so."

"It resembles lasagna, but it's far superior because it's Greek."

Phoebe shakes her head, but a smile tugs at her lips. "Not this again."

"What?" Greg pivots to look at her. "It's true. Not only is Greece the birthplace of philosophy and political science and—"

"Democracy," I offer.

"Exactly." He points at me. "See? Callie understands."

Phoebe laughs, then turns her smile toward me. "You shouldn't encourage him."

Greg winks as he unfolds himself from the floor. "Anyway, pastitsio"—he picks up Joe, who squawks at being parted from his LEGOs, and plops him in a high chair beside the dining-room table—"you're going to love it."

I take the empty seat beside Joe as Phoebe brings a steaming casserole dish from the kitchen. It's been so long since I've eaten something that hasn't come from a can, box, or drive-up window.

"So, I have a friend," Greg says, as I scoop a small portion of pastitsio onto my plate. "He's one of the guidance counselors at the high school, and he says that in order for you to attend, you'll have to take some proficiency tests to determine your grade level."

When I was about nine or ten, I was obsessed with school. I sought out books in which the characters attended school, I practiced cursive writing, I memorized the planets, and when Mom was at work, I'd spend hours playing school with imaginary students. I saw girls my age at the library and I would hover close, listening to the way they talked and wishing they were my friends. One girl, who had the palest eyelashes I'd ever seen and carried a sparkling unicorn notebook, called me "freak" for standing too close to her. Freak. Like she could see right inside me and knew about Frank. After that, I stopped wanting to go to school, because if the girl at the library could see my secret, everyone else would see it, too.

"I think you'll enjoy Tarpon Springs High," Greg continues. "I'm biased because I went there, but it's a good school. Plus, it's an easy way to make some friends and get involved in activities. Sports or music or whatever."

I've gotten over wanting to be someone's best friend, and I've managed to survive eleven years on a kindergarten education. I don't want to go, but his face radiates such hope I can't say it. I take a bite of food so I don't have to answer.

He grins. "Good stuff, huh?"

I nod, because it's every bit as delicious as he claimed, but swallowing it is all but impossible with a knot in my throat.

I can't do this.

I can't sit here and pretend I'm a normal girl when my whole life has been so fucked up. Greg and Phoebe haven't slept in the backseat of their car, or eaten all their meals from a vending machine because their mothers forgot to buy groceries. And the only monsters Tucker and Joe will ever have to contend with are the imaginary kind that are banished in the light. These people are so clean, and I feel so—

—tainted.

The need to flee overtakes me. I push away from the table and beat a retreat through the kitchen, out to the trailer, where I dive beneath the comforter and hug Toot close to my chest. The owl smells dusty, as if it's been waiting for me all this time. It's comforting and heartbreaking at the same time.

"Callie?" Greg says my name softly through the screen but doesn't come in. "You okay?"

I don't answer, hoping he'll go away.

"I've been warning myself that the real Callie might not be the same as the one I've been imagining all these years," he says. "But that didn't stop me from assuming you'd be excited about high school. Or that you'd automatically love Greek food. Or that you'd even want to be here. Anyway . . . I'm sorry."

I wait a long time—well after I hear the back door slap shut—before I get out of bed and slip on my sneakers. My unpacked suitcase is sitting beside the door, my guitar still in its case. I think about taking them and leaving, but the little bit of money I have will get me exactly nowhere.

The neighborhood is still, and the way the trees drip with Spanish moss is a little eerie. I move from patch of streetlight to patch of streetlight, unsure of where I'm headed—and try not to think about my mom. At the corner, Ada Street becomes Hope Street and continues on. It seems a good omen—hope—so I keep walking. The residential neighborhood gives way to businesses, and Hope makes its perpendicular end at Dodecanese, a boulevard lined with shops. The gift-shop windows are filled with sponges, soaps, shells, and Greek-themed tourist wear; the bakeries scented of yeast and honey; and the restaurants called Mykonos and Hellas.

Almost everything is closed, but the plucky mandolin music from a couple of open restaurants follows me, the melodies melting one into the next. My skin is stained blue in the neon glow of the gift shops, and I feel as if I'm an alien in yet another new world. I pause on the sidewalk and close my eyes. Maybe if I stand here long enough I will remember how to be Greek and I'll feel as if I belong in Tarpon Springs. Except none of this is familiar and it is not my home. I look around as if my surroundings might have changed while my eyes were shut, but it's still the same, still strange. So I cross the street.

On the opposite side of Dodecanese there is a riverfront esplanade lined with rows of fishing boats, their decks heaped with dark mounds of something I can't identify. It isn't until I reach a boat illuminated by a caged utility light hanging from the deck roof that I realize they're sponges.

Standing beneath the light, a guy around my age—no, probably a little older—strings the dark-yellow tufts on a cord like an oversize version of the popcorn garlands Mom and I used to make at Christmas. He has a blue bandanna tied around his dirty-blond curls, and when he bends down for another sponge, there's a sweat-stained spot on his gray shirt where it sticks between his shoulder blades. He glances up, and his face is something so fine and beautiful, it makes my chest ache the way it does when I hear a sad song or finish a favorite book.

If he sees me standing beyond the reach of his light, he gives nothing away. I watch, curiously, as he threads one last sponge, then secures the entire string to the underside of the roof.

"You know"—his voice is low as he knots off the second end of the cord. The muscles in his tanned arms flex—"you're kind of creeping me out, standing in the dark."

I move into the light.

His dark eyes rest on my face long enough to bring heat to my cheeks, and he gives me a little half smile that makes my heart grow wings. They beat against my rib cage as I take a bolder step closer.

"Better," he says.

"What, um—what were you doing just now? With the—" I gesture toward the garlands of sponges.

A quiet laugh rumbles up from his chest. "You must not be from around here, huh?"

"Not really, no."

"Well, I can give you the tourist brochure version," he says. "Or, we could grab a beer and I'll give you the behind-the-scenes version."

I know how this works: flirt, drink, sex. A familiar road on a brand-new map.

"What time is it?" I ask, wondering if Greg knows I'm gone.

"Eight thirty, maybe? Early."

"I really—" I look at him and he's standing on the side rail of his boat, poised to step down to the pavement if I say the word. The air between us is thick with want. Mine. His. It doesn't make sense because I don't know him. I don't even know his name. He's only the most beautiful thing I've ever seen and I'm so, so tempted. But I also know how this ends. And after everything that's happened in the past two days, I'm not sure I want to add feeling like a slut to my to-do list. "I need to go."

"Wait," he says, as I turn away. "Can I drive you . . . somewhere?"

"Not tonight," I say. "But thanks for the offer."

I don't look at him again, because if I do, I will change my mind.

Greg's house is dark when I get back, only one light still shining. I picture him and Phoebe tucking the boys in bed, reading stories and kissing them good night. I remember bedtime stories, but more than that, I remember when they stopped. After we left Frank, we lived in the empty model home in Washington State. It was at the head of a cul-de-sac with no other houses. No grass. No trees. There were only depressions along the side of the street where driveways would go. Mom would tuck me into my sleeping bag on the floor of the room with mermaid wallpaper border and tell me to pretend it was my island.

"Stay on the island so the sharks won't get you," she'd say, kissing my forehead.

Then she would go to work, leaving me alone in the dark to worry about imaginary sharks and real live men who prey on little girls.

Pushing the thoughts away, I cross the backyard. I

jolt at the dark shape of a person sitting on the step of the trailer and for a heart-rattling second I'm convinced it's Frank.

It's Greg.

"Sorry if I scared you." He stands. "But—the first place my mind went—well, I thought you took off."

"I just—I went for a walk."

"You know how we talked about rules earlier?" He runs his hand over the top of his head. "Well, one of them will be that you need to tell me where you're going and when you'll be home."

"Okay."

"And tomorrow we'll get you a cell phone so you can text me or something when you decide to go wandering, okay?"

"Okay."

He exhales slowly. "You scared the hell out of me. Don't do that again."

"I won't." The words don't mean anything. I might not be here tomorrow, and I don't owe him anything. He steps toward me, as if he's going to give me a hug. Reflexively I take a half step back, and he stops himself. The whole thing is awkward, and I just want to go inside and sleep.

"I went down to the sponge docks," I offer.

"Really?" I can't see his face light up, but his tone

shines and I can tell this makes him happy. "What did you think?"

My mind beats a path directly to the guy on the boat and how easy it would have been to sleep with him. "It was . . . interesting."

Chapter 4

The sky is still streaked with tangerine-colored sunrise clouds as I tape a note to the door of the Airstream:

Went for a walk. I'll be back.

I'm not sure how I feel about being accountable, but leaving the note seems easier than getting another ambush lecture about it later. Mom usually had no idea where I was, especially as I got older and she took more night jobs. I haunted the library by day and wandered the streets in the evening until I got tired or the town curfew—whichever came first. That's how I met Danny.

The last place we lived—God, it was only *days* ago I left there, but it already seems like some different lifetime—was a cornfield town with a handful of stoplights and a slaughterhouse at its edge. Every Saturday night—and never on Friday because Fridays were for football—kids from all over the county would make their way downtown, cruising up and down Union in their farm pickups and hand-me-down sedans, before gathering in the parking lot of the Big Chief to make plans.

The night I wandered in, Mom was working. We were a payday away from being able to fill the refrigerator, and I had just about enough cash for a small order of chili-cheese tater tots. Danny was there with his summer-sky eyes and get-in-your-pants grin. He left his friends and slid into the bench beside me. He smelled like flannel shirt and boy deodorant, and I smacked his hand when he reached for one of my tater tots.

"Ow!" He pulled his hand away as if mortally wounded, but his eyes were laughing and so was his smile. He moved closer, until his thigh was pressed tight and warm against mine, and his breath tickled my ear. "I was only trying to get your goodies."

"I know," I said through a mouth of chili-cheese. "But you weren't invited."

"What do I need to do to get an invitation?"

As it turned out, the answer was a couple of warm beers in the Big Chief parking lot.

We drove out to a gravel access road between a couple of fields and had sex in the bed of his Ford F-150.

At the time it felt good because I was the one who wanted it. I gave him the goodies. But when it was over, I couldn't help thinking about all the shit that had been hauled around in the back of that truck.

His jeans were still down around his knees, and I could see the stars looking down at me from over his shoulder when I asked him to take me home. He wasn't bothered by my request, and at the curb in front of the apartment, he gave me his number.

"Or I'm usually at the Chief on Saturday nights," he said. "But if you see me with my girlfriend, pretend you don't know me, okay?"

"I *don't.*"

He didn't get it. He flashed me his I-just-got-in-your-pants grin and drove off. I didn't call him, but the next night he showed up at the apartment when my mom was at work. And the weekend after that, I met up with him at the Big Chief and we hooked up in the back of his truck again.

I reach the sponge docks by way of Athens Street this time, and I'm met with the scent of fresh bread from one of the bakeries, luring me away from thoughts of Danny. Across the street from the bakery, a pair of old men with white bristly mustaches and black fisherman's caps sit at a table on the sidewalk outside some sort of Greek social club, smoking cigarettes and drinking coffee from foam cups. They're a living postcard.

I enter a bakery, where the cases are filled with pastries with names I couldn't possibly pronounce. *Baklava. Galaktoboureko. Kourabiedes.*

"One, please." I point to the one vaguely resembling cheesecake with a label that says galaktoboureko and order two cups of coffee to go with it. Almost immediately I change my mind, feeling silly that I'm buying coffee and baked goods for a stranger. Who might not be down here. Who might not even drink coffee. And for no other reason than because he's breathlessly good looking and we nearly hooked up last night?

"Can I make that one cup?" I ask, but the woman behind the counter has already poured two coffees and gives me a stern look that tells me I'm buying both whether I want them or not. The change she gives me from my ten-dollar bill is the last of my money.

I reach the docks and my eyes go straight to the boats, seeking out the one from last night, but it's not there. Instead, there's a big empty space. My vision blurs with tears as I sit down on a bench facing the water. Not because he's not here—crying over a stranger would be even more stupid than buying him breakfast—but because in all my ridiculous excitement, I forgot why I'm even here. I forgot about Mom.

"Hey, you okay?" A girl about my age sits down on the bench beside me. Her dark hair—nearly the same shade as mine—falls over her shoulder in a thick braid. An invisible cloud of floral scent surrounds her.

"Yeah." I wipe my eyes with the sleeve of my T-shirt. "It's just—it's really nothing. I'm fine. Do you want some coffee?"

"Ooh, yes, please!" She snatches up one of the cups and sips. "So, considering we've never met, I'm assuming you didn't buy this coffee for me. What's the story there?"

I'm not sure what to make of this girl. Clearly she has no qualms about taking coffee from strangers, or prying into their business. Or, more accurately, their lack of business.

"There's no story." I hand her the white paper bakery bag. "Have this."

She peers in, then looks up at me. "You—are my new best friend."

I take a drink of coffee and my eyes drift to the empty spot, as if the boat is going to magically appear. As she bites into the galaktoboureko, she shakes her head in a way that's slightly violent. Her braid whips back and forth.

"No," she says, her mouth full. "No, no, no, no, no." She chews quickly and swallows. "Tell me you did not buy this for Alex Kosta."

"I don't—" My cheeks get warm and how can I tell her that I didn't catch his name? "I'm not sure."

"Insanely good looking? Works weekends on the sponge dive tour?" She points a piece of pastry in the direction of where the boat should be. "And if he were here now, he'd be right about there?"

"Yes?"

"You are so lucky I found you when I did," she says. "Listen, I work with him, so I've seen the way he operates. Alex Kosta can be described in two words: man whore. Or maybe that's one word. Hyphenated?" She shrugs. "Either way, just . . . no."

I take another drink of coffee and swallow words with the bitter brew. The words that would admit it doesn't matter to me. That I'm not that discriminating. Danny is proof. So is the guy before him. And the one before *him*. I don't even remember the first guy's name, only that afterward I felt exactly the same way I did every time Frank left my bedroom. I don't know—maybe it's a good thing I walked away from Alex Kosta last night.

"What's your name?" she asks. "I'm Kat."

"Callie."

Her brown eyes widen and she clutches my forearm. "Oh my God! You're Callie! You're here!"

"Um—"

"This is so—you have no idea," she says. "You're a local legend. Every few years the newspaper runs a story about you and your mom. They speculate on where you might be, interview people who claim to have seen you, and show age-enhanced pictures of how you might look. You're much prettier, by the way, but—this is so exciting! I knew Greg rushed off to pick you up, but I didn't expect to meet you so soon! I bet you're glad to be home with your dad, huh?"

"I don't really remember him."

"Wow." Kat's shoulders sag. "I guess because I've known him my whole life, it didn't occur to me that you don't. That is so sad."

"He, um—seems nice," I offer.

"Greg? Definitely." She nods. "He's super nice. When I was little, he built me a wooden dollhouse for my birthday, with working lights and tiny hardwood floors and—you probably don't know this, but we're related. Of course, if you're Greek and you live in Tarpon Springs you're related to pretty much everybody, but your dad and my mom are cousins."

I crush the pastry bag in my fist and stand. "I need to go."

"Did I do something wrong?" Kat's eyebrows pull together.

"No."

"I know how hard this must—"

"You couldn't *possibly* know how hard this is." The words are hard. Sharp. And other, uglier words fill my mouth with a terrible taste. I am irrationally jealous because I've never had a dollhouse. Or a real birthday party. Or cousins. I am jealous that she spent her whole life knowing my father. I'm jealous of a *dollhouse*. "You don't have even the *slightest* of clues."

I make the mistake of looking back. Tears trickle down her cheeks and I am a monster girl. And the voice that came out of me was banshee shrill. I sounded like my mother.

"I shouldn't have said that." I sit down. The paper bag crackles as I pull out a napkin and offer it to Kat. "I'm sorry."

"No." She wipes her eyes, making a mess of her makeup. "You're right. I have no right to assume I know anything about your life."

Inexplicably, I want to like her. And maybe I want her to like me, too. "I didn't have to be such a bitch about it."

She gives a sniffly laugh. "You do have a point right there."

I make air circles in front of my left eye. "You're kind of . . . smeared."

Kat digs her arm into a cavernous purse and produces a compact mirror. "Yeesh, you're right. I'd better go do some repair work before the shop opens." She gestures at a gift shop beside the river. It's one of the larger shops, with a signboard out front offering sponge dive tours for fifteen dollars. "Do you, um—want to hang out sometime? Considering your narrowly averted Alex Kosta crisis, it's clear you need someone to show you the ropes around here."

I laugh. "Sure."

"Theo is hiring at the gift shop," she says. "I could put in a word, if you're interested. I mean, he's my uncle on the other side of the family, so you probably wouldn't even need to fill out an application. What do you say?"

I've never had a job before, unless you consider Mom's brief stint stocking newspaper boxes. We'd drive to the loading dock, fill up the trunk of the car—I think it was an old Ford Escort that time—with string-tied bundles of newspapers, and drive around town, swapping out yesterday's edition with the current one. She had a hard time getting up before dawn, so most of the time I did the deliveries by myself, even though I didn't have a driver's license.

I don't intend on staying in Tarpon Springs, but a job would be a better alternative to high school. Something to do. Something to occupy my brain until it's time to leave. "I'll think about it."

"Phoebe can take you shopping for school clothes," Greg says later, as we walk home from the cell-phone store. One of the things he's shared about himself is that he's an eco-friendly type who subscribes to the philosophy that if your destination is less than a mile away, you should walk. Something about reducing his carbon footprint, he said, but I wasn't really listening. I was too busy trying to figure out how to tell him I have no intention of going to school. "Cell phones I can handle, but I am clueless when it comes to clothes."

"I, um—I'm not going to school."

I wasn't anticipating the direct approach, and he looks at me as if I've sprouted a second head. I found his high school yearbook in the bookcase when I got home from the sponge docks. Greg played varsity football, captained the baseball team, and was the student-council treasurer. There's also a plaque on the living-room wall that commemorates the year he was the Epiphany cross retriever. I have no idea what that means, but clearly Greg is the type of guy who loved high school. He's a participator. I'm not surprised that my refusal doesn't even make a blip on his radar screen. "I know it would be intimidating at fir—"

"I'm *not* intimidated." I am annoyed that another person today presumes to know what I'm feeling. "I just don't want to be a freak show."

"You're not a freak show."

"Kat told me about the newspaper articles," I say. "You don't think everyone is going to want to come see the amazing kidnapped girl? 'Can she talk? Can she read? Can she eat with utensils?' "

He smiles. "It won't be that bad."

"I don't see the point," I say. "I'm nearly eighteen and I've never had dreams of going to college."

"But that's the thing, Callie. You can dream about college now if you want."

"Now?" I don't care for the implication that being with Mom somehow limited my dreams—even though it did. Or that I now have his permission to start dreaming. "I could have dreamed about college at any time, but I didn't." My words have bite and his smile fades to a frown. His disappointment makes me uncomfortable and I hate feeling like I should say something to make him happy. "I mean, maybe someday I'll change my mind, but right now . . ."

He doesn't answer right away, but he works his lower lip between his teeth, so I can tell he's going over all the angles the same way I do.

"I, um—Kat said Theo was looking for someone at the shop," I say. "I could do that."

"I don't know, Callie," Greg says. "I think high school is important, not only academically, but for getting involved and being social. I'm not saying no, but I'll need to think about it."

"I'm not going."

He sighs at the stalemate, and we don't talk again the rest of the way home.

Chapter 5

"Callie?" Kat's voice drifts into the Airstream as I sit on the couch, staring at my suitcase. It's been four days since I got here, but unpacking it would feel permanent. Settled. And that unsettles me. "We're coming in."

Before I can answer, the screen door swings open and my space is filled with Kat and unfamiliar boys. Two of them. One has a wide smile and black hair that curls up at the edge of his baseball cap. The other boy reminds me of a retriever—floppy and golden, with dark, happy eyes and a frame that's a size too large for the trailer. He has to stoop to keep his head from touching the ceiling.

"This place is amazing!" Kat flops down beside me and squeezes a silky pink-and-gold throw pillow to her chest. "You are so lucky! I would kill to have my own room, but instead I have to share it with an annoying nine-year-old."

Even though the cabinets are a little shabby, the trailer is nicer than most places I've lived. It's clean and all the homey touches—curtains, throw pillows, a couple of hanging houseplants, and a multicolored woven rug—make it clear that Phoebe put some thought into decorating it. She couldn't have guessed purple is my favorite color. Unless it's always been my favorite color and Greg remembered. With him it seems entirely possible.

"Anyway," Kat goes on. "Callie, this is Nick Adamidis, my baseball-playing physics nerd." The dark-haired one waves at me. "And this is his brother by another mother, Connor Madsen. He's our token non-Greek friend."

"Hey." His voice is surprisingly deep for someone with such a boyish face.

"So, Callie," Kat says. "The three of us are going to watch the original *Star Wars* trilogy back-to-back at Nick's house tonight and Greg already gave his permission for you to join us. Wanna come?"

"I, um—" I glance at the suitcase. What's one more day? "Sure."

"Perfect." Kat stands up and pushes Nick toward the door. "You two go outside and play catch or something while I help Callie get ready. I'm pretty sure I saw a football out there."

I look down at my red shirt. I've worn it every day because Phoebe has not had time to take me shopping and the only other one I own is a faded green T-shirt that bears the Girl Scouts logo with the words *Got cookies?* printed beneath it. Ancilla threw away the holey thermal I was wearing the night my mom was arrested. My red shirt has a small toothpaste stain near the hem, but maybe no one will notice if we're watching movies. "Can't I—"

Kat shuts the door. "We're not really going to Nick's house for movies. We're going to a party. So where do you keep your clothes?"

She reaches for my brown suitcase. As she lifts it, the handle breaks, and when the case hits the floor, the latch opens, scattering my books, journal, and the green Girl Scouts T-shirt. "Oh my God, Callie, I'm so sorry." She squats down and starts picking up the books, but my feet are rooted to the trailer floor and I want to cry.

My suitcase is broken.

"I'll buy you a new one or fix this one or find another one on eBay," she babbles. "Whatever you want."

"It's okay," I say, even though it's not remotely okay. That stupid old brown suitcase—the one I didn't even want—was a link to Mom. My way back to her.

"Are you sure?" Kat is gentle with the books as she stacks them in a neat pile, with my journal on the top.

I nod and hope the stretch of my lips seems like a real smile. "I'm sure."

"Okay, so where *do* you keep your clothes?" she asks, as she folds the T-shirt. I point to the red shirt I'm wearing and the green one in her hands.

"*That's it?*"

"Yeah."

"Wow, um—we really need to go shopping." Kat pulls at her lower lip. "Okay, I have an idea. Take off your jeans." She unbuttons the red plaid schoolgirl-style skirt she's wearing, shimmies out of it, and then hands it to me. Besides taking coffee from strangers and oversharing about her home life, she also seems perfectly at ease standing around in her underwear. "Swap me."

It takes longer for me to get out of my jeans. I haven't worn a skirt since I was a little girl and I'm not sure I'm comfortable with having so much of me exposed. Still, I make the exchange. It seems easier to do this than think about my broken suitcase. I'm taller, but we're about the same size, so her skirt fits me, and my jeans—although a little too long—fit her. She rolls up the hems.

Kat gives me the green T-shirt. "Put this on," she says, then opens the door a crack. I hear the thump of a football being passed. "Nick, I need your socks."

"They're kind of busy right now," he says. "Being on my feet and all."

She snaps her fingers. "Socks. Now."

By the time I get the shirt pulled over my head, Kat has Nick's socks in her hand. They're ankle-high white athletic-style with two green stripes around the top. She hands them to me. "Don't worry," she says. "He put them on clean before we came over."

When I'm finished, Kat walks around me, surveying her fashion decisions. "You desperately need a haircut," she says finally. My hair hangs beyond the middle of my back, a mess of snarled curls, unintentional dreadlocks, and brassy gold ends from a grown-out dye-job disguise that Mom insisted I needed. "But you look hot. In fact, I wouldn't even do makeup. Just—" She rummages around in her purse until she unearths a Dr Pepper–flavored lip balm. "Use this. It'll give you a hint of color."

"Perfect," she says, as I apply the balm. "Ready?"

"No."

She laughs as if I'm joking and pulls me out into the backyard.

"Looking good, Cal," Nick says, lobbing the football at Connor, who doesn't even attempt to catch it. Instead, he stares at me with an expression I've seen on other faces. One that makes me want to turn around, but Kat is gripping my hand and I can't. "And you look mighty fine in those jeans, kitty cat."

She kisses Nick's cheek, then uses her thumb to rub away the shine of her lip gloss on his skin. "Let's go."

Greg comes out of the house and his eyebrows pull together when he sees what I'm wearing. The skirt is shorter than anything I've ever worn. "Do you have your phone?" he asks.

I hold it up so he can see it. I'm not sure I remember how to use it, but I have it.

"Don't be late," he says, and I'm sure he's already figured out we're not going to watch *Star Wars* movies. "Call if you need me."

"So what do you think of Connor?" Kat asks, as we stand at the kitchen island in the largest house I've ever seen. It belongs to a classmate of Kat's whose parents are out of town. Except for the Ruskins' house, every place I've lived in could fit into this house, all at the same time. And nearly every window has a view of the Gulf of Mexico. She pours a generous shot of coconut rum into a blue plastic cup and tops it off with a splash of pineapple juice. The countertop is littered with half-empty liquor bottles, a variety of sodas and juices, and blue cups like hers. And mine. Except mine contains the same beer I've been nursing since we got here.

"He's—" Connor opened the car door for me when the four of us left Greg's house and stammered that I looked pretty. Not enough information to form an opinion. "He seems nice."

"He totally is." Kat nods. "He's super shy, but he *really* likes you."

I glance up and he's staring at me again. It's not predatory, the way he looks at me. Nor is it the same as the other night with Alex Kosta, when the air between us felt alive. Kat is wrong. Connor doesn't know me so he can't *really* like me. He likes looking at my face. He likes the shape of my body. There is a difference.

"You should go talk to him," she says, as Nick comes up with a fish-shaped tray filled with tiny plastic cups.

"Ladies, have a shot."

Kat picks one up and sniffs it. "What is it?"

"I call it a Pan Galactic Gargle Blaster," he says. The *Hitchhiker's Guide* reference makes me laugh. "But basically, it's vodka, lemon juice, and sugar."

She hands one to me and raises hers in a toast. "To Callie"—she leans in close to me and lowers her voice—"and Connor."

I roll my eyes.

"To life, the universe, and everything," Nick says.

The vodka makes my eyes sting, but the shot makes me feel warm inside. It makes me want to have another. A million. As many as it takes to feel this way all the time.

Nick places the fish tray of shots on the countertop and slides his arm around Kat's waist. "Wanna go in the hot tub with me, kitty cat?"

"I didn't bring a suit."

He waggles his eyebrows and pretends to leer at her. "Exactly."

She shoulder-bumps him. "Let's go stick our feet in the pool."

"That works." Nick takes her hand. "And much easier to do now that I'm *not wearing socks*."

They don't ask me if I want to join them, and I don't follow. I stand at the kitchen island like a stone in the middle of a stream. Party noise swirls around me. Shouts and splashes from the pool in the backyard. The bone-jarring thump of the bass from the stereo. The chattering of girls, clustered like flocks of colorful birds. Explosions from the zombie-killing video game rage on the large-screen television.

Connor breaks his gaze from the video carnage to look at me. When he notices Kat and Nick are gone, he hands the game controller to the guy sitting beside him on the couch and stands. His puppy-dog eyes ask permission to approach. I pull my lower lip between my teeth, debating whether I'm ready for this. Except Connor mistakes it for coy approval and a shy grin spreads across his face. I take a gulp of warm beer as he makes his way through the crowded living room. Ready or not, here he comes.

"Hey." He stands beside me. "Doing okay?"

"It's kind of loud."

Connor nods. "It always is."

"Do you want to get out of here?" I ask. "Maybe go for a walk?"

Again with the grin, his teeth so white against his tanned skin. "Sure."

He tops off my cup with fresh beer and pours one for himself. I hook my index finger around his pinkie as he leads me through the tight crowd, passing a group of girls who whisper-wonder who I am, and an older guy—one who doesn't look as if he belongs at a party full of teenagers—tells me my ass looks fine, his cigarette breath fanning my face. It's so noisy that I'm not even sure I heard him correctly, but when I glance back, he winks at me. My insides trembling, I press closer to Connor until we're out of the house. The air is cooler, and it creeps beneath my hair, unsticking it from the back of my neck. Connor shifts his grip so all of his hand is holding all of mine. His palm is damp. "Is, um—is this okay?"

He doesn't have Danny's gift for sweet talk, or the bad-boy charm Matt possessed—he was the one before Danny—but Connor's bashfulness is appealing. It's non-aggressive. Safe.

"Yeah, it's fine."

My brain rummages through my mental filing cabinet for small talk, selecting and discarding topics, as we walk down the sidewalk. Connor doesn't say anything either, and the silence stretches unbearably long. I fill the space with sips of beer and, judging by the view from the corner of my eye, he does the same.

Three houses down, we reach a vacant lot.

"Here," he says. "You can see the water a lot better from here."

At the end of the grassy lot, Connor removes his blue plaid shirt and spreads it on the ground. Beneath it, he wears a plain white T-shirt.

"You can sit on it," he says. "Kat will kill you if you ruin her skirt."

He lowers himself beside me, his legs stretched out alongside mine. The white sliver moon is reflected in fractured pieces across the surface of the water. It's so beautiful it makes my eyes glaze with tears. I don't want to cry in front of Connor.

"What's wrong?" he asks.

"Nothing." I wipe my face on my sleeve. It isn't that

I wish my mom was here to see this, because somewhere along the way she lost her wonder for the world. But it's wrong—so wrong—that I've never seen this before. I mean, the moon and stars are everywhere, but I don't remember being *here*. And it's all her fault.

"So, I was thinking—"

I press my lips against his, cutting off whatever it is he's going to say. I'm too angry to talk. And I *don't* want to think.

Connor's brain eventually realizes what his lips are doing and his arms come around me. When he kisses back, his tongue tastes of beer and orange Tic Tacs, which is more pleasant than it sounds. His hands are warm and big on the back of my shirt as he holds them there. He doesn't try to take off my clothes. Danny would have had me out of my underwear by now. Of course, Danny would have never given me his shirt to sit on and I'd have gone home with bits of grass and sand on my ass.

"Wow," Connor says as he exhales in the space between kisses. "That was—"

"Don't talk." Kissing him again, I straddle his hips. His faded jeans are soft against my thighs.

His hands hang in midair for a moment, as if he's uncertain where to put them. He decides on my lower back, right above where my T-shirt rides up, but I can feel some of his fingers against my bare skin. Again, he doesn't move his hands, doesn't reach under my shirt to unhook my bra. It's like all but his lips are frozen.

Connor baffles me. He doesn't act like any boy I've ever met. I pull my mouth away from his and reach for the hem of my shirt.

"I was thinking maybe we could—" Connor's words die an instant death as my shirt slides up over my head. His eyes flicker to my half-naked chest before he looks away. "What, um—" His gaze is fixed on something over my shoulder. Almost as if he's talking to someone else, as if I'm not even here. "Are we—?"

My face goes hot as it hits me. I've read this wrong. "I thought—" How could he not want me? He's a *boy*. This makes no sense at all. "Forget it."

I can't get off his lap fast enough.

"Callie, wait."

I don't wait. I shove myself into my shirt and run. It takes me a couple of tries, but I locate the GREG speed-dial icon on my cell phone. As it rings, I hear Connor calling my name. Not wanting to face him, I duck behind a thick shock of sea grass that decorates a neighbor's front yard.

"Can you come get me?" I keep my voice low when Greg answers. "Please?"

"Is everything all right?"

"I just—I want to come home."

"Okay." I hear his keys jingle through the phone. The immediacy of his response is reassuring. "You're at Nick's house, right?"

"No, um, I'm at a place called Pointe Alexis."

"I'm not even going to ask right now," he says. "I'll be there in about fifteen minutes."

After giving him the address of my sea grass hiding spot, I work out a text message to Kat, telling her I went home. I don't want her to worry. She texts a reply, but I don't look or answer. I slide the phone in my pocket and wait for Greg.

"Callie?" Connor's voice is closer now. I hug my knees against my chest and make myself as small as possible so he won't see me. It reminds me of the way I'd curl myself up, hoping Frank would mistake me for a pillow—even though nothing about this night is the same as back then—and I press the heels of my hands hard against my eyes to keep from crying. Connor's phone chimes, and I imagine him looking at the screen—probably at a message from Kat, calling off the search. He swears softly, and his footsteps fade away as he returns to the party.

The scene between us plays on a continuous loop in my head, the humiliation catching flame on my face over and over until I'm scorched. I don't understand what happened, why Connor didn't want me. And I don't understand why I still feel every bit as worthless as I felt after Danny, after Matt. After Frank.

I stay hidden until I see a pair of headlights coming up the street and Greg's SUV pulls into the driveway beside me.

"Are you okay?" he asks, and the concern in his voice undoes me.

I shake my head, tears creeping down my cheeks. "I don't want to talk about it."

"Callie—" Greg blows out a frustrated breath. "At least tell me if there's some idiot up at that party I need to kill."

"There isn't." The only idiot at the party was me, but I don't tell him that. "Am I in trouble?"

"The short answer is yes." Greg puts the SUV in reverse and backs down the driveway. "But we'll talk about that tomorrow."

Chapter 6

"Relax," Greg says the next afternoon, as we cross the front porch of an old house with faded gray shingles. It belongs to his mother, Georgia, and my stomach is wound yarn-tight at the prospect of meeting her—and apparently every member of Greg's extended family. My homecoming and Thanksgiving combined in one belated feast. "As soon as they start eating and drinking, they'll forget all about you."

I smooth my palms down the skirt of the green sundress Phoebe let me borrow. I'm not used to wearing dresses and it exposes more of my legs than makes me comfortable, but it has flowers embroidered around the hem that remind me of the shirt Ancilla bought me. Phoebe also gave me a pair of sandals embellished with wooden bits and said I could keep them.

"We should go shopping tomorrow," she said. "Living with three guys, it would be a fun change to go with another girl."

Even though Phoebe has always known I exist, it can't be easy to have a new person who doesn't belong to her in her household, so I said I'd think about it. I didn't tell her Kat has already appointed herself my personal stylist.

The age-scarred wooden front door opens and a woman with wiry dark-gray hair pushes Greg aside to get to me, enveloping me in a hug so tight I feel as if my ribs might crack. Her hair tickles my nose, but her scent—the rose soap smell—reminds me of making oatmeal raisin cookies and singing a song about the moon.

"Oh, my little Callista," she croons softly in my ear and rocks me from side to side in a way that feels familiar. I recognize her voice. She's my *yiayoúla*, my grandma. And while I don't exactly remember her, bits and pieces of memories are sprinkled through my mind. Even more than Greg. "We've missed you so much."

Georgia stands back to look at me—her hands clutching my shoulders—and I see my face in her wrinkles, my eyes behind her red-rimmed glasses. It's strange to go your whole life thinking your DNA is all your own, and then see yourself in someone else.

"Come." She drags me inside, into a living room

overstuffed with people—on couches, perched on the arms of chairs, standing in every available space—and shoves me into a circle of eyes. More people than I've met in my whole life are packed in this house. A baby whimpers from some other room, and a little girl about Tucker's age says, "But I don't *want* to meet her, Mommy."

"Everyone," Georgia says. "Here is our Callista, home at last."

They all start clapping, except for the little girl, who puts her hands over her ears and sticks her tongue out at me. I try to feel as if I'm part of this, but they're all strangers. Some of the elderly women begin to converge, but my grandmother fends them off as if she's my personal bodyguard.

"Let the poor girl breathe," she scolds, as if she didn't just squeeze the wind out of me herself. Behind me Greg snickers and she shoots him a stern look, which makes me smile.

Georgia keeps her arm wrapped firmly around my waist as she introduces me to more aunts, uncles, and cousins than I'll ever be able to remember. Some of the old ones have accents so thick they sound as if they arrived from Greece this morning. They touch my face with papery fingers. Verifying I'm really me, maybe? I'm not sure. It creeps me out, but I don't say anything. I smile and nod and say "thank you" a lot.

"Ma." Greg comes up with Kat at his side. I'm glad to see both of them. "Maybe it's time to give Callie a break."

"You're right," Georgia says. "And I should check on the *dolmades*. Ekaterina, you have such a pretty face. Why do you cover it up with so much makeup?"

Kat rolls her eyes, but before she can say anything, my grandmother is pushing her way through the crowd to the kitchen. My cousin links her arm through mine, and I let her lead me out the front door to sit on the porch.

"I am so hungover." She drops onto the wooden swing, making the chain shake. "Did you get in trouble?"

"I'm grounded for a week."

"Ouch." She winces. "I'm sorry. My mom didn't say anything so I assume Greg didn't tell her."

"He was thinking about it," I say. "But I talked him out of it."

"You are the best. I owe you." She bumps her shoulder against mine. "So what happened with Connor? He came back to the party looking kind of freaked out."

"I don't want to talk about it."

Her eyes narrow. "He told Nick the same thing. Did you—?"

"No."

She pushes off with her foot, making the porch swing sway. "Then it can't be that bad, can it?"

Fresh embarrassment blooms on my face. "I thought we were, so, um—I took off my shirt."

"Seriously?" She stops the swing with both feet. "Wow. No wonder he freaked. I mean, I'm a little surprised he didn't rally in the face of"—Kat gestures toward my chest—"*those*, but I think he wanted to ask you out on a date first, not go straight to hooking up."

It never occurred to me. Not once. "Oh."

"You didn't know that?"

"No."

"Wait. You've never had a boyfriend? *You?*"

"No." When you don't stay in any one place very long, there's not much opportunity to be someone's girlfriend. Also, not much opportunity to meet the kind of guy who wants you for anything more than sex. "I've only . . ." I trail off, but Kat picks up on what I don't say.

"Whoa." She sounds surprised, and I envy having the kind of naïveté that assumes if you've never really dated, you might still be a virgin. If I had grown up here, I might be. Or at least I wouldn't have lost my innocence when I was eight years old. "Well." She starts the swing again. "I think you should try again with Connor. We could double-date."

"Maybe." Connor will be a great catch for someone, but I'm pretty sure it's not me. I don't know how to be that kind of girl. He's sweet, though. Cute.

We sit a minute and Kat starts giggling. "I wish I could have seen Connor's face when you took off your shirt. I don't think he's met real live boobs before."

"Well, he has now."

She's cracking up laughing when Georgia comes out onto the porch. "There you are, girls. Callista, the dolmades are ready. Come in. Try them."

She hustles me away from Kat to the dining room, where the table is laden with a variety of Greek foods, as well as ordinary holiday fare, like turkey, cornbread stuffing, and mashed potatoes.

"Dolmades"—Georgia says, scooping an enormous portion of little green bundles onto a plate—are rice and meat wrapped in grape leaves. When you were a baby, I would feed you this and you would open your mouth the way a new bird does, wanting always more, more, more."

As if I'm still that baby, she severs off a piece with a fork and brings it to my mouth for a bite. The rice tastes like rice, but the flavor of the leaves is minty and sour at the same time. It's unpleasant, and I chew quickly to rid myself of the taste. I try not to let her see that I don't care for her dolmades, but disappointment settles in her eyes and at the corners of her mouth, and I feel as if I've failed some secret granddaughter test.

Grandchild, daughter, friend, a girl a normal boy

would date—a growing list of people I don't know how to be.

"Ah, well." She smiles and she hands me a fresh plate. "We can't stay babies forever, can we?"

I fill my plate mostly with foods I can identify and grab a can of Coke from an ice-filled plastic tub in the kitchen. As I make my way through the living room toward the porch, I hear someone say "Veronica." In a short hallway that leads to the bedrooms and bathroom, two older women—not as old as Georgia, but definitely a lot older than Greg—huddle, talking softly about my mother. I linger close to the doorway so I can hear what they're saying.

"Kidnapping is a federal offense," the fat one says, with such certainty that I wonder if she's right. "She's going to jail for a long, long time, and I can't say she doesn't deserve it."

"If you ask me, she should be committed," the second woman says. "If it wasn't for the crazy disease, she would have never done what she did."

Crazy disease?

"I'll never understand what Greg saw in that girl."

The first one snorts. "He was thinking with his *poutsa*."

I don't need to understand Greek to understand what she means, and I want to tell them that it wasn't about sex. That Greg saw what other people didn't.

But my mind snags on the words "crazy disease," and I remember what Ancilla said about Mom getting the help she needs. And the words the man in the leather jacket yelled after me when I ran away from him. I've lived with her my whole life. Wouldn't I know if my own mother was really crazy?

I deposit my plate and soda on an end table and seek out Greg. He's drinking a beer and talking to Theo, the cousin who runs the gift shop at the docks.

"We need to talk," I say.

Greg looks as if he's going to protest at first—because we're in the middle of a party—but I guess he sees the seriousness on my face because he nods. "Sure."

Outside on the porch, I ask, "Is my mom crazy?"

"No."

Greg levels his index finger at me. Defensively. As if he's had this conversation one too many times. "Veronica suffers from borderline personality disorder, Callie. It affects her moods, and can be treated with therapy and medication, but she's *not* crazy."

I remember an amber prescription bottle in her purse, but there were no pills in it. Just coins. Quarters fit in it just right and she'd let me put them in whenever we got change. "I never saw her take any medication."

"You probably wouldn't have," he says. "Her doctor had her on a mix of antidepressants and antianxiety medications, but she complained they turned her into a zombie. She said they made her feel as if she was made of nothing. But without the meds she'd swing from one extreme to another. One day everything would be fine, and the very next day she'd accuse me of not loving her enough and try to bait me into telling her I wanted to break up with her. She'd cut friends out of her life for no apparent reason. She'd get unreasonably angry about the smallest offenses. And she absolutely hated being alone."

Like the last number on a combination lock, the tumblers of my life fall into place, and all the different mothers my mother has been finally make sense. The anger inside me makes my skin feel too tight and I need to get away from here. I start down the front-porch steps.

"Callie, where are you going?" Greg asks.

"I just—I'll be back."

My sandals are too slow, so I take them off. The sidewalk is warm as I run and I don't mind the sharp bite of tiny stones against my soles. How could my mom be so selfish? Taking the pills would have kept us here. Taking the pills would have kept her from hooking up with Frank. All she had to do was *take the goddamn pills* and her life, *my life*, would have been ordinary. Happy.

I end up at the sponge docks. Mostly because it's

beautiful so near the water, but also because I don't know any other places to go. The place where Alex Kosta's boat should be is empty, but so is the bench where I met Kat. Around me, sightseers study brochures and discuss what they want to do next. The sponge-diving tour boat pulls away from the dock with a load of tourists aboard. An old couple wearing sandals with socks take turns photographing each other in front of a bronze statue of a man wearing an old-fashioned sponge-diving suit.

I reach the bench and try to sit quietly, but my head is too loud. It takes me to the Super Wash, where the tall man with the leather jacket said Mom and I were both crazy, and a brand-new fear overtakes me. What if I *am* just like her? Is borderline personality disorder hereditary? Am I crazy, too? And if I am, how would I know for sure?

The sound of an engine rumbles into my thoughts, disrupting them and making me look up. A white boat with the name *Evgenia* painted on the side in blue slides into the empty spot, Alex Kosta behind the wheel. Today, his sweaty shirt is faded green, his bandanna is red, and his face is as perfect as I remember. There is another guy with him, shorter and rounder than Alex, who helps him tie off the boat. They stand beside the boat for a minute and talk before they shake hands, and the shorter guy heads off toward Athens Street.

"If I'd have known you were going to wait for me . . ." Alex closes the distance between his boat and my bench. His eyes, I notice, aren't really dark at all. They're on the greenish side of hazel, and a tattoo wends its way down his right forearm from his elbow to his wrist, a banner carried in the beak of an old-school swallow that reads *rise free from care before the dawn and seek adventures*. Thoreau. ". . . I'd have told you I was going to be gone a few days."

"I wasn't waiting," I say, but now that I see him again, it feels like a lie. "You just got lucky."

"Yes, I did." He grins and it feels as if my bones have liquefied. If he has this effect on me, I can only imagine what he must do to female tourists. I feel an inexplicable flicker of jealousy at all those imaginary girls. Silly, because he is Danny. He is Matt. He is another name on my hit-and-run list.

He extends a hand. "I'm Alex."

Without telling him I already know his name, I let him pull me to my feet. "I'm Callie."

As we walk to his boat, we're close enough that I can feel the sleeve of his T-shirt graze the bare skin of my arm, sending a flurry of shivers down my spine. He climbs aboard first.

"Pretty dress," he says, as he helps me up and over the side. "What's the occasion?"

"I am."

His laugh is warm and slightly wicked. It should scare me, but it doesn't. Well, maybe a little, but I don't care. "Yes, you are."

"I mean, a homecoming party. For me." I watch his face for signs of recognition—for him to connect the dots between me and the Kidnapped Girl—but they don't seem to appear.

"Where were you?" he asks.

"Everywhere."

"And you came back here?" Alex shakes his head. "Well, welcome home anyway."

The boat stinks. Literally. As if I've walked into a bathroom after someone forgot to flush. I fan my hand in front of my nose, and he laughs again.

"It's the sponges," he explains, flipping the latch on a small door in the cockpit of the boat. "Until they're finished decomposing, they secrete this foul-smelling shit called gurry."

"How long does that take?"

He opens the door and steps down into a small cabin that reminds me of the Airstream, beckoning me to follow. "Three, sometimes four days."

"How can you stand it?"

Alex shrugs. "I don't really notice it much."

He reaches into a small refrigerator for a couple

bottles of beer, twists off the tops, and hands me one. We stand there for a moment, and we're both looking at each other as if neither of us can stop. And this inexplicable thing between us hangs the way humidity hangs in the air, heavy and thick.

Finally, he takes a long drink of his beer, his eyes still on mine.

"I need a shower," he says. "Do you mind?"

"Yes. I mean, no," I say, my face growing warm as he grins at my stammering. "No, I don't mind."

He takes his beer with him into the bathroom and less than a minute later I hear the shower running. I look around the cabin while I wait. The berth opposite me is made up for sleeping with blue-striped sheets and a navy comforter. On the floor, the zipper-edged mouth of a duffel bag gapes open, exposing a jumble of T-shirts, shorts, and plaid boxer shorts. An open box of brown-sugar Pop-Tarts sits on the counter. And beside me, the sink is filled with books—Burroughs, Kerouac, Bukowski, Hemingway, Thoreau, and a bunch of brightly colored Carl Hiaasen paperback mysteries—which makes me smile.

I'm paging through a Hiaasen when Alex comes out of the bathroom. His curls are wet and I watch a drop of water fall onto his bare chest and slide south until it disappears into the waistband of his shorts.

"My library," he says, and I remember I'm holding a book.

It takes him only a couple of steps to reach me. His mouth touches mine and *Stormy Weather* crashes to the cabin floor, my arms sliding up around his neck. I twine my fingers in his hair as he catches the back of my dress in his fists. Kissing him holds the same sweet relief as inhaling after holding a breath too long. I lose track of how long we stand there, our bodies pressed together. You could tell me that the sun went down and rose again the next day, and I would believe it.

Alex's mouth pulls away from mine and wanders down my neck to my collarbone. Heat pools between my thighs and my nerve endings explode in tiny fireworks as his lips brush my skin. His grip on my dress loosens, but only to lift it up over my head. His shorts come off. My bra. His boxers. My underwear. He eases me onto the striped sheets, as cool against my back as his skin is warm against the front of me.

His hand skims down between my legs, and reality gets wrapped around memory. I feel Frank's sour breath against my face and Frank's rough fingers probing where they don't belong. I grab his wrist. "Don't."

"What did I do wrong?" The voice in my ear isn't Frank. It's Alex.

"Just—don't. Please."

Confusion flickers in his eyes, but he doesn't say anything. He moves his hand away, cupping my face and kissing me until the memories melt away. Kissing me until I want him again. It doesn't take long.

"Do you have protection?" Not sure why I'm whispering.

"Oh, shit. Yes. Hang on." Alex scrambles off me and rummages through his duffel, swearing, apologizing, scattering half the contents, and his butt is so white compared with the tan of his skin it makes me laugh. "Found one." He holds up the foil packet. "You know, in my head this goes much smoother."

"You've thought about this?"

"I've been in a boat in the Gulf of Mexico for five days with another dude." He returns to the bed. "I've thought about this a *lot*."

"With me?"

"Yes. With you."

Sex is so different with Alex. On a purely physical level, there's more kissing and less grunting, more touching and less groping. And when it's over I feel as if I'm shining bright enough to light a room.

"I should probably go." Right now I don't feel like I'm trash waiting to be discarded, but I want to leave instead of being asked to go.

Except Alex is tangled around me, his face against

my neck, and he makes no move to let go. “Is there somewhere you need to be?” His voice is sleepy and content.

Greg and Phoebe are probably wondering where I am, and I may have offended my grandmother by walking out of her welcome-home party, but I have no intention of returning. “I guess not.”

“Hungry?”

“Yes.”

“Good.” His lips brush against my neck, making me squirm. “When I get feeling in my legs again we’ll go get food.”

This wanting me to stay—and me not wanting to leave—is new and unexpected. “Yeah, okay.”

Chapter 7

Alex and I don't speak as we walk up Dodecanese toward the parking lot. We've returned to being the total strangers that we are. His curls are matted down from dozing off with damp hair and my dress is wrinkled, and it feels as if everyone we pass can tell what we've been doing. Sex was the easy part. Thinking of things to say afterward is harder. Except I don't feel uncomfortable not talking to Alex. He doesn't make me feel as if it's necessary.

We reach a chalky white pickup truck that's more dented than smooth, and the wheel wells are starting to rust. Alex opens the passenger door for me.

"I wouldn't lean against it," he says, holding it open as I get in the truck. The dark-red vinyl seat is hot, so I wedge my hands beneath my thighs to keep them from burning. "It's been known to fly open."

I shift away from the door as he slams it shut and walks around to the driver's side. He starts the engine and slides his arm along the back of the bench seat. Not exactly putting his arm around me, but not exactly not, either. It occurs to me that he might be lying about the door, but there are tiny points of heat where the tips of his fingers touch my skin and I don't bother caring.

"What are you hungry for?" he asks.

"Anything but dolmades."

Alex laughs. "Greek food is for the tourists. I was thinking maybe pizza?"

"Yes."

As he drives through Tarpon Springs, I check my phone for messages. Greg is not happy I ran off, so I send him a text that I'm getting something to eat and will be home right after. He replies that this is not how grounding works, but I don't respond. Kat's message informs me that I missed the arrival of Nick and Connor at the party, and that I should come back. I don't answer that one, either.

The pizza place is inside a small Italian grocery with two small aisles of pasta, sauces, cookies, sweets, and Italian wines, and a deli counter filled with meats and cheeses. The walls are covered with New York memorabilia—sports team pennants, autographed photos of various celebrities, framed newspaper clippings about 9/11, and a large framed photo of the New York

City skyline at night. Our table is one of only three and it has a candle in the middle, but with the deli counter three-deep with takeaway customers, it's not a romantic candle.

A beefy guy wearing a white apron smeared with dried blood comes out from behind the counter to take our order. "You want the usual?"

"Yeah," Alex says. "And a pitcher?"

The waiter-slash-butcher looks at me with one eyebrow raised. "You got ID?"

Mom taught me how to drive, but I never tested for a license, so I don't have any identification at all. For all practical purposes, I'm nobody. I shake my head. "A Coke is fine."

"How old are you anyway?" Alex asks, after the guy shuffles away.

"Seventeen."

"Really?" His eyebrows hitch up a little. "Huh."

When Matt found out I was only fifteen, he rolled away from me, called me jailbait, and told me to get the hell out. The trailer park where Mom and I were living was about two miles from his apartment, so I walked to the diner where she worked. When she asked what I was doing wandering around town in the middle of the night, I lied and said I couldn't sleep. I'm not sure she believed me. Not when I could still smell his sweat and cologne on my skin and hair.

"I'm not going to tell anyone." I focus on the fork he taps against the tabletop. "It doesn't have to be an issue."

"It's not an issue." He shrugs. "I'm a little surprised is all. You look older."

"How old are you?"

"I'll be twenty-two in April."

"My birthday's in May."

On the wall behind him is a photo of the restaurant owner—I'm guessing, but it seems likely because he appears in other pictures as well—shaking hands with one of the New York Yankees.

"Have you ever been to New York?" I change the subject.

Alex picks up and puts down the glass shaker of grated parmesan cheese and shakes his head. He's got one curl that's all askew and I tuck my fingers into my palm to keep from reaching out to smooth it down. "I've never really been anywhere but here."

"Where would you go if you could go anywhere?"

"Australia, Polynesia, Central America, the Caribbean, the Galapagos—" He ticks them off on his fingers easily, as if this is a list he's had plenty of time to think about. "Hell, I'll even go to the Keys if it means diving that doesn't involve me cutting sponges off the ocean floor."

"That's what you do?"

The butcher returns with a bottle of beer and a can of soda. "Pizza'll be ready soon."

"It's a family business," Alex says. "It used to be me and my dad, but my mom got sick, so now it's just me. I don't mind doing it, but—never mind. Not important. Why'd you come back?"

"I didn't have a choice."

"Why?"

"My mom got sick, too." I'm skirting the truth, but this is as close as I want to come with a guy I barely know. "So I had to come live with my dad."

Frankly, I'm surprised he hasn't put the pieces together. How many teenage girls named Callie come home to Tarpon Springs to live with their dads after living everywhere with their sick moms? Especially when Kat claims I am a local legend. But if Alex has figured it out, nothing in his face gives it away. He leans back on his chair. "Tarpon Springs isn't a bad place."

I laugh. "Yeah, I can tell how much you love it."

The corner of his mouth tilts and my stomach does an elevator drop. "I still plan to escape someday," he says. "But definitely not today."

Alex takes me to the sponge docks when we're finished with our pizza. He offers to drive me home, but I don't want Greg to see me getting out of some strange guy's truck. Not when he's already upset with me.

"Thanks for the pizza," I say, as Alex opens the sticky door for me, its hinges groaning. I'm pretty sure he was lying about it flying open unexpectedly.

"Do you want the leftovers?"

I'd never heard of putting carrots or asparagus or *capicola*—I didn't even know what kind of meat that is—on pizza, but it was the best thing I've ever tasted, so it's a tempting offer. Except Greg would definitely wonder how I managed to walk to a pizza place that far from Georgia's house. "You keep them," I say.

"I was hoping you'd say that." He grins and my whole body goes weak.

I'm not sure what to say next. *Thank you for sleeping with me and not treating me like a whore? Thank you for not being ashamed to go somewhere with me in public? Thank you for kissing me as if you meant it?* I mean, I had sex with a stranger, followed by pizza. I don't think there are etiquette rules for that.

"I, um—I'd better go."

"Are you sure you don't want me to drive you?"

"I'm sure," I say. "But thanks."

For a moment, I feel like I'm a character in a book,

the girl hoping the boy will tell her he'll call. Except I'm not sure I want Alex to say it because I don't want it to be a lie. Turns out I have nothing to worry about because he doesn't. Instead he says, "I guess I'll see you around."

As I walk home, I'm not sure what to make of the afternoon. Maybe Kat is right about Alex. Maybe sex and pizza is his standard operating procedure. Maybe he tells every girl he'll see her around. Maybe he's not so different from Danny after all. And maybe that means that I'm not so different, either. I fell for it.

Greg and Phoebe are sitting on the front-porch swing as I come through the gate. I climb the steps and Phoebe stands, giving Greg's shoulder a gentle squeeze before she goes into the house. She offers me a grim smile, which makes me think maybe this is going to be serious.

"Have a seat," Greg says.

I sit beside him on the swing.

"Listen," he says. "I understand that after living with your mom you're used to having a lot of freedom, but—"

"What if I'm like her?"

He holds up a hand and frustration shadows his face. "Let me finish."

"No, Greg, this is important," I say. "What if the reason I take off the way I do is because I have this borderline personality thing, too?"

"Running away when you're angry or scared isn't

really symptomatic of borderline, Callie," he says. "If anything, it's a learned behavior. You run away because that's what Veronica always did."

"But how can you be sure I don't have it?"

"I can't," he says. "But by the time your mom was your age, she was already on medication because she was experiencing mood swings that would make her do—"

"Crazy things?"

He sighs. "Impulsive things."

Having sex with random strangers is not exactly well-thought-out behavior, but under the circumstances I don't think Greg needs to know about this.

"I loved your mom so damn much," he says. "We were only married for three years and I didn't want a divorce. I sure as hell didn't want to start a custody war, but Veronica was convinced I was going to keep you from her. And the thing is . . . if she hadn't taken you when she left, I don't know if she'd have made it alone."

We sit for a moment and a car drives past, the tires bumping on the brick-paved street.

"Do *you* think you have BPD?" he asks.

I consider all the times I was the Greg in my mom's life, listening to her ramble about grand plans of becoming a chef—when she couldn't even cook—and being dragged along when she decided to go to New York City. We slept in the car for the two days we were there and she almost lost me in Times Square when she let go of my hand, distracted by a rare Sonic Youth album in a record-store window. I remember days when she wouldn't get out of bed and I'd eat cereal for every meal. I don't act the way she acts, but I can't shed the fear that the things I do are my own brand of crazy.

"I don't know."

"Do you want to see someone?" he asks. "Even if you're not borderline, which I really don't think you are, it might be good to talk to a professional about—well, about whatever."

And have someone verify it? "No."

"Okay. So. Miss Tzorvas . . . ," he says and I have to remind myself he's talking about *me*. Callista Tzorvas is as new as the names Mom and I made up. Greg says it with a measure of seriousness that makes me think we've returned to the punishment portion of the conversation. "I've spent twelve years worrying about where you were and what was happening to you. Now that you're here, I don't want to keep worrying so much. So I expect you to tell where you're going and when you'll be home, got it?"

I nod. "Yeah."

"I'll give you a free pass for today," he says. "But the original grounding still applies."

I've spent most of my life in one room or another

with only my imagination to keep me company, so I can't explain why the thought of spending the rest of the week in the Airstream with nothing to do bothers me.

"Have you thought any more about the job?" I ask.

"About that—" he says, and I brace myself for bad news. "I talked to Theo today, and he said the job is yours if you want it."

"Really?"

"Yeah, well, you can thank your grandma for that," he says. "She suggested that it doesn't make sense for you to play catch-up in high school when you can get your GED and work for Theo. So you start the day after tomorrow, but only if you sign up for the exam."

I'm overtaken by an urge to hug him, but I can't make my arms do that. Not yet. Instead, I reach over and squeeze his hand. "Thanks, Greg."

He smiles at me in a way that makes me think it's almost good enough.

Chapter 8

The next morning I'm reading about borderline personality disorder on the Internet when I hear a knock at my door. I minimize the website and close the laptop. Kat is standing on the other side of the screen, her hair twisted up in a pair of low knots, and she has half a dozen long necklaces draped around her neck. She's also holding two paper to-go cups of coffee.

"Hey," she says, as I push open the door for her. She steps up into the trailer and hands me the cup without the lip-gloss stain on the rim. "You left the party so suddenly yesterday and when you didn't answer my texts, I got kind of worried. Is everything okay?"

"Yeah."

Her dark eyebrows pull together as she places her cup on the table. "Are you sure? What happened?"

"I heard some women talking about my mom and—I don't know. I had to get out of there."

Kat falls onto my bed, laughing and rolling around as if she's having a seizure, which is not quite the response I expected. I'm not sure what's funny about those women talking about my mom. Maybe this is a joke I don't get. After a few seconds, she leans up on her elbows. "So *that's* why Yiayoúla Georgia went ballistic on Carol and Gloria. And when she was done telling them off, she threw them out!"

"Really?"

"Carol kicked up a fuss about taking her nasty spaghetti salad and Gloria made Yiayoúla Georgia get her Tupperware container out of the dishwasher," she says. "And both of them said they'd never speak to her again, but she was like, *Whatever, bitches.*"

"She *said* that?"

Kat laughs. "Well, no, I embellished a little there. But it was still pretty epic. Your grandma is so cool. I wish mine were more like her. It's hard to believe they're sisters."

"I didn't mean for any of that to happen."

"Please." She waves me off as if it's nothing. "It isn't a proper family party unless someone goes home pissed off. Give it a couple of weeks and it'll be over. Anyway, I'm glad you're okay."

"Thanks," I say. "By the way, Greg is letting me take the job."

Kat flails again and when she sits up, her knots are half-undone and my once-made bed is a mess. "This—is so awesome!"

Still, her excitement is infectious and a kind of happiness bubbles up inside me, and even though I feel guilty about it, I can't stop myself from smiling.

"We need to go shopping. I mean, Theo makes us wear T-shirts from the store when we're at work, but you need shorts and jeans and—" Kat eyes my too-often-worn red top. "You need everything, Callie."

"Phoebe is taking me today."

She tugs at her lip a couple of times. "Okay, you know, Phoebe is awesome and dresses great—for a mom. Seriously, my mother? Wears *mom jeans*. But this is your fashion future we're talking about. You can't entrust it to just anyone, especially not someone who spends her day hanging out with toddlers."

"What does that mean?"

"This is why you need me, Callie," she says. "You're a blank canvas. Let me paint you. Wait—that sounded creepy, didn't it? Trust me, okay?"

"Okay."

Kat jumps to her feet. "Let's go now."

"I'm grounded, remember?"

"Let me handle this."

She leaves the Airstream and returns a few minutes later wearing a lip-glossy grin. She gives me two thumbs up. "It's a go."

"How did you—?"

"I reminded him you've been wearing the same two shirts since you got here," she says. "That because I am your age, I am far more qualified to take you shopping. And if he lets me take you to the mall, I won't charge him the next time I watch the boys. Guilt and free babysitting are *gold*. I did promise to have you back by four, though, so let's get moving."

Leaving Kat in the trailer, I take my towel and a change of clothes into the house for a shower.

". . . I'm just saying I think you should insist she see a therapist," I hear Phoebe say, as I go into the bathroom. She and Greg are in their bedroom. Her voice is kind, but I can hear the insistence in it. "You can't be sure that she hasn't inherited Veronica's problems, and who knows what other sort of psychological damage she might have suffered living the way they did?"

"I know my own daughter." His conviction makes me want to cry.

"But you don't," she says. "Not really. Look, I knew Callie coming back to Tarpon Springs could be a reality, and I'm okay with that. I really am. But I would feel more comfortable about her being around the boys if I knew she wasn't . . ."

I quietly close the door to the bathroom so I don't have to hear what she's going to say next. Even if she doesn't use the actual word, it still hurts.

The warm water from the shower cascades down on my head, washing away both the tears and the happiness I felt earlier. I tilt my face up to feel the spray and wonder—for the smallest of moments—how it would feel to drown. I wouldn't be anyone's problem anymore.

Greg is leaning against the wall beside the door when I come out of the bathroom. "You, um—probably heard—"

"That your crazy daughter can't be trusted with the boys?" I interrupt. "Yeah, I caught that."

"She didn't mean it that way."

"Really? Because that's *exactly* how it sounded."

"She's . . . overwhelmed," he says.

"She's had *years* to prepare," I say, hearing my mother's voice come out of my mouth again. "While my life was ripped right out of its socket and dropped in the middle of a bunch of strangers, so excuse me if I don't care that *Phoebe* is overwhelmed."

My shoulder bangs against him as I push past Greg and go out to the trailer. I don't feel any better for having said what I did. If anything, I feel worse, because

I *do* care. I don't want my presence to make Phoebe feel stressed out. Don't like Greg having to play the peacemaker between his wife and his daughter. Hate that every time I raise my voice, it's as if I'm channeling my mom. But most of all, I hate that Phoebe might be right.

"Let's get out of here." The slap of the screen door matches my mood as I enter the trailer and hurl my wet towel at the sink. It misses and falls to the floor.

"Callie, what's wrong?" Kat asks, following me across the backyard. Her car keys jingle as she hurries to catch up.

"Nothing I want to talk about," I say. "Let's go to the mall and you can do your blank-canvas . . . thing."

"It's not a thing," she says, unlocking her car door. "I want to help you. I want to be your friend."

"Why? So you can tell everyone you know the kidnapped freak?"

"Callie!" Tears pool in her eyes and I wish I could reel the words back into my mouth. I keep saying the most hateful things to her.

We get in the car at the same time and I sit silently, my face burning with shame, as she digs through her purse. She pulls out her wallet, and I can see anger trembling in her fingers as she flips through the little plastic pockets of ID cards and photos.

"This—" She shoves the wallet at me. Beneath the clear plastic is a picture of two little dark-haired girls, wearing identical pink bathing suits and splashing in a small inflatable wading pool. As I look at the photo, I can easily hear the squeals of delight and imagine them eating Popsicles afterward, rivers of red and orange trickling down their baby-fat arms. I don't know if it's an authentic memory or a product of my imagination, but it feels real. "This is you and me when we were four. When we were best friends."

I am slime.

She turns the wallet around and smiles at the picture. "Of course, I don't remember it very well, and when you're four, even the next-door neighbor's dog is your best friend. But I've spent all these years imagining what our friendship would have been like if your mom hadn't taken you. In my head we had sleepovers and took gymnastics lessons and had first dates with twin brothers, which is hilarious because I don't even *know* any twins. And when you came home, I hoped—"

"God, I suck."

Kat inhales a snotty breath, then laughs. "Ew. That was gross," she says, fishing a tissue from her purse. "Not gonna lie, I'm looking forward to doing my blank-canvas *thing*, as you so eloquently put it, but not because I want to be friends with the freak show. I want to be friends with my cousin again. Also, you *don't* suck. So, shut up."

When Kat drops me off a few hours later, I have so many bags that she has to help me carry them all. The whole experience was exhausting—especially trying on dozens of pairs of jeans because Kat was on a mission to find the "perfect" pair—but it's a wondrous feeling to have clothes and shoes and books that belong to me. That no one else has worn—or read. She picked out jewelry for me, suggested decorations for the Airstream, and insisted on makeup, although I don't usually wear much. And even though Kat assures me that all these things are a fraction of what she owns, it's more than I could ever imagine.

"I can't get over your hair," she says, as I fold a pair of denim shorts into a drawer. She's repeated it about a million times since I had my hair cut earlier at the mall, but now the tangles, brassy ends, and dreadlocked bits are gone, and the curls are full and soft. It doesn't even feel like my hair. "It looks amazing. I'm so jealous."

"Thanks. For—everything," I say. "And I'm sorry about what I said earlier."

"Ooh! That reminds me." Kat ignores my apology and rummages through the pile of bags for the small one she said was a surprise. Inside is a box of tiny white star-shaped Christmas lights. "Every girl needs a string of these for her room," she says. "Not only are they beautiful, but when you have fairy lights, you're never completely in the dark."

The lump in my throat won't let me speak, but she doesn't wait for a reply. Instead she hands me one end of the string. "Let's hang them now."

We loop them around the curtain rod on the window beside my bed. It takes only a minute and when we finish, Kat plugs her end into the outlet. With daylight still streaming in through the window, the stars are pale yellow and weak.

"Well, okay, they don't seem very special at the moment," she says. "But later? They'll be spectacular."

Chapter 9

Following my ugly outburst in the hallway earlier, I'm dreading dinner. Although I'm not certain I owe Greg and Phoebe an apology for my feelings, I should probably apologize for being such a bitch. I don't want to face them, though, so I drag my feet until the last minute, looking at my new shirts, paging through books I can't wait to read, and smelling the new pomegranate-scented body wash that came from the store selling nothing but lotions and soaps.

There is no one in the kitchen when I go inside, but it's still warm from the oven and I hear voices in the dining room. I round the corner, going through the doorway, and stop abruptly.

Alex Kosta is sitting at the dining-room table.

He looks up and his eyes go wide for a split second,

then he levels that devastating grin at me and my whole body feels as if it's about to spontaneously combust, leaving me a pile of embarrassed ash on the carpet. What the hell is he doing here?

"Hey, Callie." Greg's tone is pleasant, as if this morning never happened. Right now, though, I think I'd prefer an uncomfortably silent meal with him, over one with the last person to see me naked. "I didn't get a chance to tell you this morning that we'd be having company for dinner. This is Phoebe's brother, Alex."

Oh my God. Her *brother*? Has he known all along?

Alex stands politely as I come around the table to the empty place beside him. Although his eyes follow me the whole time, his expression is inscrutable. It's only his neck below his curls—flushed pink the way my face must surely be—that gives away his embarrassment at the awkwardness of this moment.

"Nice to meet you," he says, as I sit down, and I'm torn between wanting to punch him in the mouth, and wanting to drag him under the table and kiss his face off. Instead, I mumble a hello and turn spreading my napkin on my lap into an Olympic event.

"Callie, your hair looks gorgeous," Phoebe says, breaking bits of roasted chicken into a small bowl of mashed potatoes and gravy for Joe.

"You look like Super Mario," Tucker says.

Alex laughs as he takes a dinner roll and hands me the basket. "Do you mean Princess Peach, buddy?"

Tucker nods. "Yeah, only Callie's hair is not yellow and she doesn't wear a pink dress that's long."

Joe giggles and points a tiny finger at me. "Peach."

"I'd take that as a compliment," Greg says. "Tuck doesn't have a broad basis for comparison and Peach *is* pretty cute, as far as video-game girls go. And if Joe agrees? It's some seriously good hair."

All of them are looking at me and it makes me want to hide. "Thanks."

"Kat didn't go crazy with my credit card today, did she?" Greg asks.

I think about all those bags. It never occurred to me that she was paying for everything with his money, but of course, it makes sense. How else would she have been able to afford it all? "I, um—"

"I'm kidding, Callie," he says. "Did you get everything you needed?"

"I think so."

The room goes quiet for a moment, the only sound the clinking of silverware against plates.

"Alex," Phoebe says, "Callie's going to start working for Theo tomorrow at the shop. Maybe after dinner you could give her a crash course in sponges, so when the tourists ask questions, she'll be able to answer."

"Yeah, sure," he says. "No problem."

Another silence falls, broken only when Joe points and calls me Peach again. Everyone chuckles nervously and fails to make eye contact. This is a million times worse than the dinner I'd imagined.

"So, Alex, what happened to your face?" Phoebe asks.

It's only then I notice a deep pink splotch—a bruise so new it hasn't had the chance to turn black and blue yet—on his cheekbone.

"Bumped into a fist," he says. "But you should see the other guy." He laughs it off, but his eyes are grim. He's hiding something, but I don't think Phoebe notices because her mouth is too occupied with frowning.

"You know Mom would not approve of this behavior," she says. "You should be in college, not wasting your life and getting in bar fights."

"Well, I'm not." The muscles in his left arm flex and he puts down his silverware. "Did you invite me over to nag me again? Because I've got some leftover pizza back on the boat."

I focus on buttering my dinner roll.

"I just worry about you," she says.

"Don't," Alex says. "I'm fine."

"Mom asked about you today. She misses you."

"Phoebs—" There's a warning in his tone and he looks as if he's ready to push away from the table.

"I'm sorry," Phoebe says quickly. "I'm sorry. Don't go. Please."

Alex doesn't leave, but the rest of the meal seems to stretch into forever. The tension zig-zags across the table, connecting us all like an invisible spiderweb. When we've finished eating and there's no more excuse not to talk, I stand and start gathering the plates. "I'll do the dishes."

"Thank you, Callie." Phoebe removes Joe from his high chair. "Come on, little man, time for a bath."

As I fill the kitchen sink with soapy water, I hear Greg tell Tucker that it's his bath time, too.

"Can Uncle Alex read me a bedtime story?"

Alex's response is muted, but from the delighted sound Tucker makes, I can guess the answer. A few moments later, Alex comes into the kitchen with the remaining plates. "So that was all kinds of awkward, huh?"

I scrub at a bit of food stuck to one of the plates but don't look at him. "Did you know?"

"No." He adds the plates to the water, then takes a drying towel from one of the drawers. He stands beside me and I can feel the warmth from his body spanning the space between us. "But when Phoebe asked me over for dinner to meet Greg's daughter, Callie, I finally put it all together."

I rinse a bowl and shove it at him. "You really expect me to believe that?"

"Yeah, I do." The bowl drips water onto the floor as he looks at me. "I've been sponging full-time since I was seventeen, and for the past year I've been working two jobs. I don't even have time for my *own* life, let alone time to pay attention to all the little details of Greg's life."

I wonder if I should be insulted that he considers me a little detail, but I decide I'm kind of flattered that he's the only person for whom my coming back here is not a big deal. I hand him the next plate. "Why did you lie to Phoebe about your face?"

His eyebrows pull together. "What makes you think I was lying?"

"I've spent a lifetime keeping secrets," I say. "I know a lie when I hear one."

Alex puts the plate on the counter and hooks his finger through a belt loop on my new jeans, pulling me against him. Someone could walk into the room at any minute, but when his mouth finds mine, caring isn't even a consideration. He lifts me onto the counter, wedging himself between my knees.

"We should not be doing this," I whisper, sinking my fingers into his curls.

"No, we shouldn't." He slides his hands up my thighs

to my hips, his thumbs grazing the bare skin at the top of my jeans, under the hem of my shirt. "We should get out of here."

My mouth is about to form the word "yes," when the sound of giggling boys drifts out from the bathroom. Alex pulls away from me, blinking as if he's surfaced from sleep. He runs his fingers through his hair, making that one curl spring out in a random direction. "Wow."

I reach up and put it in place. "You forgot about story time, didn't you, *Uncle Alex*?"

"Completely." He slides me down from the countertop, holding me against him. He draws his thumb across my lower lip as if he's thinking about kissing me again. I hold my breath, waiting to see if he does. "We could still make a break for it," he says.

"We could—"

Alex releases me and bends to pick up the towel he dropped. There are damp handprints—my handprints—on the back of his T-shirt, and I feel an inexplicable surge of possessiveness, as if I've marked him as mine. Which is ridiculous, because soon the prints will be dry and no one will ever know. I return to the task of washing the dishes and, except for still being able to feel the imprint of his lips on mine, it's as if we weren't just making out.

"—only I'm grounded from the last time we, um—"

He laughs. "Already?"

Tucker shuffles into the kitchen a short time later wearing space-themed footed pajamas and carrying a book about Spider-Man. Alex scrubs a hand over his face and only I hear the groan.

"Spider-Man, again?" He swings Tucker up onto his shoulders. "Come on, buddy, let's go pick out something we haven't read yet."

I finish up the dishes by myself and stand alone in the kitchen. I consider joining Greg and Phoebe in the living room, where I can hear them discussing which on-demand movie they should watch. I don't want to sit through any more awkward silences. And when I think about Alex, reading bedtime stories to Tucker and Joe, I'm not sure I can maintain the charade of pretending we've never met. So I slip out the back door.

The fairy lights glow strong and white now that it's dark outside. It's odd that such a small thing can make such a big difference, but Kat was right—the lights make everything seem softer, prettier, and they keep the darkness at bay. I think about reading one of my new books—maybe the Hiaasen novel I bought so I can understand why Alex keeps five of them in his sink—but I don't. I think about taking my guitar out of its case, where it's been since I arrived in Tarpon Springs—but I don't do that, either. I strip down to my bra and underwear—new ones that didn't come in a sack with seven other pairs—and lie on my bed, looking up at the string of electric lights and remembering the feel of his hands on my skin. I trace the edge of my lower lip with my fingertip, but it's not the same as kissing.

I'm not sure what time it is when I hear a soft knock on my door, but all the lights in the house are off so the whole family is probably asleep for the night. I don't bother getting dressed because I'm almost certain I know who it is.

I let him in.

"Jesus, Callie." Alex stares at me and there's something in his eyes I can't name. It makes me nervous and live-wire exposed, and I reach for him to make him stop looking at me that way. As his arms come around me, he whispers in my ear, "You are so damn beautiful."

My face flushes, but in the glow of the fairy lights I don't think he can tell. "You don't have to say that."

"I know."

My new bra has a clasp in the front instead of the back, but as he kisses me, Alex seems to already know this. He slides the bra off and lets it drop to the floor, then does the same with my underwear. This is not the same as last time when our clothes were being shed quickly, and at the same time. He's still wearing jeans and a T-shirt, and it makes me uncomfortable. I yank the end of the sheet around me, holding it closed over my nakedness. "Take off your clothes."

He laughs a little, then his face goes serious when he sees my hand shaking. "Callie? What's wrong?"

"I would feel better if you took off your clothes."

He probably thinks I'm a complete freak, but I can't tell him that Frank would remove my pajamas and sometimes open his pants to rub himself, but he never, ever took off his clothes. I wouldn't blame Alex if he left right now and never returned. Except he tilts his head and looks at me as if I'm a puzzle he's trying to solve—and then he takes off his clothes.

We have to start all over from the beginning, and I'm not sure why he even bothers when he could easily go find someone less damaged to have sex with him, but Alex kisses me and slides his fingers through my hair in a way that makes me feel as beautiful as he claims I am, until I release my grip on the sheet.

"You wanna get ice cream?" he asks later, as I lie with my head on his chest. My eyes don't want to stay open, so I close them and listen to the thump of his heartbeat as it returns to its normal pace beneath my ear. His fingers move through my hair, making me shiver.

"Now?"

"Why not?"

"What if Greg finds out?"

"He's asleep and we'll be quiet."

Now that I'm thinking about ice cream, I can't unthink it. "Let's go."

Alex uses the bathroom to clean up while I put on my clothes. When we're dressed, we sneak out of the trailer and hug the dark perimeter of the yard, crouching like spies—and trying not to laugh—until we're away from the house.

"My truck is up on Grand," he says. "I parked up there earlier, then doubled back on foot."

"Resourceful."

"I have my moments."

We reach the truck and he drives down Pinellas to the Sparta gas station. Alex goes inside first and leads me to a low white freezer chest filled with ice-cream treats, like Klondike bars, ice-cream sandwiches, and rocket pops.

My favorite is the ice-cream sandwich. Mom and I get them sometimes as a special treat, and she was the one who taught me that the best way to eat them is to lick away the ice cream until it's only a thin layer inside the chocolate sandwich.

"What are you going to have?" Cold air blasts out as

Alex opens the door and selects a Drumstick ice-cream cone. My hand reaches for the ice-cream sandwich, but it occurs to me that I don't have to choose it because Mom and I always do. I can get whatever I want. Instead I take a Drumstick.

We get to the checkout counter when I change my mind. "Wait."

I go back for the ice-cream sandwich.

As we sit on the dropped tailgate of Alex's truck under a streetlight in the gas-station parking lot, he licks the peanut bits off his Drumstick, oblivious to the inner turmoil I'm suffering over ice cream. And now that the frozen sandwich is in my hand, paid for and unwrapped, I don't want it. Tears prickle my eyes, and I hate that I'm making something as simple as choosing ice cream more complicated than it needs to be. And I hate that I seem to cry all the time. I'm so tired of crying.

"I'll be right back." I hop down from the tailgate, go inside the store, and buy a Drumstick. I throw the ice-cream sandwich away.

Alex doesn't comment on my weird ice-cream-buying habit as I hoist myself onto the tailgate. "Ready for your sponge identification lesson?"

"Really?"

He leans back and slides a blue milk crate toward us. Inside are sponges.

“This one is the easiest,” he says, pulling out one with a stem and about a dozen long knobby-knuckled fingers. “It’s the finger sponge. It’s not used for anything except decoration, and tourists love it.”

The next one resembles a bowl, with a hollowed-out center and a flat bottom.

“Grass sponge,” he says. “The small sizes are used for painting and, I guess, for putting on makeup, but the pot-shaped ones are really popular in the store. People put plants in them.”

He drops it into the crate and draws out another. “Wire sponges are mostly used for insulation, so you don’t really have to think about this one because we sell these to industrial customers.”

He tosses that one over his shoulder and brings out two more that look similar to each other.

“Wool and yellow sponges are fairly interchangeable, but the wool is softer. Wool sponges are for personal stuff, like taking a bath or shower, and yellow sponges are the household ones for washing dishes or whatever. You can use grass sponges for all that stuff, too, but tourists want to think they’re getting something special so we make the distinction.”

“Finger, wool, grass, wire, and yellow,” I repeat.

“Yep.” Alex pops the last bit of Drumstick in his mouth and brushes his fingers on his jeans. “And if you forget, wing it. Tourists are going to believe anything you say because you're beautiful and you're Greek. So you can tell them a grass sponge is a wool sponge and they won't know the difference."

He hands me the wool sponge. "For you."

"I've smelled these things on your boat." I crinkle my nose and hand it back. "I'm not sure I want that thing touching me in the shower."

Alex laughs and swaps it for the finger sponge. He presents it to me like a bouquet of flowers, pulling it out from behind his back with a flourish. "Sponges are better than flowers," he says, as if he's read my mind, "because they'll never die. They're already dead."

I take the sponge. It's quite pretty, really—like a winter tree bowing to the breeze—and it's the closest thing I've ever come to getting flowers from a boy. Or any gift at all. Still, I laugh it away, so he can't see that it means something. "Thanks."

"There's more where that came from." He gives me an exaggerated wink. "Of course, I'd have to dive down and harvest them, so—just hang on to that one, okay?"

"Is sponging really that bad?"

"Not really." He leans on his hands and looks up at the sky. It's kind of hard to see with the lights of the gas station, but the moon has expanded since the last time I paid attention to it and it's peeking around the edge of the Sparta sign. "I've always loved it. I mean, being underwater is—I don't think I can even explain it in a way that will make sense. I'm a lot more comfortable in the water than I am on dry land. But my crewmate Jeff doesn't dive. He handles everything on deck, which is cool, but I *never* have the option of not going down. I can't be tired. I can't be sick."

"What if you *are* sick?"

"No sponges, no money," he says, glancing at his watch, a wide brown strap lashed around his wrist. "So unless I can't breathe, I go. And speaking of going . . . we should probably head home."

I don't want to go yet, but we're well into tomorrow and I start work in only a handful of hours. "Yeah."

Alex parks the truck down the street from Greg's house and lets me out on the driver's side so he won't have to slam the passenger door. "I'd walk you home." He keeps his voice low. "But under the circumstances—"

"It's okay." I nod. "Thanks for—"

He cuts me off with a kiss that makes my toes curl under and my heart feel as if it's going to climb right out of my chest and throw itself at his feet. It's an entirely new feeling.

"I, um—" he says, getting back into the truck. "See you later."

I stand there for—I don't know—maybe a minute,

wondering what is happening between Alex Kosta and me. Just when it feels as if this might be something more than nothing, he pulls away. He doesn't make me feel as if I'm just another piece of ass, but maybe he's just better at this game than Danny or Matt or—Adam. I remember now that the first guy's name was Adam and he played guitar in a park, busking for change. He charmed me with a little song he made up on the spot with my name in it, and at thirteen I lost my virginity to him in his van.

It's a distinct possibility that I am a terrible judge of character.

I sneak over the fence, being careful not to trample the flowers, and press myself into the shadows until I'm inside the Airstream. I place the finger sponge on the little shelf above my bed and crawl in, not bothering to even take off my clothes. Alex's scent lingers on my pillow, and I fall asleep with the ghost of his fingers moving through my hair.

Chapter 10

Eight o'clock arrives much too quickly. I jolt upright when my alarm goes off and squint at the numbers, convinced they must be wrong. But it is official—the four hours of sleep I've had are all I'm going to get. My insides vibrate with tiredness as I drag myself out of bed, gather my bathroom supplies, and go into the house.

Greg, Phoebe, and the boys have gone to the early service at the Greek Orthodox church, so the house is empty. On the drive to Tarpon Springs from the airport, Greg told me I was welcome to attend church with them, but I have no interest in God. Especially when it seems he's never really had any interest in me.

When I'm washed, dried, dressed, and caffeinated, I walk down to the shop. As I pass Alex's boat, I wonder if he fell asleep thinking of me the way I thought of him. But mostly I wonder if he's lucky enough to still be sleeping. The shop is already open when I get there and Theo is counting money into the cash register.

He looks up and smiles. "Hey, Callie, I'm Theo. Pick out a shirt." He gestures at a tiered wooden display filled with T-shirts in a variety of colors and styles. All of them have *Tarpon Sponge Supply Co.* printed on them. "The first one is on me. If you want more, which you probably will, you'll get the 50 percent employee discount. Same goes with jewelry. It's always good if you wear stuff from here, because if the customers see how good it looks on you, they'll want to buy it."

"Okay."

I choose a bright-turquoise T-shirt with a red scuba diver swimming across the front.

"Changing room's behind that curtain." He closes the cash drawer. "And when you're done, I'll show you around."

It takes only about an hour to learn all the ins and outs of the shop. We sell T-shirts and sponges, along with hemp and leather jewelry, hippie-style dresses, sunglasses, and handmade goat-milk soaps. My job is to help customers find whatever they need and to ring them up after they've found it. I also sell tickets for the sponge-diving tour boat docked beside the building.

Simple stuff. Theo tells me that if I do a good job, he'll let me open and close the shop and make the bank deposits. Those sound like extra responsibilities rather than rewards, but I don't point that out.

"Do you know anything about web design?" he asks.

"No."

He drops a book about designing websites on the counter beside me. "I'll pay you extra if you can figure out how to get our website up and running."

I have no idea how I'm going to accomplish this, but extra money is extra money. "Okay."

"When Kat gets here, I want the two of you to go out on the eleven o'clock boat," he says. "I don't expect you to be an expert on sponges and sponge diving, but it doesn't hurt to have a working knowledge for when customers ask questions."

A couple enter the store with their preteen daughter in tow.

"Hey, folks," Theo greets, stepping out from behind the counter. "How are you today?" He's so at ease with strangers. I hope he doesn't expect me to be able to do that.

From my post at the cash register, I watch the mother wander slowly along the baskets of sponges, pausing occasionally to pick one up and squeeze it. The daughter makes a beeline to the T-shirts and unfolds six different styles before deciding she doesn't want any of them. Leaving the shirts in a jumbled pile, she heads for the spinning rack of jewelry. Her hand freezes on the display and her mouth drops open, her eyes pointed at the open doorway.

I turn my head to see what she sees.

Alex stands in the opening looking as if he's just stepped off the boat from Greece. He wears an ethnic-looking tunic-style shirt with an intricate flower design embroidered along the neck and a pair of loose-fitting white pants, and his curls are perfectly messy. On anyone else this look would be trying too hard, a silly costume, but on him—I have to check my own mouth to make sure it's closed. He casts his beautiful smile at the girl, who goes as pink as her tank top.

"Here's our diver now." Theo drops an arm around Alex's shoulders before he has a chance to smile at me. If he was going to smile at me at all. "Alexandros is second-generation Greek and has been sponging since he was twelve. He'll be on the eleven o'clock tour boat. If you haven't gotten your tickets yet, Callista"—Theo says my name with an accent that makes me seem more exotic than I am—"still has a few available."

The couple debate quietly for a minute and then come up to the register to buy the tickets, while their daughter steals glances at Alex in the mirror as she pretends to try on necklaces. Judging by her expression, I think we're both disappointed when he walks out.

After the tourists are gone, Theo says he needs to run an errand.

"I won't be long," he says. "Think you can handle it?"

"I'll be fine."

"If you get robbed—"

"Really? What are the odds?"

He laughs. "Good point. Be back soon."

I'm folding the mess the girl left behind on the T-shirt display when Alex returns. He comes up beside me. "Hey," he says. "When will your grounding be over?"

"Next weekend, I think."

"I was thinking—"

"Callie!" Kat blows into the store like a breeze and whisks me away from Alex as if he's not even there, leaving me to wonder what he was going to say. *What was he thinking?*

She's wearing a simple navy-blue dress that skims her knees and is ultraconservative compared to the skinny jeans and short shorts she usually wears, and her makeup is lighter than normal, too.

"Ugh, I know," she says, pulling me toward the dressing room. "My mom will not let me wear anything even remotely cute to church. Must. Change. Immediately."

I glance over my shoulder at Alex, who gives me a two-fingered wave and leaves.

"What did he want?" Kat asks, from the other side of the closed curtain.

"Nothing," I say. "He was just saying hi."

She snorts, and I wonder if there is something in their common history that makes her hate him—beyond her perception that he's a man whore, I mean. Why does she care? But I don't ask. Not here.

Kat emerges a couple minutes later wearing a pale-yellow Tarpon Sponge Supply Co. T-shirt, denim shorts, and leather sandals. Her lips are slicked with her signature rosy gloss and her lashes spiked with mascara, making her the girl I recognize.

"Good shirt choice." As she selects a shell necklace from the jewelry rack and fastens it around her neck, I notice she's wearing a black cord around her wrist with an evil eye bead knotted in the middle. "That color looks amazing with your skin tone."

"Where did you get that bracelet?"

"Oh, you can buy evil eye bracelets everywhere around here," she says. "Mine was one of those stretchy, elastic kinds with beads all the way around, but I wore it so much the band disintegrated. I saved one of the beads and threaded it on a cord. If you want one, you can get one right across the street."

I reach into my pocket and pull out my matching bead. "I've had it as long as I can remember, but I don't know where it came from."

"We got them from Greg," Kat says. "I don't really remember it either because we were little, but apparently he brought us down here one day and we begged for them until we broke him down."

"That's it?" Most of my life I've thought this stupid bead actually meant something. I can't believe it was just a trinket to pacify a pair of demanding four-year-olds.

She laughs. "They're not magic or anything. It's just an Old World superstition. But how cool is it that we both still have them?" Kat plucks mine from my palm. "I'll string it for you. Then we'll match again."

It feels strange letting it go, but I don't take it back. "Theo says we're supposed to go on the eleven o'clock tour. He wants me to familiarize myself with sponging."

Kat rolls her eyes and fishes her cell phone from the pocket of her shorts. "Wonderful." She texts someone as she talks. "We'll have front-row seats for the Alex Kosta show."

A trio of older women come into the store to buy tickets for the tour, followed by a group of German high school students with a couple of adult chaperones. While I ring up the tickets and some T-shirts for the

Germans, Kat tries to sell a chunky bar of honey-almond soap to the older ladies.

"It's magic. I swear," I hear her say, with the same outgoing charm Theo uses. "I might look seventeen, but really? I'm thirty-five."

One woman nudges her friend and says, "If this soap could make me look seventeen again, I'd go after that Greek boy outside. He's a hunk." As the trio giggle, Kat turns toward me and makes a face as if she's gagging. She also makes the sale.

Theo returns right before the tour, and Kat and I head outside to wait for the boat to board. Alex is getting his picture taken with his arm around the woman who called him a hunk, which makes Kat groan. "God, he's so annoying."

Her cell phone buzzes. She looks at the screen and smiles. "I hope you don't mind, but I invited Nick and Connor to go with us. I figured if we had company, it would be less lame."

I really don't want to see Connor, but it's too late. I spot his floppy hair above the crowd of German teens as he and Nick make their way toward us.

"Hello there, Kit Kat." Nick greets her with a kiss, while Connor hangs back. He offers me a tentative smile and I counter with one of my own, but neither of us speak.

A couple of men move a boarding ramp up alongside the boat, which is a replica of the original boats from when they first started diving for sponges in Tarpon Springs. Or at least that's what it says in the brochures we keep on the desk in the shop. The boat is lined with benches for passengers and the deck is covered by a canvas canopy for shade. Alex stands in the middle, his casual Greek outfit replaced by an old-fashioned one-piece dive suit with a heavy brass collar and weighted shoes strapped to his feet. Kat chooses a stretch of bench for us near the stern of the boat—as far away from Alex as we can be—and Connor sits beside me.

All around us, tourists are snapping photos with their cameras and phones of the Anclote River, of the sponge docks from the boat, and of Alex. It's so odd that he's a tourist attraction, but he is—and he makes the most of it, flashing his knee-weakening grin at every female on the boat, posing for pictures, and answering questions even though the tour hasn't even started yet. He leans in to listen as if their questions are special and intimate, and the stupidity of my thinking I might be something more makes my face hot.

"About the party—" Connor interrupts my embarrassment.

"I don't want to talk about it." I keep my voice low. "I'd rather forget it ever happened."

"Oh, um—okay."

Alex glances up from talking to a little boy, taking in the sight of me sitting beside Connor. I don't think he heard me, but he looks away before I can read the expression in his eyes.

"So, how's the new job going?" Connor asks.

"The first two hours have been good," I say. "But I might need the rest of the day to know for sure."

I realize I'm being rude to him at the same time that Kat elbows me. I start to apologize, but the captain cuts me off, welcoming everyone to the boat. He begins his practiced spiel about the origins of sponge diving and how experienced Greek divers were brought from the Dodecanese Islands to Tarpon Springs more than a century ago, after sponges were discovered on the floor of the Gulf. As the boat motors down the river, he describes the different types of sponges, handing out samples of each variety for the tourists to examine. Alex and I make eye contact, and the corner of his mouth twitches in a tiny grin. I drop my head, letting my hair fall forward, hiding my smile from Connor and Kat.

When we reach a bend in the river, the captain puts the boat in neutral and another old man wearing a Greek fisherman's cap helps Alex put on the bell-shaped windowed helmet, locking it to the collar around his neck with large brass wing nuts. To the back of the helmet, he attaches a hose connected to an air compressor. Like an astronaut walking on the moon, Alex takes heavy steps to the bow of the boat. Armed with a small rake-like tool and a mesh bag, he descends a wooden ladder into the water and floats for a moment as the captain explains that he has to release the air in the suit to sink to the bottom.

All the tourists stand and move to one side of the boat so they can watch. Their camera shutters click and one guy is even videotaping as Alex waves for the cameras, then slowly disappears below the surface. The water is murky, so we can't see him, but the captain tells us Alex is walking along the bottom of the river.

"This is totally fake," Kat whispers. "Sponges don't even grow in the river, so the ones he brings up have already been harvested."

Right after she says it, the captain repeats the same fact to everyone, adding that real sponges grow too far offshore for a proper tour, and that the old-fashioned suit has been retired in favor of wetsuits and dive masks. Still, the passengers cheer when Alex comes up with a preharvested sponge at the end of his rake. He puts it in the mesh bag, then makes his way back to the boat. The old man with the Greek hat helps him on board the boat and immediately removes the helmet. Alex wasn't in the water very long, but his curls are damp with sweat.

The captain turns the boat back in the direction of the sponge docks and Alex is swallowed up by a crowd of people who want to take his picture and get his autograph.

"So, Callie," Kat says. "Since you're grounded, how about if Nick, Connor, and I come over and watch movies at your place? Nick has a portable DVD player we can hook to your little TV."

"I'll have to check with Greg."

"Text him," she urges.

I take out my phone and type: *Kat wants to come over tonight with Nick and Connor to watch movies. Please say no.* I feel guilty, but I'm not interested in spending my evening with Kat trying to fix me up with Connor. A moment later, Greg replies: *Maybe next weekend. Kat has school tomorrow.*

I turn the screen in her direction and she groans. "Gah! It's as if he's in league with my mom. You're so lucky you don't have to go to school."

The boat returns to the dock and we're the first ones off. As Kat kisses Nick good-bye, Connor touches my arm.

"I know things are weird," he says. "But do you think maybe we could go out sometime . . . on a date?"

My brain says "no" and the word is there in my mouth, waiting to be set free, but his eyes are so hopeful and I don't want to be rude to him again. "I'll think about it," I say. He gives me a wide smile and I wish I'd just said no. "I've got to get back to work."

"So how'd it go?" Theo asks, as I come into the store.

I give him a thumbs-up. "Wool, grass, yellow, wire, and finger."

"You're a champ," he says.

I buy hummus and a Coke from the restaurant next door and take my lunch break on my favorite bench, sitting on the back the way my mom used to do it when we waited for the school bus. Alex walks over and climbs up beside me. I offer him a torn-off piece of pita, which he dredges through the hummus.

"Thanks," he says.

"Sure," I say. "Your sponge-dive thing is impressive."

He shrugs. "It's money. How are you liking the shop so far?"

"It's money."

Alex laughs. "What would you do if you could do anything?"

No one has ever asked me that question before. "I don't know if I'm good at anything," I say. "When I was little I wanted to work in a library."

I expect him to laugh, because being a librarian is

not the most glamorous job I could have named, but he doesn't. "I want to get my dive master certification and go—"

"To Australia, Central America, the Galapagos, Polynesia, the Caribbean, and maybe even the Florida Keys." I tick them off on my fingers the way he did and the corner of his mouth tilts up. "You should," I say. "You should go everywhere you want to go."

"Someday." He stands up and aims his thumb over his shoulder at his boat. "But right now, I'm gonna go grab a quick nap. Wanna join me?"

"Yes." I'm so tired and, despite watching two more boatloads of tourists fawn over him, Alex is still such a temptation. "But I have to work now."

"It's an open offer," he says, stepping up onto the side of the boat. "If you ever need a place to hide out or take a nap, the combination is the numeric version of my name."

"*L* and *X* are double digits," I say, doing the math in my head.

"I'm sure you'll eventually work it out."

"I already have." I stand and brush the pita crumbs off my shorts, then walk over to the boat. He steps aside and I click the numbers 1-3-5-6 into place on his combination lock. It opens.

"So smart." His lips beside my ear make my nerves

light up, and I can feel his fingers through the fabric of my shirt as he touches my lower back. "Sure you don't want to join me?"

I look through the doorway at his bed and I'm not sure at all. "I, um—I have to go."

"No problem." He drops his hand away and I want it back. "Another time."

When I reach the shop, Kat is straightening the T-shirt display.

"You looked pretty cozy with Alex," she says without looking at me.

"If offering him some hummus is cozy, then okay," I say.

"On his boat?"

"Since you seem to have been watching the whole time, you already know I was on the boat for about twenty seconds." I throw a stray wool sponge in its proper basket and wonder how this is any of her business. "Does this need to be an issue?"

"I'm just looking out for you," she says. "Excuse me if I don't want to see you get hurt."

I could tell her I've been hurt in ways she can't imagine, in ways Alex Kosta couldn't even begin to accomplish. I could also tell her that even in my nonexistent experience when it comes to friendships, I'm pretty sure looking out for someone shouldn't be the same as telling them what to do. But I'm not trying to pick a fight with her, so I keep my mouth shut. When she drives me home at the end of our shift, there's a silent thread of anger connecting us and neither of us does anything to cut it.

Chapter 11

Greg is sitting on the front-porch steps, a plate balanced on his thigh and a sweaty bottle of beer beside him. Through the open door, I can hear Pearl Jam's "Corduroy" on the stereo. Nostalgia overtakes me and being angry with Kat fades to nothingness, replaced by a twisting guilt I'd forgotten to feel and a sadness so sharp it takes my breath away.

I did it again.

I got so caught up in silly drama that I stopped thinking about Mom.

"Hey, Cal," he greets. "How was your first day on the job?"

"It was okay, I guess." I sit down beside him and incline my head toward the house. "I didn't know you were a Pearl Jam fan."

"Not hard-core the way Veronica was, though." There's a wistfulness to his voice, as if maybe we were both thinking about her. When I see him with Phoebe it's easy to forget that he once loved Mom, too.

"She calls me a blasphemous child for not worshipping at the altar of Eddie Vedder."

"There *is* a certain sacrilege to that." He takes a sip of beer. When he sets it down, the wet label slips sideways. "There's an extra burger in the kitchen for you if you're hungry. Phoebe and the boys are visiting her folks."

"You didn't go?"

"Not today." His smile is not strong enough to make it up to his eyes. There's something that needs to be said, and it makes me wonder if he stayed behind so he could say it. Whatever it may be, I don't want to hear it right now. I stand.

"I'm going to go get that burger."

On my way through the living room I pause at the stereo. On the floor is a shoe box filled with CDs, the lid dusty and the tape pulled away as if the box hasn't been opened in a while. I squat down to riffle through them. Nirvana. Soundgarden. Alice in Chains. Hole. The soundtrack of my life with my mother.

The CD changes as I'm building a cheeseburger and the house fills with the melancholy twang of Mazzy

Star's "Fade into You." It was my favorite song when I was small, and whenever I wanted to listen to it, Mom would ruffle my hair and call me her little hippie chick. It was the first song I taught myself to play on my guitar. Every word—every note—rips another hole in my heart and I can't stop the tears that run down my cheeks faster than I can wipe them away.

"Callie?" Greg comes into the kitchen with his empty plate. "What's wrong?"

"I miss her."

He takes a deep breath as he hands me a towel that I use to wipe my face, then blows it out slowly. "Okay, I was going to wait until you had a chance to eat, but . . . I got a call today from Veronica's father. Your mom was extradited this past week, and her parents posted bond Friday."

"Extradited? What does that mean?"

"It means kidnapping in Florida takes priority over stealing a license plate in Illinois," he says. "So she was brought here to face charges, her parents bailed her out of jail, and she's free until her court date."

"Really?" Excitement takes hold of my stomach. "Where is she? When can I see her?"

"They, uh—they wired the money Friday and haven't heard from her since," he says. "I hate to say this, but she's probably already gone."

No. My mom wouldn't be here in Florida and not contact me. She'd find me. Except doubt creeps in as I remember the night she was arrested and the cold chill in her voice when she told me not to tell the sheriff's officer anything. What if she thinks I betrayed her? What if she thinks I had a choice? What if she left me behind?

"I, um—" I push my plate away, wishing Greg had been able to wait to tell me until after I'd eaten. My appetite is gone. "Thanks for telling me."

"If you need anything—"

"Thanks," I say. Except I don't know what I need. Or how to feel.

He nods and pulls a box of aluminum foil from a drawer. "I'll wrap this up in case you get hungry later, okay?"

The sweet, simple gesture makes me feel like crying again. "Thanks."

I walk out to the Airstream, but I don't know what to do with myself. It's early and the afternoon sun is still high enough in the sky to count. Too early to sleep. And too early to sit in my room and drive myself crazy wondering where my mom might be. I change out of my work T-shirt and leave a note for Greg on the trailer door:

I have to run, but not away. Even though this will

probably extend my grounding, I need to move. P.S. Yes, I have my phone.

I tell myself I'm not going to the docks. I'm not going to go looking for Alex. But my feet—or maybe a part of my body slightly higher up than my feet—propel me toward Dodecanese. Visitors are still poking through the gift shops and sitting clustered around tables on restaurant patios as I round the corner from Athens Street.

Alex's boat is gone.

I'm not surprised. Well, maybe a little surprised that he left without telling me. Except Alex is not mine and I'm not his, and he doesn't owe me any explanations. Still, it doesn't prevent a tiny bud of disappointment from breaking the surface of my heart.

As I walk home, I send a text message to Kat: *Movie night is a go . . . if you still want it to be.*

I don't really want company, but I don't want to be alone, either. Thirty minutes later Kat flops down on the couch in the trailer, pulling me down with her. "So glad Greg changed his mind." She leans her head against mine. "Sorry I gave you a hard time about Alex," she whispers. "I forget that just because you haven't lived here doesn't mean you can't see him for what he really is."

I wonder which of us—or if either of us—is seeing Alex for what he really is, but with Nick and Connor huddled over the television as they connect the DVD player, I can't ask. "What are we watching?"

"Only the best movie ever," Nick says.

He sits down on the other side of Kat and she tilts away from me to him, curling up under his arm with her head against his shoulder. Connor stands awkwardly by himself—there's not enough room for all four of us on the couch—before sitting on the floor, leaning against the couch between Kat's legs and mine. His shoulder touches my knee and it sends a warm flutter down my spine. It's not the same as with Alex, but it's still nice.

The best movie ever turns out to be the original *Star Wars* film, the one we were allegedly going to watch the night of the party. I might not be as current on popular culture as other teenagers, but even I've seen it. More than once. The scrolling *A long time ago in a galaxy far, far away* . . . text has barely crawled up the screen before Kat and Nick are making out as if Connor and I aren't there.

I slide to the floor beside Connor. "Do they do this a lot?"

"Yeah, pretty much," he says.

"Did you bring any other movies?"

He shakes his head. "Sorry."

I stand and walk over to the door, motioning

Connor to follow me out to the backyard. "Wait for me at the picnic table, okay?" I say, and he nods. "I'll be right back."

Greg and Phoebe have a variety of board games stashed in their entertainment center. I imagine them having friends over for drinks and a few rounds of Apples to Apples. They seem like the kind of people who would do that. I don't know the rules to most of the games, but at the bottom of the drawer is an old checkerboard and a plastic bag of checkers.

I unfold the board between us and upend the checkers onto the picnic table. Connor smiles. "Prepare to be annihilated," he says.

I claim a black checker and return the smile. "You wish."

We don't talk about what happened at the party. We don't really say much, except to talk a little smack between moves and gloat over successful jumps. At some point during our first game the weirdness evaporates. We still don't have much to say to each other, but it feels as if we've moved past my shirtless debacle.

We're nearly finished with the game and my annihilation—as he'd predicted—is impending when Kat and Nick come out of the trailer. Her braid has come half undone, and her lips are puffy and lip-gloss-less.

"Hey! Why'd you leave?" She sits too close to me,

the way she always does. She's a space invader. It doesn't bother me too much, though.

Connor closes his eyes and makes exaggerating kissing noises through puckered lips, making Kat giggle. I separate the checkers and push the red ones across to his side of the board.

"Another game?" I ask, and he nods.

"Sorry." She crinkles her nose, and she looks so cute and happy that I feel a rush of affection for her. "We got a little carried away. You're, um—you're not mad, are you?"

Kissing Alex in the kitchen when Greg and Phoebe were right down the hall was . . . irresistible. And not because there was a chance we could get caught, but because not kissing him was inconceivable at the time. So, I don't know. I guess I understand that Kat and Nick have an inability to keep their lips off each other. If Alex had been at the docks earlier, I can only imagine what we'd be doing right now. Also, I wonder if I'm supposed to be thinking about Alex when I'm playing checkers with Connor. I file that away to consider another time and nudge Kat with my elbow. "Next time, pick a movie we haven't seen."

Greg comes outside. If he's surprised to see everyone after I asked him to say no, he doesn't mention it. He joins us at the picnic table, asking Kat, Nick, and Connor about their classes and teachers, and reminisces about when he attended Tarpon Springs High. I feel a little left out—and maybe slightly curious about high school—but not enough that I regret my decision not to go.

They stay until it gets too dark to see the checkerboard and Phoebe returns with the kids. Greg gathers up the game while I walk around front with Kat and the boys.

"Thanks for inviting us over." Kat links her arm through mine. "And next time I promise we'll watch the movie."

"Deal."

She throws her arms around me and even though I'm not sure I'll ever get used to the demonstrativeness of this family, I hug her back. "I'll see you at the shop tomorrow after school," she says.

Connor lingers as Kat slides into the passenger's seat of Nick's green sedan. "I was wondering—" Connor runs his hand up into his hair, then pats his bangs down against his forehead. His nervousness is kind of endearing. "Do you want to go to the movies Saturday night? Without Kat and Nick, I mean."

Alex resurfaces in my mind, but I remind myself that if I don't warrant an explanation, neither does he. I'm not sure how I feel about Connor. I guess I like him. Enough, at least, that he would be a good choice for my first real date. Enough to want to say yes.

So I do.

The next two days drag and I spend most of my time perched on a stool behind the cash register, studying the Dummies book between customers. I'm struggling to decipher the language of web design, and my inability to understand it, let alone master it, frustrates me. It doesn't help that we're always busy, but Theo explains we're "in season" and that the flow of tourists won't slow until after Easter.

Wednesday is my day off. I planned to sleep late, but my body has already gotten used to waking up early. As I lie in bed, I look around the Airstream. It's strange how much I've accumulated in such a short time. How easy it is to start sending roots down into my personal soil. A weed of guilt sprouts in my metaphorical garden, making me feel as if I don't deserve to own fairy lights or long silver necklaces or a finger-sponge bouquet. And when did I start thinking about my own mother as a weed?

I throw off the covers, gather my shower supplies, and head to the house.

"Morning," Phoebe says, as I come into the kitchen.

Tucker sits in his booster chair, his mouth stuffed with pancakes. Joe gives me a bashful grin and calls me Peach. I have a feeling this nickname is going to stick.

Phoebe and I haven't spoken much since the day I overheard her worrying about my potential for mental illness, but I don't want to be rude. "Hi."

"If you're interested"—she places a plate of cut-up pancakes in front of Joe—"I brought my bike home from my parents' house. It's old, but it might make getting around a little easier until you get your license."

This feels like a gesture. An apology, maybe? If not, a bicycle is still a useful thing to have, and it's been a very long time since I've had one. "Definitely. Thanks."

She smiles and I wonder if she thinks this makes everything between us good again. Does it? I'm not sure. "I'll have Greg clean it up when he gets home from work."

"I can probably do it," I say. "I kind of want to find a bookstore today."

"There's one downtown," Phoebe says. "It's really nice, but they don't have a huge selection like the big store at the mall. I can drive you there if you can't find what you need in town."

"I'll think about it."

"I'm free all day."

I nod. "Thanks."

"Want some pancakes?" She angles the pan so I can see the golden brown circles. My traitorous stomach rumbles.

"Yeah, okay." I sit down beside Joe, who touches my cheek with sticky fingers. I turn my face and pretend to chomp his hand. His eyes go wide and my heart sinks to my stomach, afraid that I've frightened him. And verified that I can't be trusted around Phoebe's babies. Except, when he realizes his hand is still intact, Joe giggles. Belly giggles. Infectious giggles that make Tucker laugh and his mother smile.

"Again, Peach," Joe says. "Again."

I play the game over and over, until Phoebe brings me a steaming plate of pancakes. "Eat your breakfast, Joe," she says.

"Joe eat," he says. "Peach eat."

We don't talk as we all sit at the table, but Tucker zooms his fork around as if it's an airplane and delivers a running monologue as his pancake plane crashes into his mouth. It's really annoying and I have to bite my tongue to keep from telling him to shut up—but he keeps the silence from being uncomfortable. When I finish eating, I rinse my plate and continue on my way to the bathroom for a shower.

Phoebe's bike is on the front porch. It's a flat-tired blue cruiser style, coated in a layer of sticky dust. After

I wipe it down with some dish soap and the hose, she offers to drive me up to the gas station to put air in the tires.

"You don't have to go through the trouble of getting the boys all loaded up for me," I say. "I can walk."

She puts on her sunglasses and digs through her purse for her keys. "It's no trouble. I'm going to take them to the park."

I put the bike in the SUV while she fastens Tucker and Joe into their car seats. Phoebe drops me off at the Sparta station, and as I pump air into the tires I remember the way Alex's knee touched mine as we sat on the tailgate of his truck in this parking lot. How one little contact point could conduct so much heat. I wonder if he's thinking about me right now and—if he is—does it make him blush the way it does for me?

From the gas station, the bookstore is only a block away. It's a small storefront, tucked between an antique shop and an Irish pub. On the sidewalk outside the bookstore is a sandwich board with a Mark Twain quote chalked on it in blue lettering. I bet they change the quote daily and use different colors of chalk. It looks like that kind of place. I lock the bike to a one-hour-parking sign and go inside. The store has the dusty, papery scent of old books, and right in the middle of the floor is a salmon-pink, *L*-shaped vinyl couch littered with throw pillows sewn to resemble giant Scrabble tiles. Someone has arranged four of them to spell "shit," which makes me smile.

The store carries both new and used books, but the sections are arranged illogically. Instead of alphabetical fiction by the author's last name and nonfiction broken into categories, the shelves are tagged with snarky labels—*vampire novels that don't suck (no pun intended)*, *books no one should read (but you probably will anyway)*, and *books by dead white guys*. There's also a shelf called *authors who committed suicide*, and I wonder what criteria go into deciding if Hemingway is a dead white guy or an author who committed suicide. I'm unsure where to look for a book on taking the GED exam, but I find it with other study guides on a shelf labeled . . . *in the real world all rests on perseverance (goethe)*. It's not a new book; there are penciled notes in the margins and it's dated to last year's exam. Do study guides change significantly from year to year? I'm willing to risk five dollars plus tax the answer is no.

The sole employee in the store is a pale-skinned girl in her twenties, sitting on the checkout desk with her black-denim-clad legs dangling over the edge, reading a paperback. She's wedged between a small spinner of artsy postcards and a *now playing* display featuring a CD by a band I've never heard. Beneath the *now playing* sign, scratched in black pen, it says *as selected by real people, not corporate assholes with bad taste.*

She tears herself away from the page and looks at me through black-rimmed glasses that magnify the way her black eyeliner is slicked along her lashes, cat-eye style. Her earlobes are stretched around black plugs, a silver ring is looped through her lip, and a script-y tattoo on the inside of her wrist says *be here now*. "All set?"

"Yeah."

She doesn't comment on the GED study guide but eyes the paperback I found on the *they won awards for a reason* shelf in the teen section. "I approve."

Despite the judgmental book categories, so-cool-no-one-has-heard-of-it music, and a bookseller—the lanyard draped around her neck says her name is Ariel—who feels the need to critique my selections, I love this place. I feel at home among the books and could see myself curled up in the *L* of the couch with a book on a rainy day. Or, maybe working here.

Ariel bags up my purchases, then squats to change the music. On the far end of the counter, right next to the door, is a stack of job application forms. I slide my fingertips over the line where my name would go and picture myself shelving books. It's startlingly easy to imagine. They may not be hiring and it's possible they wouldn't even hire me, but I take an application and shove it in my bag on my way out.

Phoebe and the boys are still at the park when I get to the house. I lock the bike to the fence beside the Airstream and go inside. As I take my books from the bag, I catch the faint scent of vanilla and cigarettes in the air, making my heart stutter. It's my mom's signature scent—cheap drugstore vanilla body spray and Marlboro Reds.

As if she's—

I rush from one end of the small trailer to the other, flinging open the bathroom door as I pass. Pulling aside the shower curtain.

—she's not here.

It's only my imagination.

Except, on the counter, there's a cigarette stubbed out in the purple candle I bought with Kat. I pick it up and smell it. Marlboro Red.

Mom was here.

The bushes outside are unmoving—as if, like me, my mother would hide in someone's landscaping—and of course she's not going to be lounging on Greg's porch steps. Why would she stay long enough to smoke a cigarette, but not long enough to wait for me? I whirl around, my eyes narrowed as I look closer for something. Anything. A note, maybe. Or, a message that only I'll understand. Except the message she's left makes my heart slide into my toes. She didn't come to see me.

The laptop Greg gave me is missing.

My stomach curls in on itself, and I wonder if this is how the Ruskins felt after we lived in their house. Violated. Unsafe. I'll lock the trailer door tonight because I don't want her sneaking in when I'm sleeping. My face burns with shame that I feel this way about my own mother, but also—how am I going to tell Greg? I don't want him to know it was her, but I don't want to lie about what happened to the computer. I hate that she's put me in this position.

Chapter 12

"Does this come in green?"

Alex is back, and I watch through the open doors as he and Jeff load sponges into the back of Alex's pickup truck. Today he's bandanna-free, his bangs pulled back with an elastic the way a girl might wear her hair. Except there is absolutely nothing feminine about the way he looks, and I love how comfortable he seems in his skin.

It pains me to tear my gaze away from him to deal with the customer who has been nagging me with questions for the past fifteen minutes. I want to tell her that if the T-shirt she's waving at me came in green, it would be there among the dozens of available styles. No, that purple dress doesn't come in gold. No, we don't have more necklace colors in back. No, you can't have three sponges for ten dollars because the place down the street is selling them for that price. I shake my head—again. "I'm sorry."

Theo comes into the store and flashes me the "you're not trying hard enough" look I've been getting all week. He goes over to the woman and by the time he's done schmoozing her, she comes to the register with a T-shirt that's not green *and* a dress that's not gold.

"Callie," he says, when the customer is gone, "I know you're new to all this, but you really need to work it a little more. Make the sales."

"I'm sorry." I've attempted to compliment the customers the way Kat does, but the words always trip over my tongue and taste insincere. And although I *am* Greek, what it means to *be* Greek is an alien concept, so I can't use it to my advantage the way Theo and Alex do. "I'll try harder."

He sighs as if he doesn't believe me. "Go ahead and take your lunch break now. I'll cover you, and Kat should be here by the time you're done."

It feels as if I'm being punished.

My bench is empty, so I go there with my daily hummus and Coke. When Alex sees me, he says something to Jeff, hands him the keys to the truck, and they do one of those complicated guy handshakes. Jeff glances in my direction as he climbs into the cab and drives away. The whole exchange unsettles me somehow. Maybe because it feels as if I've answered some sort of silent booty call and now even Jeff knows what's going to happen next. And maybe I'm embarrassed because I wouldn't mind being something more than Alex's booty call. Still, that doesn't stop me from stepping aboard the boat and following Alex down into the cabin.

"Hi." His arms come around me and he pulls me against him.

I thread my fingers through his curls as he lowers his face. His mouth is almost on mine when my own hoarse hello comes out. Just before he kisses me, he gives me that grin that makes my knees go rag-doll limp.

"I've been thinking about you all week." Alex's mouth is against my neck as his hand slides under my T-shirt. His skin tastes faintly of salt and sweat, and any hesitation I had about being nothing more than a booty call dissolves.

I'm pulling my shorts back on—and four minutes past the end of my break—when he asks me what time I get off work.

"Five." I'm not worried about Theo, but I'm afraid that Kat has started her shift and she'll be watching for me. That my T-shirt won't hide the bite mark on my collarbone.

"Do you want to come over later?" His eyes follow

my movements, as if I'll disappear if he looks away. Ironic, considering he was the one who disappeared without a word. "I'll get Chinese and maybe we could watch a movie or something."

"I, um—" I pull my shirt over my head so I can escape his gaze for a second or two before I have to tell him the truth. I look at the floor when I say the words. "I kind of already have—plans."

"Oh." His eyebrows pull together, as if it hadn't occurred to him that I'd be busy.

"You just left, so I thought"—the cabin grows smaller and I'm not sure how to end that sentence—"you could have called or something."

"No, you're right." Alex looks away and I hate that. I could break my date with Connor. God, I *want* to break my date with Connor so much. But that wouldn't be right. I don't want to be that kind of girl. "I didn't really think about it. So, it's cool. Maybe another time."

"Definitely. Absolutely. Yes." Too many words are coming out of my mouth, but I hope that one of them might be the spark to reignite whatever it was I saw in his eyes before. I want him to suggest we do something tomorrow night instead, but he leaves me hanging.

"Okay, well, I have to go. I'm already late from break," I say. "So, I guess I'll see you later?"

"Sure."

But as I let myself out of the cabin and walk to the store, I keep looking back. Not sure about anything at all.

Kat is helping customers when I come in. She smiles and waves at me in a way that makes me think she's been too busy to worry about me. Which is good, because I'm too busy trying to figure out what just happened with Alex to make up an excuse.

"Oh my God, Callie, why didn't you tell me Connor asked you out?" She comes over to me as I'm reorganizing the jewelry spinner. "I had to hear about it from Nick."

"I guess I forgot."

"How could you forget?" She bounces on the balls of her feet and her charm bracelet jingles. "This is so exciting! What are you going to wear?"

"Probably jeans and maybe a plaid shirt."

"Good call." Kat bobs her head as if my lack of planning is a plan. "Understated yet cute. Maybe with one of the lace-trimmed tank tops underneath and—ooh, that necklace with all the keys. And those brown leather sandals. You'll look—um, you look as if you're about to puke. What's wrong?"

"I don't know." I hang and rehang the same necklace twice, just so I don't have to look at her excited face. "I'm not sure about this."

"Why? Connor is the nicest guy I know."

"It's just—I'm not feeling it."

"I used to think Nick was completely annoying. But one day during our freshman year, he sweet-talked the lunch lady into giving him an extra peanut-butter cookie and then gave it to me. It was such a dumb little thing, but"—she shrugs—"that did it for me. Give Connor a chance. He might surprise you."

I work my lower lip between my teeth. I wish I could be honest with her about Alex, but she wouldn't understand, especially when she wants this thing with Connor to happen. It's in her face, in her voice. And I don't want to fight with her anymore. "Yeah, okay."

Theo lets us leave work a little early, and as we walk to Kat's car I can't help but sneak a glance at the boat. Alex stands on deck, stringing sponges the way he did the first night I saw him, and I have to quell the urge to tell him I want to eat Chinese food and watch movies with him. Disappointment thumps with every heartbeat when he doesn't even look up.

It feels like an event when the whole family walks Connor and me to the front door and waves from the porch as we get in the car. Everyone's expectations seem to be riding on my shoulders, and I feel like I'm going to get this wrong.

"You, um—you look nice," Connor says, pulling away from the curb. "I like your hair."

Kat wove the front into two small French braids and ribboned them together in the back. It's pretty.

"Thanks." He's wearing a distressed polo-style shirt and faded jeans, and his cologne is sporty and slightly strong, as if he just put it on. "So do you," I say.

He fiddles with the radio as he drives, scanning up and down the frequencies until he finds the right song—something hard rock I don't recognize—and glances at me to make sure his choice is okay. I smile, but I've got nothing to say. Playing checkers in Greg's backyard was easy because we didn't have to talk, but now . . . this is awful.

"I, um—" I turn down the volume on the radio. "I don't really know how to say this, but—"

"You don't really want to go out with me, do you?" His voice is quiet and I can hear the disappointment running through it.

I slide my finger along the frayed spot on my jeans. "How did you know?"

"I could kind of tell." He brakes to a stop at a red light. "I mean, the first time I asked, you said you'd think about it. That should have been a bigger hint. I guess—I don't understand why you said yes if you're not interested."

"Kat was so excited and I've never been on a real date before, and I thought you'd be . . ." I search for a flattering word. *Comfortable. Nice.* Those words suck. ". . . safe."

Why didn't I say "fun"? What guy wants to be told he's *safe*? As proof, Connor's nose crinkles as if I've used a profane word. Then he sighs and the sound punches me in the stomach. I would have avoided all of this if I had just said no.

"Not gonna lie." He looks up through the windshield at the traffic light, as if he can't wait for it to change so he can drive away from this moment. "I feel like an idiot because, well . . . for once it seemed as if I had a chance with a girl who is completely out of my league."

"I'm not."

Connor shrugs. The light changes and he makes a left.

"We can—"

"Yeah, I know. We can hang out." He sounds tired and slightly sarcastic. I guess I can't blame him for that. "Be *friends*."

"I'm sorry."

He parks in front of the bookstore. Just up the street I can see the lighted marquee of the movie house hanging out over the sidewalk. "Do you still want to go to the movie?" he asks.

"Not really, no."

"Me neither," he says. "Do you want me to take you home?"

I shake my head. "I don't really want to have to explain this to Kat yet."

Connor nods. "She already started planning a double date to homecoming, so—yeah, that's not going to be fun."

I open the passenger side door. "I'm really sorry."

"We're cool." He offers me a smile that has sadness at the corners and his fist for a bump. I touch my fist against his, then get out of the car. "See you later, Callie."

He drives away and I consider going into the bookstore and curling up on that comfy couch until my imaginary date is over. But as I reach for the door handle, the hipster girl with the black glasses turns the closed sign toward me and points at her watch.

Ten minutes later, I'm at the sponge docks.

On my way to Alex's boat, I pass a small restaurant with a handful of tables arranged on the sidewalk. At one of the tables, a blond girl with freckled cheeks picks at the label of her beer bottle as she flashes a bright smile at the guy across from her. At Alex.

I lower my head so my hair will cover my face, but the damn braids hold most of it back. I walk fast, hoping they won't notice me, but the flat soles of my sandals slap on the pavement as I pass.

"Callie." I hear Alex call after me. "Hey, Callie. Wait."

So. Stupid. So. Stupid. So. Stupid. My footfalls call me out. So stupid. So stupid for going out with Connor. So stupid for coming here for Alex. For thinking I could fit in here. For thinking I could be someone else. I could go faster without these shoes, but I don't want to waste time stopping to take them off. Even though I have nowhere to go, I want to flee my embarrassment as quickly as possible.

He catches up with me on Athens Street, his hand wrapping around my upper arm. "Wait."

"Let go of me." I look down at his fingers. "Now."

He releases my arm, shoving his hands deep in the pockets of his jeans, and his voice drops low. Soft. Melting. "Please."

So stupid.

"I have this terrible habit of picking the wrong guys. Ones who don't give a shit about me." My shoulders sag as I lean against the brick of the building behind me. "I broke my date for you."

"I gave you the combination to my boat."

"Yeah, but then you just left and I thought you didn't want—"

"I gave *you* the combination to my *boat*," he repeats, and the weight of the words hit me.

"Oh."

"Yeah. Oh."

"You really shouldn't give the combination to your boat to strange girls."

The corner of his mouth tilts up and I get this intense longing to kiss him right there on that little crease. He reaches out and touches my neck, his fingertips curling around the back and his thumb resting against my wild pulse. He takes a step closer. "Did I give it to the wrong girl?"

I lick my lower lip and shake my head. "No."

His other hand comes up on the other side of my neck and his mouth brushes feather-soft against mine. Fleeting and—oh, how I want more, more, more. "Let's go to the boat."

"What about your friend?"

"That's all she is, Callie. We were just having a beer while she was waiting for her boyfriend to meet her for dinner." His fingers slide down my arm until they reach my hand and he pulls me gently toward the dock. His palm is rough against mine, but I don't mind. "C'mon. You still want Chinese?"

"Sure," I say, leaving out the part where I already ate dinner.

On the boat, Alex rummages through a pile of takeaway menus until he finds the grease-stained yellow flyer from the Great Wall restaurant. He hands it to me. "What'll you have?"

I sit down, handing him the menu without looking at it. "Maybe just an egg roll?"

"That it?" He digs his cell phone from the pocket of his jeans. "You sure?"

"This time."

Alex grins as he makes the call, ordering an egg roll for me and moo shu chicken—my favorite—for himself. Mom and I never order anything but kung pao chicken because that's what she likes.

"So where'd you go just now?" Alex cracks open the cap on a bottle of beer and offers it to me. I shake my head as I tuck my knees up against my chest. He drops down beside me and props his bare feet on a milk crate.

I rest my cheek on my knee. "Thinking about kung pao chicken."

"You like it?"

I've never told Mom how much I hate it. "Not even a little."

"I'll keep that in mind," he says, catching one of my curls between his fingers. "For next time."

I want to reach out and touch him, too, but I don't. I'm not sure why. "Will there be a next time?"

He looks away and takes a sip of beer, and I wonder if he's swallowing the words he was going to say. But then he looks back at me with those green-side-of-hazel eyes and says them. "As many as you want."

I can feel the heat blossom in my cheeks and he laughs in a not-mean way. I look past him, out the doorway to the deck where the dark garlands of sponges hang. "So I think you said something about watching a movie?"

"That was before you turned me down," he says. "I mean, I have a couple of things we can watch, but they're kind of old."

"That's okay. What do you have?"

He opens a sliding hatch behind our heads and takes out a short stack of DVD cases. I shuffle through them. "*Princess Bride*, *High Fidelity*, *Road House*, *Coyote Ugly*, and—" I side-eye him. "*Kinky Kittens 6*?"

"We can skip that one." Alex snatches the case and sends it spiraling out through the cabin doorway. It lands with a thump on the deck. "Not much plot."

"Well, yeah. After *Kinky Kittens* one through five, what more is left to be said, really?"

He laughs. "Exactly."

I fan the remaining DVDs like a hand of cards. "Which is your favorite?"

Alex pulls *High Fidelity*. "Have you seen it?"

"No."

"You have to." He pulls a small combination TV/DVD player out from a storage compartment beneath his bed and plugs it into the orange extension cord that runs out to an outlet on the dock. As the disk is synching up, he props a couple of bed pillows against the bulkhead and settles against them. He pokes my thigh with his toe. "Come here."

I shift backward between his legs until my back is against the wall of his chest. The brush of his stubbled cheek against my temple makes me shiver and he wraps his arms around me. His hand slides beneath the collar of my shirt, his fingers resting on my collarbone. It strikes me as both an unusual and perfect place for a hand to be.

"All good?" he asks.

I feel as if I'm inhabiting some other girl's body, as if something this excellent could not actually be happening to me and that at any moment the universe is going to clue me in to the joke. "All good."

He reaches overhead and switches off the light.

We stay in this position until the delivery driver from the Great Wall arrives. Alex unwraps himself from me and pauses the DVD before going out on deck to pay for the order. He returns with a stack of takeaway containers. "There are a couple of TV trays in the storage locker opposite the head." He tilts his chin in the direction of the locker.

I unfold the trays in the middle of the cabin and he spreads out the food. I take my wax paper bag of egg roll and sit down again, as Alex opens the foam carton of moo shu chicken and the greasy fried scent takes me back to the hallway of our last apartment and those little Dora the Explorer shoes outside our neighbors' door. We'd still be living there if Mom hadn't gotten the stupid itch to leave. She wouldn't have been arrested. I wouldn't be here and she wouldn't have stolen my computer.

"Can I have some of that?" Even though I can't think of anyplace I'd rather be than right here with Alex Kosta, I'm angry. Eating some of his moo shu chicken feels as if it's a perfect *Fuck you, Mom*.

"Sure." His eyebrows pull together as he looks at me. My eyes hurt and I feel as if I'm going to cry. "You okay?"

"Yeah, I just—I need to use the bathroom."

I sit on the closed toilet lid and try to shove my mom out of my head, but it's hard when it feels as if she's out there somewhere watching me, judging me. And my head is a jumbled mess because I want to be with her again. I do. But living with Greg is better than I thought it would be. I have a real bed—even if it's in a trailer—and home-cooked meals, and little boys who touch me with sticky fingers and call me Peach. I enjoy having a job, even though I'm still not sure if I enjoy the job I have. All of it makes me feel as if I'm being disloyal to Mom. As if I don't care. And that's not true at all.

"Hey, Callie." Alex's voice is on the other side of the thin wooden door. "I forgot to tell you that to flush you need to pump the red handle first."

"Okay, thanks." I blow out a breath and look at myself in the dirty mirror on the wall. The eyeliner Kat applied is smudgy, so I run my knuckle beneath my lower lashes to clean it up a little before opening the door.

I can see the concern in his eyes, but I ignore it as I spoon some of his moo shu chicken onto a pancake and pretend I'm totally fine. "So why does Kat hate you?"

"She, um—she had a crush on me for a long time," he says. "Even back when we were kids. I knew about it, but she's too young for me."

"I'm the same age as Kat."

"That's different," he says, but doesn't elaborate on what the difference is. "A couple of years ago, she asked me to take her to homecoming and I turned her down. I told her I've always considered her like my little sister."

I wince.

"Yeah." He scrunches up one side of his face. "Didn't go so well."

"I can see that," I say. "She wouldn't talk to me after she saw me share my lunch with you the other day. I don't really get that. I mean, if she's happy with Nick, why does she care what you do?"

Alex shrugs. "She doesn't want me anymore, but she's still mad that I didn't want her. Best I can tell, it's a girl thing."

"I have a feeling I'm not very good at being a girl."

He leans over and his scruffy face tickles my neck, making me squirm. His voice is low as he says, "You—are exceptionally good at being a girl."

We share all the food. Alex eats half of my egg roll, and I find room for a moo shu pancake filled with chicken and plum sauce, rolled into a little Chinese burrito. And after the empties are stowed in the trash, I settle against him again to finish watching the movie. Except I have a hard time paying attention when his thumb is wandering across my collarbone and his lips keep touching my hair. At least I think they do. It feels that way. When I lift my face to look at him, he kisses me and the movie fades to background noise.

Alex works open the buttons on my shirt, kissing me between each one. When it's on the floor, he slides my tank top over my head. He tugs off his own T-shirt and sends it to the growing pile of clothes, then pushes me backward until I'm lying on the berth. My jeans and underwear come off together and I lift my hips so he can slide them down. He kneels down on the cabin floor and strokes his thumbs along my thighs, easing them apart. His lips brush against the inside of my knee.

"What—" The words clog my throat and my heart ricochets around my chest like a drugstore Super Ball. "What are you doing?"

"I'm not going to hurt you, Callie." His jaw grazes my skin and the stubble from four days of not shaving raises goose bumps across my entire body. His grin says he's pleased with himself, but the muscles in my thighs are stone as I await the words that Frank always said. That it will feel good. That I'll like it. Except Alex says his own words. "If you tell me to stop, I will stop."

He touches me with his fingers. So gentle. As if I'm something so fine. I'm scared and shaking so hard and he keeps asking me if I want him to stop, but I don't want him to stop. Then he touches me with his mouth and I melt.

When his body finally moves up over mine, my cheeks are damp with tears because I never believed it *could* feel good or that I *would* like it. Right now, in this moment, the absence of shame is shaped like Alex Kosta and I don't want to let go of this feeling. Of him. Ever.

"All good?" he asks quietly, later, when he's cleaned up and we're half-dressed. The TV has reverted to the movie menu, prompting us to watch the movie again.

I nod against his chest, and this time when I feel his lips against my hair, I know for sure. "All good."

I dream about Alex.

He comes into my room and I'm wearing a Hello Kitty nightgown. I'm seventeen—not a little girl—so it barely covers me, the bottom ruffle falling just below my hips. He lifts the hem, but I'm not afraid because it's Alex, who whispers that he's not going to hurt me. Except when he touches me he turns into Frank, who laughs his phlegmy smoker's laugh and tells me he always knew I liked it. That no one will ever want me because I'll always be his special girl.

I break free from the circle of Frank's arms and stumble out of bed. I snatch up my shirt from the floor and pull it on, holding it closed with my fist, covering myself as I look for my jeans. "Where are my pants?"

"Callie." Someone is saying my name. It's not Frank's voice, but I ignore it anyway. I have to get out of here. Away from him.

"I need to find my pants." The words are soaked with tears and desperation.

"Callie." Reality snaps into focus as Alex grabs my shoulders. "What the hell is going on?"

I blink once. Twice. My heart rate is crazy fast and

I touch his face to make sure he's real. "It was only a nightmare."

"Only?" He brushes his fingers along my cheek and they come away wet. "You were *crying* in your sleep."

"It was pretty terrible." I dry my eyes on the collar of my shirt.

"Do you, um—do you want to talk about it?"

"No." My skin feels as if ants are marching beneath the surface. I don't want to think about the dream, let alone share it. Not even with him. Especially not him.

"You probably think I'm the weirdest girl you've ever met."

"I think . . ." He rests his chin on top of my head and there's a kind of security in the hollow of his neck. ". . . that we all have stories we don't tell. If you want to share it, you will. Or, you won't."

"Thanks," I say. "What time is it?"

"Not sure. Three, maybe?"

"Three? Are you sure? Shit. I'm so dead." I wriggle into my jeans and stuff my feet into my sandals. My cell phone has dozens of voice mails and text messages from Greg, Kat, and even Connor. This is so bad. "Shit."

Alex dresses quickly and grabs the keys to his truck. "I'll drive you."

"Drop me around the corner?"

"All things considered . . ."

"Yeah."

Under any circumstances the ride to the house would be short, but tonight it feels even shorter. Alex pulls alongside the curb around the corner and looks at me. "I feel like a dick for making you deal with Greg by yourself."

"You're not." I lean over and kiss him quick. Because if I linger, I will have even more reason not to want to get out of the truck. "And I'll be fine."

"Here." Alex slips something into my hand, and it isn't until I'm away from the truck that I look down and find a plastic-wrapped fortune cookie in my hand. I'm tempted to open it right now, because what I need most is good fortune, but there's no time.

I round the corner, and when I reach the house all the lights are blazing and Greg is sitting on the front-porch steps. He springs forward when I come through the gate and I brace myself for an explosion. Instead, his arms wrap around me.

"You scared the hell out of me tonight." His hug is both fierce and gentle, the same as the tone of his voice as he speaks. "And I'm so angry that I don't trust myself to have a rational conversation. Just—thank God you're okay."

"I'm sor—"

"Theo knows not to expect you tomorrow. We'll talk then." He cuts me off and lets me go at the same time, and I kind of wish he hadn't. "Right now I think you should go to your room and stay there."

Disappointment shimmers off him like a hot road on a summer day and I feel like picking a fight with him so he'll be angry instead of disappointed in me.

"It's not a room," I retort. "It's a trailer in your backyard."

But as I circle around the side of the house to the Airstream—that I really love, regardless of what I say—I don't feel any better for having said it.

Chapter 13

My cell phone vibrates me awake five hours later, and I have to dig through the blankets to find it. The little screen says it's Kat calling, and I don't want to answer. I'd rather turtle my head under the covers and hide from reality a bit longer, but she will be relentless. "Hello?"

"Oh my God, Callie." Her voice blasts through the receiver. "I have been going out of my mind. *Where were you?*"

I scrub the heel of my hand against my eye, dislodging the crust, as I think about what I'm going to say. I can't tell her about Alex. Not only because I'm afraid of her reaction, but because we reached a different place last night. It's new and it's mine, and I'm not ready to share it with anyone. "I just wandered."

"For that long?"

"I've been homeless almost my whole life, Kat. A few hours is not a long time."

The line is quiet as she considers the reality of my past, and in the background I can hear her mom telling her she needs to get moving.

"You could have told me about Connor," she says.

"I wanted to, but you were so excited about it," I say. "And he's nice, so I really wanted to like him, but I don't. At least not in a way that counts."

"Callie." She sighs and I feel as if I've let her down in the same way I let Connor down. "You don't have to date someone because I say so. You can tell me the truth, you know. That's what friends do."

"I'm sorry."

"Listen," she says. "My mom is nagging me to get in the shower, so we'll talk more at work. Want me to pick you up?"

"I'm not going to the shop today." Something crackles at my toes. I reach down and find the fortune cookie, shattered within the plastic. "Greg hasn't yelled at me yet."

Kat winces. "That could get ugly. He was crazy worried last night."

"Yeah."

"Let me know how it goes," she says. "Love you."

She disconnects before I can say good-bye. I tear open the cookie wrapper, fishing out the fortune. My lucky numbers are 6-13-25-32-48, and printed on the front it says: *You have the power to write your own fortune.*

Thanks for nothing, fortune cookie.

I fall backward on my bed, but I'm only there a couple of minutes before I hear Greg calling me through the screen and knocking on the door. "Good morning, Callie." He doesn't sound angry, and it's disconcerting. "Time for breakfast."

I grab a pair of shorts and my old Girl Scouts T-shirt and duck into the bathroom, wondering when the other shoe is going to drop. When I come out, Greg is holding the candle with Mom's cigarette butt. Shit. I forgot to throw it away.

"You smoke?" he asks.

"Um—no," I stammer. "I mean, once in a great while when I'm stressed. Hardly ever. Almost never, really."

"I don't know if you're telling me the truth or not," he says, as I follow him out of the trailer and across the lawn. "But if you're smoking, you need to stop. Not only because I don't want it around the boys, but because it's so bad for you."

"Okay. I mean, I'm sorry."

"So this is how our day is going to go," he says. "First, breakfast with Phoebe and the boys, then you and I are going to run an errand, and after that, you'll be doing some yard work for your grandma. Weeding, mulching, mowing—"

"Is slave labor part of my punishment?"

He laughs. "Slave labor is part of belonging to a family."

Which leaves me wondering what, exactly, my punishment will be.

Phoebe is scrambling eggs as we come into the kitchen. Tucker and Joe are sitting on the floor, playing with a little farm set of wooden animals. When he sees me, Joe extends a sheep toward me. "Play, Peach."

"There's time," Greg says, going to help Phoebe with breakfast.

I sit cross-legged on the floor, and Joe wriggles his way into my lap and tilts his head so he's looking at me upside down. He smells like baby shampoo, and I get the urge to bury my nose in his hair and just inhale that innocence. "Sheep."

"Baa," I say.

He laughs, grabs a cow from the set, and resumes the upside-down position. "Cow," he says, and I know what's expected of me.

"Moo."

We do this with each animal—duck, horse, pig, goat, chicken—until I have a lap filled with wooden livestock and Tucker whines that we're not sharing. Joe gives me a sly smile, as if this was his plan all along, and I give him a secret squeeze of solidarity. Except when I look up, Greg is watching and smiling, so I guess it wasn't so secret.

"You can play more after we eat," Phoebe tells Tucker. "Breakfast is ready."

Tucker scrambles to his feet and I slide Joe from my lap to stand. He raises his arms, his little fingers making grab hands at me. "Up."

I deposit Joe in his high chair and sit beside him as Phoebe and Greg bring breakfast to the table. Breakfast is pleasant, but I'm on edge. The specter of last night hovers and my stomach twists itself into a knot that makes eating homemade scrambled eggs and bacon not nearly as satisfying as it should be, and I wonder if this isn't punishment in itself.

After breakfast, Greg and I ride our bikes across Tarpon Bayou to a waterfront construction site on Chesapeake Drive. Sitting on the lot is a faded blue house on stilts with a set of wooden stairs leading up to the front porch. The windows and doors are missing and there is new plywood jutting out from open spaces in the roof where dormers used to be.

"What is this place?" I ask as I follow him up the stairs.

"This is one of my projects." We walk through the space where the front door should be, into a scaffolding of studs and half-hung walls. "The outside has those great old Florida beach-house bones, but the inside was really cut up and impractical. It's kind of hard to picture right now, but there will be two bedrooms right up here in front, and back there"—he points to a big space with huge window openings overlooking the bayou—"will be a combined living room, dining room, and kitchen. And beyond that, another porch."

I don't know anything about architecture, but the preexisting house is pretty big. Not mansion-size the way they are out at Pointe Alexis, but a lot bigger than Greg's cramped cottage.

"Let's go upstairs," he says.

The stairs are built of plywood and there is no handrail yet. Our footsteps echo as we climb to the second floor.

"This is my favorite part because I love the original wood and the slanted ceiling," Greg says. "We're blowing out the front dormer window to create an office space, but this—" He leads me through the two-by-four framework of a new wall. "This will be *your* room."

His words stop me in my tracks. "My room?"

He pulls a folded set of blueprints from his bag. "Phoebe and I bought this house two years ago, at the same time we bought the cottage, and I've spent the better part of last year altering the existing design to something a little more updated."

I kneel down and unfold the drawing. Greg squats beside me.

"See this part here?" He touches some lines on the paper. "I added it last week—just for you." He walks over to one of the walls and spreads his arms wide. "Right here I'll be building a reading nook with bookcases all the way around it so you can sit in here and read. And out there, where the dormer window used to be, will be your own personal deck."

Greg goes blurry as my eyes fill with tears, and I feel both happy and sad at the same time because I want to deserve this, but I don't feel as if I do. Not after everything I've done. He comes over to me and takes me gently by the shoulders. "You have *always* been a part of my family, Callie. Always a part of my plans."

"I didn't mean what I said about the Airstream," I say. "I like it a lot."

He smiles. "I know."

"But this is . . ." I close my eyes and imagine a wall filled with books.

"C'mon." He walks between wall studs out onto the

beginnings of the deck and sits, his legs dangling over the edge into the empty air below. I join him.

"Here's the thing," Greg says. "I am so completely out of my depth when it comes to you that I don't know what to do about last night. Tucker and Joe are easy because they're little. Whenever Tuck figures out a way around one of our parental roadblocks, Phoebe and I are still smart enough to think up a new one. But you—" He shrugs. "I remember being a teenager, so having to parent one scares the hell out of me. Especially one who has done a pretty good job of taking care of herself."

I shade my eyes and look out at the bayou. It hardly seems possible that this view could be mine. That this room will be mine. "I didn't mean to stay out that late."

"It's not only the staying out too late, Cal," Greg says. "You left with Connor Madsen and came home hours later alone, without a single call to anyone to let us know where you were. How do you expect me to feel about that?"

"It's just—this is new for me, too," I say. "Mom always worked nights, so I've never had to answer to anyone. I wasn't purposely ignoring your rules. I just lost track of time."

"Where were you?"

"I, um—I was with someone." The words surprise

me. I wasn't expecting to reveal anything this personal to him.

"Someone who is, apparently, not Connor."

"Right."

"Do you—are you—?" His face is pink and he pinches the bridge of his nose. "God, this is not a question I ever thought I'd have to ask, but if you're, um—are you being careful?"

My own cheeks get warm. Mom and I had the sex talk years ago. It was after Frank, so she was kind of too late, even though he didn't have actual sex with me. But it's a never-in-my-wildest-dreams scenario to be discussing birth control with Greg. Despite the weirdness of the moment, it feels, maybe for the first time since I got here, as if he's really my dad. "Yes."

"If you need Phoebe to take you to her doctor, I can ask her."

I nod. "That would be good."

Greg hoists himself to his feet, then helps me up. Right there, where it's as if we're standing in the sky, he hugs me and tells me he loves me. My cheek against his T-shirt brings back a thin slice of memory, of him hugging me when I was little. I was jumping off the porch steps of wherever we were living when the three of us lived together. I had no trouble on the first step or the second, but when I tried from the third, I fell and skinned my knees and palms. Greg was there to pick me up and wipe away the tears. My arms circle around him and so quietly that I'm not sure he'll hear me I whisper into his shoulder. "Thank you."

He kisses my forehead, which makes me think maybe he did.

I follow him back down the plywood staircase, trying harder now to picture what this house—our house—will look like when it's finished. He talks about drywall and bamboo flooring and other things that mean nothing to me, but I don't mind.

"So this boyfriend of yours—" he says, as we walk our bikes out to the street.

I climb onto my bike. "Just trust me, okay?"

Greg sighs. "I'm really not comfortable with this, but—okay."

He turns off at Ada Street—after telling me that he plans to install a propane tank this afternoon so I can shower in the Airstream—and I ride on alone to Georgia's house. When I coast to a stop at her front walk, she's already puttering in the yard, wearing floral gardening gloves and a pair of rubber clogs. When she hugs me, she smells of dirt and grass and lipstick. It's a pleasant combination.

"Did you get yourself all sorted out the other day?" The gloves she hands me are blue and much larger than the ones she's wearing, and they're a little scratchy inside. She leads me to a stack of mulch bags.

"I guess so."

"If I can throw in my two cents," she says, "I suspect you're not much like your mother at all, Callista. You may go off on your own to work through your thoughts, but the difference is—and this is important—you come back."

I never thought about it that way.

"You're like your father in that regard, and"—she gestures at the top bag and indicates that I should spread it around the low shrubs along the front porch—"I suspect that you're not running away so much as you are running to something. Or, someone."

My thoughts go immediately to Alex and, as if she can read my mind, Georgia smirks. She reaches up and puts her gloved hands on my face. "Your cheeks give you away, *matákia mou*."

"What does that mean?" The bag of mulch is heavier than I expected and I stagger over to the shrubs with it.

"It means 'my eyes,'" she says. "Not literally, but—it's like saying you are the apple of my eye."

"What about 'korítsi mou'?" I ask, repeating the words Greg used at the sheriff's office in Illinois, as I tear open the bag of mulch and upend it on top of the old mulch. I'm not sure I'm even saying the words correctly. "What does that mean?"

"The literal translation is 'my girl,'" she says. "But it implies that the girl in question is loved and held dear. It's used by parents. Now, if a young man were to say *latría mou*, which means 'my darling,' he loves you . . . or he's trying to charm you out of your underpants. Either way, he's serious about something."

I distribute the dark and earthy-smelling mulch around the bushes and laugh that Alex didn't need to trot out Greek terms of endearment to get me out of my underpants. But it's a good laugh, not one rooted in I'm-shit-in-the-back-of-someone's-truck shame. "I'll keep that in mind."

The work is sweaty, but it doesn't take long before the mulch is spread and the weeds are pulled. Georgia did most of the weeding herself and confessed she paid a neighbor boy to mow the grass so I wouldn't have to do that part. I feel as if I got off pretty light on my punishment, but—I don't know. I guess I get what Greg was trying to tell me.

"I'm having lunch today with my friend," my grandma says, as we peel off our gloves. "Would you like to come with me?"

"I don't want to impose."

"I wouldn't invite you if it was an imposition," she says. "And Evgenia wants to meet you."

The name feels familiar, but I can't place it. "Okay."

I wash up in Georgia's bathroom, finger-combing my hair to work out the tangles and sniffing the underarms of my T-shirt to make sure I don't smell foul. I look as if I've been working in someone's yard and the end of my nose is a little pink from the sun, but I hope her friend won't mind.

The tiny stone house with an old-fashioned sailing ship carved into the wooden front door is within walking distance, and not far from the sponge docks. On the way, Georgia teaches me how to say hello and thank you in Greek, making me repeat the words over and over until I have the pronunciation down cold. We're greeted by a salt-and-pepper-haired man, barrel shaped and broad enough to nearly fill the doorway.

"Georgia!" He kisses my grandma on both cheeks. "Good to see you! This must be your granddaughter. We've been looking forward to meeting you." His hand swallows mine as he shakes it. "Come in, come in! Please, sit."

He ushers us into a living room barely bigger than my Airstream. Although the drapes are drawn, lace curtains push back the sunshine and cast a gloominess over the room. It smells as if the whole room could use a good shaking. Seated on the couch is a woman—Evgenia, I presume—whose mouth is slack, and when she looks at us, I think she might be blind because her eyes don't appear to be focused on anything at all.

"Evgeniki." The man squats and pats her knee. She swings her head in his direction, but her expression doesn't change. "Georgia is here to see you. You remember Georgia."

She nods as my grandma sits beside her on the couch. I perch on the edge of a faded brown chair.

"I've brought my granddaughter, Callista," Georgia says. "She's been helping me with my garden today. Callista, this is my dearest friend, Evgenia, and her husband, Nikos."

I wave, then feel stupid. What if she can't even see me? I attempt a Greek hello. "*Yia sou.*"

Evgenia claps her hands and says something, but her jaw is stiff and the words are unintelligible. They sound more gibberish than Greek or English.

"Use your board." Nikos hands her a white dry-erase board and red marker, then turns down the volume on the television. Georgia watches over Evgenia's shoulder as she scrawls some words on the board. From my upside-down vantage point, I can't read them, but I'm pretty sure they're in Greek. So I couldn't read them right side up, either.

My grandma smiles and looks at me. "She says you have grown into a beautiful young woman."

"I, um—*efharistó*." Thank you.

Yiayoúla nods her approval and nudges Evgenia

with her elbow. "I'll make a Greek of her yet. Even if she doesn't like my dolmades."

"I'll leave you ladies to talk." Nikos stands, then bends over and gives his wife a tender kiss. He strokes her cheek, and the sweetness of the gesture makes me smile. "Call if you need me."

The conversation between Georgia and her friend alternates between silence as Evgenia writes and a flurry of words in English and Greek as my grandma talks. If you couldn't hear the squeak of the marker on the whiteboard, you'd think Yiayoúla was talking to herself. With nothing to add, I look around the room. It's not fancy and the furniture is old, but well kept and clean. Lived-in and loved.

Hanging on the wall is a picture of a much younger and thinner Nikos, his hair fully dark and his face without a mustache. He's standing with a skinny blond boy—whose legs are disproportionately long compared to the rest of him—beside a white boat with *Evgenia* painted in blue on the side. Alex. Evgenia is Alex's mother.

I walk over to the picture. Beside it is another photo of Alex. In this one he is older and broader, and in the water, surrounded by a group of other boys. His arm is held aloft with a white cross in his grip.

"That is Evgenia's son, Alex. Phoebe's brother."

Georgia comes over to me and slips her arm around my waist. "But you already know this, don't you?"

I don't look at her for fear my cheeks will give me away again. If they haven't already. "Yeah, he, um—he came over for dinner once, and he does the sponge-dive tours on Sundays."

She points to the picture of Alex in the water. His whole face is smiling and even then—whenever *then* was—he was steal-your-breath beautiful. "Each year in January, we celebrate the baptism of Jesus in the Jordan River," she says. "One of the annual traditions is the Epiphany dive, when the archbishop throws a cross into Spring Bayou and the boys dive in after it. It's thought to bring good luck for the coming year to the boy who retrieves it. Alex won it that year and your father won it when he was sixteen, too."

That was the year my mom got pregnant with me. Not so lucky for Greg, who ended up a father before he turned seventeen.

Behind us I can hear the squeak of Evgenia's marker. We turn around to see her holding the board up. It says: *Alex is good boy. Proud of him.* A tear catches in one of the lines of her face and rolls down her cheek. She misses the son who never visits, and my heart breaks for her.

My grandma laughs to lighten the mood. "Haven't

you done enough matchmaking?" She turns to me. "It was Evgenia's idea to fix up Greg and Phoebe, so now she thinks she's an expert."

Evgenia laughs as she wipes her eyes and cheeks with a tissue, then rubs out the words on her board to write fresh ones. *Lunch now?*

Georgia helps her up from the couch and walks her into the kitchen, where they assemble sandwiches for me and Georgia and mix up a milk shake of chocolate nutrition drink and banana for Evgenia. Yiayoúla explains that her friend suffers from progressive supranuclear palsy, a degenerative disorder that is slowly eroding her motor skills, including walking and talking.

"It's become very hard for her to swallow," my grandma says as the blender whirs. "So her meals are nearly all liquid. Nikos and Phoebe do what they can to make sure her nutritional needs are met, but it's not enough. She's getting weaker and more susceptible to illness. Eventually she'll catch pneumonia and her body will be unable to defend itself, and she'll die."

My sandwich turns to dust in my mouth as she talks so frankly about death. Everything hits me at once— why Phoebe wants Alex to see his mom, and why he refuses. It's hard to look at her face, almost expressionless, and know there is sorrow and fear behind it. Alex is pulling away, preparing himself for the inevitable.

But what I don't understand is how he can bear being apart from his mother. If she were sick, there is nothing I wouldn't do for my mom. She *is* sick and I have kept terrible secrets to protect her.

After lunch, Georgia helps Evgenia into bed for a nap and Nikos returns a few minutes later. He looks in on his sleeping wife, then thanks us for coming over. "Georgia, I don't know what I'd do without you and Phoebe. Caring for Evgenia is a full-time job."

"It's a blessing you have a strong, capable son to run the boat, eh?" His thick eyebrows nearly touch as he frowns, but before he can say anything, my grandma pats his shoulder and cuts him off. "Call me if you need a break. I've got nothing but time."

As we walk down Mill Street, Georgia laces her fingers through mine. "Last evening I was visiting a friend of mine who owns a soap shop on Athens Street when I happened to see a young couple kissing on the sidewalk."

My eyes go wide. If she knows—

"Relax." She waves her hand. "Your father has no idea. But, my silence comes with a price." She laughs. "That makes me sound so sinister, doesn't it? Not so much a price as a very big favor in exchange for keeping your secret."

I have nothing of value to offer her. Nothing of which I'm aware. "What?"

"Convince Alex to go visit his mother."

"But—I can't do that," I protest. "Phoebe brought it up at dinner and he got mad at her."

"Well, of course he did," Georgia says. "She's his sister and she was nagging him. You, Callista, are a beautiful girl, and beautiful girls can always persuade boys to do things they don't want to do. Also, you're smarter than he is. You'll figure it out."

Chapter 14

I'm curled up on my couch with the novel I bought downtown at the bookstore and a blanket against the chill that's settled into the December evenings—something that surprises and delights me about Florida—when I hear a soft tap at my door. Alex called me from the dock a little while ago to tell me he was leaving, but maybe he's come over to say good-bye in person. I smile to myself as I unfold and go to the door.

It's my mom.

I pull her inside before anyone sees and close the outer door. There are no lights on in the house, but for all I know, Greg is watching from the window to make sure I don't sneak out again.

"Mom, what are you doing here?"

She looks worse than the last time I saw her. The

dark roots of her hair are bleeding into the platinum, and the fairy lights deepen the bruise-colored half circles beneath her eyes. Her signature red lips are too present on her washed-out face. I wrap my arms around her, but she feels different to me. Slight and insubstantial, an autumn leaf that could whirl away in the breeze. And she doesn't hug me back.

"This is a real nice setup you've got here." She touches a dangling vine on the philodendron hanging above the sink, then skims her fingertips along the countertop to the book I was reading. "Is this all it took to win you over to his side, Callie? Some books and a couple of expensive gadgets?"

"It's not like that." Except when she says it like that it makes me wonder if I *have* been seduced by *stuff*.

She picks up my cell phone and cocks her head at me. I can look up things on the Internet with that phone. It was expensive. "Oh?"

"Mom—"

"You left me there in jail." The phone clatters when she drops it on the counter. "And went off with him as if I didn't even exist."

"That's not true," I say. "I didn't have a choice. He's my father."

She lights a cigarette and I wince, thinking about the mini-lecture I just received from Greg about my pretend smoking habit. Then I feel bad for worrying about what he thinks. Maybe she's right. She blows out a stream of smoke. "There's always a choice, Callie."

"What could I have done?"

"Well." She drops down on the couch and props her feet up on the table. The black velveteen of her favorite ballerina flats is worn thin and the heels are rubbed down to nothing. "You're still here, aren't you?"

I've hidden some of the pocket money Greg has given me in the body of my guitar, and I have my pay from the gift shop now. There's no reason why I couldn't leave.

"I'm sorry." I sit down beside her, not sure why I'm apologizing. I could ask her where she thinks I could have gone on my own, or how I would have found her, but this is my mother. She believes all of this is somehow my choice. And even though I know it's her personality disorder that makes her believe this, I can't silence the tiny voice in my head that agrees. "Aren't you worried that you'll be caught?"

Her face softens and she gives me a grin that dimples her cheek. "You should know by now that I'm excellent at not being found. And anyway, I won't be here much longer. As soon as I have enough money for us to start over, we can get out of here."

"How much did you get for the computer?"

"Fifty bucks."

"Can you get it back?"

She laughs. "Why would I want to do that?"

"Because it was mine," I say. "You stole it from me."

She reaches out and touches my hair. It's comforting and familiar and I want to press my head into her hand for more. I want her affection back. "We can go to Colorado the way we planned or"—I see the excitement flicker to life in her eyes as she ignores my question completely—"anywhere. We can go anywhere we want, Callie. We can be *free*."

Free.

"I, um—" In the short time I've been here, I've found a job, a friend—even as turbulent as our best-friendship has been so far—and a parent who grounds me when I mess up. Greg's been a safety net when I fall. And that's a kind of freedom I would have never expected. But none of this is what she wants to hear. I smile and rest my head on her bony shoulder. "Sounds good, Mom."

My cell phone buzzes with an incoming text message. She reaches for it and I see Alex's name flash across the screen. "Ooh, *Alex*," she teases. "Let's see what Alex has to say."

"Mom—" I make a grab for the phone, but she holds

it out of my reach as she fumbles for the button that will reveal his message. I stand and lunge for it, ripping it from her grasp.

Her eyebrows lift.

"Interesting." Her voice is soft as I pocket the phone without reading his message, even though I'm dying to know what he said. "Is he Greek?"

I never told her about any of the other guys I've been with because they weren't worth mentioning, but now—Alex might be worth it, and I'm afraid telling her will ruin everything. "He—he's nothing."

"Obviously." She laughs and stubs out her cigarette in the candle again. I make a mental note to get rid of it before Greg sees. "Be careful with those Greek boys, though. They'll break your heart."

Except I know better. I've seen the photos in the red leather album that tell a different story about who's heart was broken.

"I have to go to work in the morning," I say. "You can stay with me tonight if you want, but you should probably be gone before Greg and Phoebe get up at seven."

Leaving her sitting on the couch, I go into the bathroom to read Alex's text.

It's dark out tonight and the sky is thick with stars. I think you'd love it.

I lean against the bathroom wall and close my eyes, trying to picture what he sees. Imagining him at the wheel of his boat as he heads out into the dark water of the Gulf of Mexico. I look out my little window but the sky is obscured by trees and houses. I send a message back, just four words.

I'm sure of it.

The phone buzzes again.

I'm about to lose signal, but don't make any dates this weekend.

My mouth spreads to a mile-wide smile, as I answer.

Too late. Unless you've got plans with someone else on Saturday night.

Buzz.

I'm all yours.

I stand there, attempting to think of a clever response, but my brain has abandoned my head and taken off for the party my heart is throwing in my chest. *I'm all yours.* I can't stop smiling as I brush my teeth and change into my pajamas. *I'm all yours.* I arrange my face into a less incandescent expression so Mom won't ask questions, but by the time I come out of the bathroom, she's already tucked beneath the covers of my bed.

Typical.

Most everywhere we've lived she's chosen the best sleeping space, claiming that because she worked, she needed a good night's sleep. That usually left me with the too-short couch, or the uncomfortable foldout sofa, or the sleeping bag on the floor. That was the worst, especially when it was cold. Although the Airstream's couch converts to a full-size bed, I climb in beside my mother, something I haven't done since I was very small. She rolls onto her side and faces the wall, giving me what little room is left.

"Mom?"

"Yeah, baby?"

"I've got money," I whisper. "If you can get my computer back, I'll give you some of it. Just—please?"

I wait, but she doesn't reply, except for the deep, even breaths that come with sleep. I shift so my back is against hers, stealing a little comfort from the soft vibration of her snores. Except my happiness that she's here is eroded by worry that Greg is going to discover her in his own backyard, and I can't sleep. What am I going to do when she's raised enough money to leave? My life is complicated now and I'm no longer so certain I can just walk away from my dad. And this time I'm old enough to have a choice.

I draw Toot up under my chin and stroke my finger across the soft wales of a brown corduroy patch, the way I used to do when I was a little girl. It's as soothing now as it was back then and I finally fall asleep.

When my alarm goes off the next morning, Mom is already gone.

"I can't ask Kat because she's already left for school." Phoebe's cell phone is wedged between her ear and shoulder, as she scoops oatmeal into a bowl on Joe's high chair tray. He dips his fingers into the steamy mush. "Use your spoon," she says, before returning to her call. "Are you sure you can't come home? What about your mom? Do you think she could watch the boys?"

Tucker wriggles off his chair, saying my name over and over until it becomes a string of sound—calliecalliecalliecallie—and attaches himself to my leg. "Pick me up."

"Greg—" Phoebe stops abruptly when she sees me, and I feel as if I've walked in on another private conversation about me. "I just—"

She's quiet as she listens to whatever it is he has to say. I imagine he's defending me because he does that. Pretending I'm not paying attention, I reach down for my little brother. As I hoist him up, I groan and strain, as if he's too big for me to lift. "You must have grown a million inches last night, Tuck. Or have you been eating *rocks*?"

He giggles. "Yes. I ate a *stalagmite* for breakfast." He

draws out the syllables in "stalagmite," with a note of gravity in his voice. I love that about him.

"A *stalagmite*?" I finally lift him completely into my arms and feign a breath of relief. "You have to be careful not to overdo it on the stalagmite munching, buddy. You might end up stuck to the ceiling."

"Callie." His puts his hands on my cheeks to make sure I'm looking at him, that I'm paying attention. "Stalagmites. Are the ones. On the floor."

I know this, but it completely knocks me out that he knows, too. "They are? Are you *sure*?"

He nods.

"Well, either way," I say. "It's important not to eat too many rocks, because then I wouldn't be able to lift you. And that wouldn't be good at all."

I put Tucker back in his seat, where his bowl of oatmeal is waiting and Phoebe is staring at me. "Greg, I'll call you back," she says and disconnects the call. "Callie—"

"I can watch the boys." I keep my voice level so I don't sound like my mother. "I know you think I might be crazy and I get that my past is a mystery, so it makes sense that you don't trust me, but—"

"It's not that I don't—"

"Yes, it is," I interrupt. "You're their mom and you want to protect them." Unexpected tears make my eyes burn, and I'm surprised that what I feel is jealousy. Tucker and Joe will always know what it's like to have someone in their corner. "I don't know if there's something wrong with me, but if there is, I can't feel it. All I know is that I would never, *ever* do anything to hurt them."

Phoebe looks at me for a long moment, as if she's searching for a sign, for that one thing that will make me trustworthy. If she sees something, I can't read it in her face.

"Okay." She takes a deep breath and releases it slowly. "Here's the deal: my mom fell down, and even though my dad doesn't think it warrants a trip to the hospital, I'll feel better if I know she's all right." She gathers her purse and the keys to the SUV. "There's a list of emergency numbers on the side of the fridge. I don't think I'll be very long, but if you need any help at all, call Gre—call your dad."

"I will."

"Please don't let me down."

Her eyes hold mine and I want to promise that nothing bad will happen while she's away, but it's not a promise I can make. Bad things don't announce themselves. All I can do is assure her that I will do my best. That I will be better than my mother. "I won't."

"Be good for Callie." She kisses the boys, then offers

me a smile that's offset by the lines of worry between her eyebrows. "Thank you."

Phoebe's SUV is down the driveway and gone when panic sets in. This is different from playing with Tucker and Joe while their parents hover in the background. I don't know the first thing about caring for little boys. What made me think this was a good idea?

Kat is already in class, but I send her a text message anyway. *I'm babysitting. What do I do?*

A couple of minutes later, I'm stirring sugar into my bowl of oatmeal when my phone rings.

"I'm calling from the bathroom," Kat says. "I told my history teacher I started my period. What's going on?"

"Phoebe had an emergency with her mom, so she left me alone with the boys. We're eating breakfast right now, but I'm not sure what happens next."

"Oh, this is an easy one," Kat says. "Wash them up, then let Tucker pick out a DVD. That will keep them busy long enough for you to clean up the kitchen. Then check Joe's diaper—"

"His diaper?"

"Yeah, you might have to change it."

"Oh, God."

"Not gonna lie," Kat says. "It's horrendous. I've been babysitting since I was twelve, and the smell of baby poop still makes me gag. Also, don't forget that the tabs go in the back and attach in the front. It'll make sense when you see it. The first time I ever changed Tucker's diaper, I put it on backward."

"Anything else?"

"That's about it," she says. "Oh, you might remind Tuck to use the potty. He has accidents sometimes. Aside from that, between the television and LEGOs—piece of cake."

It doesn't sound easy, but I'm grateful anyway. "Thank you."

"Anytime," she says. "Anyway, I'd better get back to class. Good luck and I hope Phoebe's mom is okay."

I turn back to the table to find that Joe has rubbed oatmeal in his hair, and Tucker spilled orange juice down the front of his T-shirt.

"It's wet, Callie." Tucker tugs at the hem, trying to pull the damp spot away from his skin. "I want it off."

"We'll put on a clean shirt after breakfast, okay?"

"No, now." The serious little man from before is replaced by an irrational, whining toddler. "It's yucky."

"God, Tucker, it's just juice," I snap. "It's not going to hurt you."

His bottom lip juts out, and I sigh.

"Fine. Come on."

Leaving Joe in his high chair, Tucker and I go to the

bedroom, where we swap the damp shirt for one with Batman wings across the chest. He scampers back to the kitchen and we finish our breakfast, accompanied by his nonstop narrative about how his oatmeal is an island, he's a pirate, and his spoon is digging for buried treasure.

After I wash up the boys, I park them in front of an animated movie, do the dishes, and then sit down on the floor with them. Joe worms his way onto my lap and leans back against my chest. There's an oat still stuck in his hair. As I pick it out, he makes a grunting noise and his face turns bright red.

"Uh-oh," Tucker sing-songs. "Joe is pooping."

"Poop," Joe agrees.

Even through his diaper and little stretchy-waist jeans, I can feel the warmth against my thigh and the smell creeps up between us. I dread having to change him and consider pretending I didn't notice he'd soiled himself until Phoebe gets home, but if he smells this bad now, it can only get worse with time.

I carry Joe into the bedroom and put him down on the changing table. Tucker follows, repeating the word "poop" and giggling every time.

"Okay, Joe." I unsnap the inseams of his jeans, revealing his chubby little legs. The smell is even more intense now and my stomach roils. "We need to do this really fast, so hold still for Peach, okay?"

He grins and points at my face. "Peach."

Tucker climbs onto his bed and starts bouncing, arms outstretched as he proclaims himself Batman, Defender of the Universe.

I tear open the Velcro tabs at Joe's waist and peel back the diaper. A wave of stink curls up my nose and I feel bile rise into the back of my throat. How does Phoebe do this every day without throwing up? How do I get the diaper out from under him? I think about texting Kat, but I don't have enough hands available and I need to clean up Joe before I puke. I lift him by the feet and whisk the dirty diaper into the trash pail.

"Mommy always makes it in a ball first," Tucker says, as he bounces.

I ignore him, swabbing at Joe's dirty bottom with a handful of baby wipes as Tucker informs me his mother doesn't use that many wipes and that she always straps Joe down so he won't roll off the table.

"Oh my God, Tucker, shut up!" I snap. "I'm not your mommy."

He doesn't stop bouncing, but his bottom lip pokes out and I feel bad for yelling at him as I manage to fasten the clean diaper around Joe—being careful not to put it on backward—and snap up Joe's jeans.

"Okay, Tuck, let's go back out and finish watching the movie, okay?" I smile at him, trying to show that

I'm not mad at him anymore, but he looks at me with wary eyes.

He bounces once more and leaps off the bed, shouting that he's flying through Gotham City. Tucker falls as he lands, hitting his head on the corner of a wooden toy box. At first he is silent and I think he must be okay, but then he lets out a howling cry. I put Joe down and kneel beside Tucker. There's a spot on the edge of his forehead where he made impact—red in the center with an instant bruise around it. It's not bleeding, but it has already started to swell.

"I want Mommy," Tucker wails, his words punctuated by gasping breaths as he tries to push me away. "I don't want *you*. I want Mommy."

He won't stop asking for Phoebe, and I don't know what to do. It looks like an ordinary bump on the head, but what if he has a concussion? What if he's bleeding internally? I don't want to have to call his mother and tell her I messed up, and I don't want to call 911 if it's really just a bump, but how can I be sure?

"Oh, God," I whisper. "What do I do?"

Greg comes into the bedroom—like the answer to some unsaid prayer—and my brother practically throws himself across the room. In his father's arms, his sobs reduce to sniffles.

"What's going on?" Greg asks, pushing aside Tucker's

hair to look at the spot. I focus on my bare feet, my face hot with shame. "What happened?"

Tucker sucks in a shuddering breath. "I bumped on the toy box."

"What were you doing when you bumped on the toy box?" Greg holds Tucker's face in his hand and looks first into his left eye, then the right, checking for signs of a concussion. I should have thought of that.

"Flying across Gotham City."

"Were you jumping on the bed again?"

Tucker nods. "But Daddy—"

"Are you allowed to jump on the bed?"

"No."

"I didn't know," I offer.

Greg puts Tucker down. "You're okay, buddy. Go out to the freezer, get the bunny pack, and I'll check on you in a couple of minutes."

"Bunny pack!" Tucker shouts, his tears forgotten as he rushes out of the room. Joe toddles after him, leaving Greg and me alone.

"I'm so sorry," I say. "I didn't mean—"

"It's not your fault, Callie," Greg cuts me off. "It's just a bump."

"Yeah, but I promised Phoebe I wouldn't let her down."

He pulls me into a hug and kisses my forehead. "You

didn't let her down. Tucker did. He's not allowed to jump on the beds."

"But—"

"Look, accidents happen all the time," he says. "When you were . . . oh, maybe seven months old or so, I put your baby seat on the kitchen table. I turned my back for just a second and you rocked forward. The seat fell off the table, landing facedown—*your* face down—on the floor." Greg rakes his hand through his hair. "When I turned you over, there was blood on your mouth and I couldn't tell where it came from. I completely freaked out and rushed you to the emergency room, where I was sure they were going to tell me you'd suffered permanent brain damage and send me to jail. Three hundred bucks later, it turns out you tore that little flappy skin thing inside your upper lip."

I stick my tongue in the space between my gums and my upper lip and touch that connection. "It's called a frenulum," I say.

Greg smiles the way I smiled when Tucker said "stalagmite." "The point is, Cal, what happened today could have happened on anyone's watch. Even Phoebe's."

"I didn't know what to do," I say. "If you hadn't come home—"

"Well, it wouldn't hurt for you to take a first-aid class so you feel more confident, but you're a smart girl. You'd have figured out that it wasn't serious."

"So, did Phoebe send you to check up on me?"

Now it's Greg's turn to look at his feet. "Yeah, well— I'm sorry about that. She was worried, so I told her if I could get away from the office, I'd come."

Through the open door behind him, I can see Tucker watching the movie, reciting the words along with the characters as he holds a blue rabbit-shaped ice pack against his forehead. Even though it doesn't feel great that Phoebe and Greg didn't completely trust me with the boys, I'm relieved my dad was here when I needed him. Again.

"No," I say. "I'm glad you came."

"How about we pretend I was never here?" Greg asks. "Maybe let Phoebe think you handled it all on your own?"

I smile. "Deal."

He leaves and I return to the living room, settling on the couch with Tucker and Joe. They both fall asleep before the movie ends, Tuck slumped against my shoulder and Joe's face snuggled into the side of my neck. I can feel his soft breath against my skin. It feels kind of . . . peaceful.

The ending credits are rolling when Phoebe comes home.

"Hi." She keeps her voice soft and low so she won't wake the boys. She peels Joe away from me, kissing his hair as she cuddles him against her. My shirt is damp with baby sweat, but he doesn't wake as she carries him into the bedroom.

I scoop up Tucker and put him down for a nap on his rumpled-from-jumping bed. He mutters something about wanting to watch the movie, but falls back asleep before he's fully conscious. Phoebe lifts the side rail so he won't roll out and gives him a kiss. These little things make it impossible for me not to like her. Her love comes out in all the tiny details and makes me long for everything I never had.

"What happened to his head?" she asks, as we walk back out into the living room.

I tell her, hoping she won't be angry with me. Instead, she shakes her head and a tiny smile flickers across her lips. "Aside from that," I say, "and maybe some oatmeal in Joe's hair, everything else was fine."

Phoebe chuckles. "If we survive Tucker's childhood, it'll be a miracle." She twists her braided ring around her finger. "Anyway, I really appreciate your being here when I needed someone. Thank you. I've been judging you based on your mom and that's not fair."

"Yeah, but you don't really know me," I say. "So I guess it makes sense."

"I'd like to know you. If that's okay?"

I nod. "Sure."

We fall into an awkward silence.

"I should, um—" I aim my thumb over my shoulder in the direction of the backyard. "Theo's expecting me at the shop soon. I should probably get ready."

As I head for the door, Phoebe says my name and I turn back.

"Did Greg stop by?" she asks.

I consider telling her the truth so she can feel bad for not trusting me, but I shake my head instead. She looks a little relieved as I lie. "Nope."

Chapter 15

"I love Christmas," Kat says, as we loop sponge garland around a fresh evergreen decorated with multicolored starfish, plastic crustaceans, bleached sand dollars, and white lights. All along Dodecanese, the holiday decorations are going up today, as if we've crossed some invisible Christmas meridian, leaving regular December behind. The utility poles are ringed with strings of lights, a life-size plastic Santa stands outside the door to one of the soap shops, and even the pilings along the dock are circled by a glittering red-and-green garland. "The best part is the break from school, but I love the music, the decorations, picking out just the right gifts for people, and even the Christmas Eve services at church. You should come."

The holidays have always been hit or miss when it

comes to my mother. Some years she'd go all out—decorating a Christmas tree, visiting Santa, and hanging stockings near the window, since we didn't usually have a chimney. Other years—ones I now recognize as years when she was depressed—we'd have nothing at all. Once she wore her pajamas from December 24 until New Year's Day. My holiday feast was a packet of microwavable maple- and brown-sugar oatmeal, and by the end of the week her hair was shiny with oil and she smelled so bad I couldn't sit beside her. I didn't mind the oatmeal so much, but I felt like a ghost whenever she looked through me as if I wasn't even there.

The best Christmas—also the worst—was when we lived with Frank. He took us to a Christmas-tree farm out in the country, where we chopped down the biggest tree on the lot. He tied it to the roof of the car with twine, and when we got back to the house, Mom put on holiday music. We sang along with Brenda Lee as we decorated the tree, and for Christmas Eve dinner, Frank fixed baked ham and my favorite cheese potatoes. I went to bed that night buzzing with anticipation of what I'd find under the tree on Christmas morning. But when I woke up, not even the American Girl doll whose dark brown curls and brown eyes matched mine could erase the memories of what happened in the night.

We left a month later. It was sudden and immediate

because Mom was having what must have been a manic episode. I was building a snowman in the front yard when she came out of Frank's house with our suitcases already packed. As I followed her to the car, my mittens soggy from the snow, I asked about my doll.

"We don't have time for your stupid doll." She slammed the trunk and snapped that I needed to get in the car before Frank came home from work because it was his car.

As we drove to the bus station, I started to cry. Mom thought it was over the doll, and she made a promise—that she never kept—to buy me a new one.

"Just like it," she said. "Or, an even better one."

But it wasn't about the doll.

I was crying because I was so goddamn happy to be leaving.

"What do you want for Christmas?" Kat asks, interrupting my memories.

I want traditions. Eggnog. Peace on earth, goodwill toward man. I want to kiss Alex Kosta under the mistletoe. I want memories untarnished by ugliness. I want all of that without feeling guilty about wanting it. And I want my mom to get help—although peace on earth is probably a more realistic goal.

"I don't know." I stick my finger between the pincers of the plastic crab I'm holding and swing it back and forth. "Maybe I'll ask Santa to help me design a website, so Theo will stop asking me if I've finished it yet."

Kat's eyes roll back and she shakes her head at me. "Dude, why are you still torturing yourself over learning code? This is not something you need to know, especially when the Internet is full of do-it-yourself website builders. Google it and move on. Do you want to go Christmas shopping this weekend? We could go down to Tampa after work on Friday."

"Okay." I nestle the crab on one of the branches. "The idea of Christmas shopping is a little—"

"Surreal?"

"I've never really done it before. I mean, it was always just me and my mom, and I didn't have enough money to buy her anything."

Kat smiles wide. "It's kind of exciting, huh?"

"Yeah."

"So, beside your mom, who are you going to buy presents for this year?" She wriggles beneath the tree and plugs the cord into the outlet. As I settle the last crab into place, the lights flicker on. Our ocean-themed Christmas tree is one of the prettiest things I've ever seen.

"Well, you, Greg, Phoebe, Tucker, Joe, Yiayoúla, Al—" I catch myself before I say Alex's name. "And, um, maybe something for Theo."

Kat doesn't seem to notice my misstep. "That's cool,"

she says. "Maybe you can help me pick out a present for Nick. I'm totally stumped."

"Sounds good."

I gather up the empty decoration boxes and stack them in a corner of the back room. It's about time for my lunch break and I've been thinking it might be time to try something other than hummus and Coke. When I come out, my grandma is standing in the middle of the shop, admiring the tree. She's wearing a pair of jeans with a celery-green cardigan open at the neck to reveal her fine clavicle bones, and again it strikes me that I am a younger version of her.

She smiles when she sees me. "There's my sweet girl. I've come to take you to lunch."

"And me?" Kat makes puppy-dog eyes and tucks her hands up under her chin like paws. "I'm hungry, too."

Yiayoúla pats her cheek. "Next time, Ekaterina. There are things I need to discuss with Callista."

Kat shoots me a "what does that mean?" look and I answer with an "I have no idea" shrug, although I suspect my grandma wants to talk about Alex and his mom. I was hoping she'd forget, but it seems like she has a very long memory.

"Bring me back a Coke?" Kat asks, and I nod as I follow Yiayoúla out onto the street. She tucks her hand in the bend of my elbow and leads me to a narrow restaurant that smells of char-grilled meat and olive oil. We're seated at a table near the back and my grandma waves off menus, placing our order in Greek.

"Today we try something different. A specialty." She folds her hands primly on the table and gives me a look loaded with questions.

"I'm not going to do it." I don't look at her as I unwrap my silverware. "You can tell my dad that I've been seeing Alex if you want, but his relationship with his mom is none of my business."

Yiayoúla doesn't say anything, and it feels as if the volume in the restaurant has gotten louder. In her silence I can still hear what she wants from me. I scrape the tines of my fork down the place mat, leaving score marks on the paper as I avoid her eyes. She unfolds her napkin and places it on her lap as the waitress returns with glasses of water. It all feels so heavy.

"It's not fair," I say, when the waitress is gone.

My grandmother's slender shoulders rise and fall. "Life isn't fair."

Fury sweeps through me the way the dust storms whirled through that tiny crossroads town in New Mexico—and oh my God, I've forgotten its name. How could I have forgotten already? Pieces of me are falling off, getting lost.

I put down my fork.

"I've had a whole life of not fair," I say, meeting her eyes. "And then I came here and thought maybe, for once . . . except everyone just wants more from me than I can give. Greg expects the daughter he's always imagined. Kat wants slumber parties and double dates. And you—you keep pushing me to be Greek when I'm not even sure what that means yet. Can't I just be me until I figure it out?"

"Oh, Callista, of cour—"

"Alex accepts me the way I am," I say. "You have no right to ask this of me."

"Ordinarily, I would agree." Yiayoúla touches her hand to her heart. "And if you want the truth, I love the way you told me off just now. You're a stronger girl than you've been given credit for, I think. But . . . this is not ordinarily. Evgenia doesn't have much time, and she can't bear the thought of leaving this world without saying good-bye to her son. And because she is my best friend, I'm going to make it happen."

"He'll hate me."

"Not forever," she says. "He cares about you for the very same reason you care about him. He's not going to let that go."

I think about the transient boys. The ones who didn't really want me, let alone try to keep me. "That's not how life works."

"Of course it is," she says. "The good ones are the ones who are smart enough to stick around. And despite what the rest of the world thinks it knows about Alex Kosta, he is one of the very best." I look away and my cheeks grow warm. Yiayoúla reaches across the table and squeezes my hand with her cool fingers. "It will be okay. I promise."

"I still don't understand why I need to be a part of this," I say, as the waitress approaches with our lunches. "I mean, why can't you just take her down to the tour boat on a Sunday afternoon when he can't escape?"

"I like the way you think." Her smile is devious. "If you and I are the conspirators, Alex will blame us, not Evgenia. Yes. We'll do it this weekend."

"Great." There's no enthusiasm in my voice as I answer, and even less when the waitress sets a plate piled with tentacles on the table in front of me. There is absolutely no way I'm eating *octopus,* even if it tastes like proverbial chicken. "I'm sorry, but I really, really don't want this."

The waitress looks to my grandma for approval.

"Box it up," Yiayoúla says. "I'll take it home for later. Bring Callista whatever she wants."

"I, um—I'll have some hummus, please. And two Cokes."

The first time I wake up, I'm slumped over the table in the Airstream with my face stuck to a page of the GED study guide. The exam is coming up, and I'm nervous about the math segment because kindergarten addition and a battered old textbook can only carry you so far in life. I'm strong in language arts and social studies, and I've managed to reason my way through the science practice questions, but I'm having difficulty solving for *x*.

The next time I wake, it's three in the morning and my mom slides under the blanket beside me, wrapping her arm around my waist. As I settle back into the comfort of her embrace, my sleepy brain spins her presence into something that feels like a dream. Except her hair is drenched in the scent of cigarettes, and she's beer-breathy as she whispers through my hair that she loves me, so I know it's really her.

"Mom, you can't keep coming here," I whisper back.

In the stillness between us, I hear a car drive past on the next street over and a distant dog barks once, then again.

"I always wanted hair like yours." Her voice is soft and hoarse, her tongue thick with alcohol. She strokes my head. "So wild and beautiful."

"If you get caught, you'll be sent back to jail."

"This time will be different," she says. "You'll see. We'll settle somewhere nice. Maybe by the ocean.

Somewhere you can make friends and maybe get a job, or even go to college."

I roll over to face her. In the dim light, I can see the sadness wedged in the fine lines around her eyes and mouth, so I don't mention that I already have all those things right here, right now. I press my forehead against hers. "Is there somewhere you can stay . . . you know, until we leave?"

I don't know if this is truth or lie, but it feels false in my mouth. Her lips spread into a dreamy smile and my next heartbeat is spiked through with guilt.

"I had a room at a motel with someone I used to know"—she closes her eyes and her words get slow and sleepy—"but that fell through. I'll find something, though. Don't worry."

"Greg is renovating a house over on Chesapeake." Even as I'm saying it, I know this is a bad idea, but I can't bear seeing her looking so lost and alone. I don't want her sleeping in dirty motels with strange men. "There might be construction workers on-site during the day, but you could sleep there until, um—until we've got enough money to go."

She kisses my forehead. "I don't know what I'd do without you."

Her face goes soft with sleep, and it's here in this moment I'm overcome with love. She can't handle jail.

She needs to go to that imaginary someplace where she can settle down and not be looking constantly over her shoulder. I think for a while about the money I have stashed in the guitar. I doubt it's enough to buy even a cheap car, but there is enough for bus fare and some food. If I give it to her, she can leave.

We can leave.

I dream I'm locked in a jail cell with thick iron bars across the front like a cage, at the end of a long gray hallway. The concrete floor is cold under my bare feet, making my toes go numb, and my too-short Hello Kitty nightgown offers no protection from the shivers that shudder through me. In the corner of the cell is the dark form of a person I can't identify. All I know is that I am afraid.

At the other end of the hall is a door, and I can hear distant muffled conversation coming from behind it. It's white noise, a continuous and steady sound that doesn't waver when I call for help.

"I don't belong here!" I shout, wrapping my hands around the bars. "I want to go home."

The door opens and the chatter grows louder, spilling into the hallway as my grandma comes in. She's speaking Greek as she walks toward me, but I understand every word.

"This is your home now, Callista," she says. "We are your family."

She morphs into my mother as she continues down the hall, the tap of her footsteps echoing off the smooth, sterile walls. Mom is carrying my guitar case and the brown tweed suitcase I threw away after it broke. Her lips are painted bright red, making her teeth look so white, and she's wearing the sparkly barrette in her hair that she always says makes her feel like Courtney Love.

Behind her, the door swings open a second time and the chatter gets louder again for another moment as Alex enters the hall. He's wearing his old-fashioned dive suit without the bell helmet, and his footsteps boom as his metal shoes meet concrete, the sound bouncing off the walls and hurting my ears.

"Callie, wait," he says. "Wait for me."

Mom stops. When he catches up to her, her arm slithers around his waist and she snuggles up against him.

"No!" Panic rises up inside me as I realize he thinks she's me. "I'm here, Alex. I'm right here."

"I've got the money." Mom lifts the guitar case, indicating she knows where I've hidden my stash. "So we can leave whenever you're ready. Go someplace nice. Maybe Colorado. You can learn to ski."

"Alex, please." The words come out as a whimper. A plea. "Don't leave me."

Without even looking in my direction, they turn back in the direction of the door. Alex walks out of his heavy boots, leaving them in the hall. His dive suit falls away, crumpling like a hollow person on the floor.

They disappear behind the door and I'm alone with my fear. Until I feel Frank's hand on my shoulder. His smoky breath whispering that he's going to make me feel so good.

I wake up the third time when the first light of morning squeezes through the crack below the curtain and warms the back of my eyelids. My cheeks are tight with the dried tears I shed in my sleep. It's barely seven and my mom is gone again.

I get out of bed and open the closet where I keep my guitar. It's there. I open the case, remove the instrument, and shake it until the rubber-banded bundle of cash appears behind the strings. My insides go soft with relief and then tighten again with guilt for thinking the worst about my mom. I get annoyed all again when I spy a yellow page, torn from a phone book, with an ad for a pawnshop circled in red. It's lying on top of the built-in dresser between my hairbrush and a tube of lip balm. I was hoping she'd get my computer back, not make me go buy it.

Joining my dad, Phoebe, and the boys for breakfast is comforting after an unhappy night. The heat from the stove cuts the chill from the air, and Tucker's nonstop chatter sweeps the darkness like cobwebs from the corners of my brain.

“Big plans for your day off, Cal?” Greg asks.

The pawnshop ad is tucked in the pocket of my jeans. Even though I know I’m going to have to pay for my own computer, I’m getting it back. I pour syrup on my plate of waffles.

“There’s a first-aid class at the Methodist church. I might check that out.” It’s a half-truth. I saw a notice for the lesson in one of the free weekly papers we have on the counter of the shop, but wasn’t planning to attend until after I take the GED exam.

“Good idea.” Greg takes the syrup bottle from me. “I was thinking that tomorrow night we’d go get a pizza—just the two of us—and then go take a look at the house. They’ve made a lot of progress this week. Almost done.”

A bit of waffle stumbles on its way down my throat and I cough, my heart beating in double time at the thought of him finding Mom at the new house. And I realize—I have no way to warn her. I can only hope that she won’t be there when we arrive.

Chapter 16

The pawnshop is close enough for me to ride my bike. It's a hole-in-the-wall kind of place, with a doorbell that sticks on the first of two notes and the dry, burnt-toast smell of old, dusty things. Inside, it's as if someone erected a building around a yard sale: shelves and aisles overflowing with stereo systems, power tools, televisions, lawn mowers, bicycles, and musical instruments. Handguns and rifles hang on the wall behind a glass counter filled with rows of watches, rings set with a variety of gemstones, and dozens and dozens of gold necklaces. I step over the handle of a leaf blower as I look for the computer aisle, imagining my mom in this place trying to charm the broker into giving her more than he thinks my laptop is worth. She's always loved places like these. Says they have character.

Obsolete desktop computer models sit beside newer laptops, but as I scan the shelves I don't see mine. A man comes into the aisle. He's older, his hair graying at the temples, and he's liberally doused in the same cologne Frank put on in the morning. By the time he came to my room at night, it was faded and sour, but I remember the way the new scent would linger in the bathroom after he went to work. The memory brings an itch to my feet and I think about leaving. But this man is wearing a polo shirt with the name of the shop stitched on the chest.

"Need help?"

"I, um—I'm looking for a specific laptop." There's a tremble in my voice as my heart struggles to calm itself down. "One that would have been brought in about a week ago by a woman with short super-blond hair and"—I gesture at my mouth—"really red lipstick. It's, um, white—"

"I remember." He nods. "Sold it. That model always goes quick."

I'm not surprised the laptop is already gone, but I can't stop the sinking feeling I get. Greg doesn't spend much time in the Airstream, but every time he comes out for a little visit, I worry *this* will be the time he notices the computer is missing. I can't hide it forever. "Could I, um—can I give you a number to call if you get another one?"

The man gives me the "wait a minute" sign with his index finger. "Hang on."

He goes into the back, leaving me alone with the lingering and unsettling scent of his cologne. Five minutes later, he returns with a white laptop that from the outside looks the same as mine.

"This one's newer." He opens the lid. The keyboard is identical, but the track pad doesn't have a button along the bottom the way mine did. Still, it's close enough that Greg might not notice. He'd have to sit down to use it to see the difference. "Just came in last night."

"How much?"

"Two-fifty."

I press the power button to boot up the computer. The pawnbroker just stands there, and though I don't look at him, I can feel him watching me. I don't like it, but I think he's keeping an eye on his merchandise, rather than on *my* merchandise. The laptop comes to life with a familiar chime. I open all the programs and type out a few nonsense sentences to test the keys: The quick brown fox jumped over the lazy dog. The only thing we have to fear is fear itself. Help, I'm a genie trapped inside this computer! Set me free and I'll grant you three wishes!

That last one makes him chuckle a little.

I turn off the computer. "Would you take one hundred?"

"Two-fifty. Firm."

Two hundred and fifty dollars means I won't have much to spend on Christmas presents, but Mom didn't leave me much choice. I hand over the cash and he gives me the laptop, the power cord, and a dirty pink neoprene carrying case that I throw in the trash on my way out of the store. Then I feel bad for tossing away a carrying case just because it was dirty. Who have I become that castoffs aren't good enough for me? I go back to fish it out of the trash, but the pawnbroker is watching, which makes me feel suspicious and stupid, and the broken door chime keeps going off every time I open the door. Finally, with my face as pink with embarrassment as that dirty old laptop case, I just leave.

It's still early and I have no other plans, so I stash my new computer in the wire basket attached to my bike and ride to the bookstore. The breeze cools both my cheeks and the irritation I'm feeling toward my mom.

The chalkboard sign outside the bookstore is empty, and I'm greeted by angry, bone-rattling bass as I open the door. The throw pillows on the couch spell SUCK IT, and Ariel is standing on a stepladder, shelving books in a new section called *asses for the masses*. Most of the books in the section are legal thrillers and mysteries by stratospherically famous authors, so the implication is not lost on me. I'm not sure it's a statement she should be making when she's trying to sell these books to customers. Then again, I'm the only one in the store.

"Hey!" She has to shout over the music as she hops off the stepladder. She leans over the checkout counter to lower the volume. "Need any help?"

I shake my head. "I'm just kind of looking."

"Did you bring your application?"

"What?"

"I saw you take one the last time you were here," she says. "Are you going to apply for the job?"

"I don't know." A sigh escapes me. "I mean, I have a job right now with a family business—"

"God, I know how that works." Ariel hoists herself onto the counter, the zipper tabs on her green plaid bondage pants rattling against the wood. Her black T-shirt looks like it got caught in a shredder, but she pulls off the look. "My mom owns this place and I worked here through high school. Then I went away to college and I thought I'd escaped Tarpon Springs forever, and yet"—she lifts her arms like a TV game-show model—"here I am."

She wants to escape. Alex wants to escape. I wonder if I'd lived in this town my whole life if I'd feel that way, too, instead of being the girl who wants to stop moving and just stay in one place for a while.

Ariel spins the artsy postcard display, making it wobble and squeak. "I need to get the hell out of here."

"Would your mom be upset if you left?" I don't think Theo would mind if I quit, but family is important to Greg. He might be disappointed. Yiayoúla, too. And I think Kat wouldn't understand at all. But, really, the only thing the gift shop has going for it is its proximity to Alex.

"Well, I think she's like any mom. She'd probably keep me forever, if she could." Ariel laughs. "But I think she'll be relieved to have her shop back to normal."

"Why does she let you do all this?"

She shrugs. "It's kind of our thing. I work for cheap and she leaves me alone to do what I want. But when I'm bored, this is the result."

"Well . . ." I look around at the handmade signs. They're a nice touch and I think Ariel has the right idea—just not the best execution. "*I* think it's funny, but I can see how customers might be insulted by the suggestion that their favorite books suck."

"Oh, I'm fully aware," she says. "What my mom needs is someone who is *invested*, who will keep her from turning it into a haven for little old ladies who read bodice-ripper romances, but isn't, you know, *me*. Someone like . . . you."

"What makes you say that?"

"You just strike me as a book girl."

"A book girl?"

"The last time you were here, you looked for the books you wanted instead of whining about not being able to find them, the way most customers do." She lowers herself off the counter. "I'm Ariel, by the way."

"From *The Tempest*?"

"Thank you. God, just—you have no idea how many people assume I'm named after *The Little Mermaid*. What the hell was my mom thinking?"

"It could be worse," I say. "She could have called you Dogberry or Elbow."

"You know your Shakespeare." She smiles. "I like that."

"I'm Callista." I try out my full name, but then change my mind. "Callie."

"Nice to meet you," she says. "Anyway, think about the job, okay? I've got a good vibe about you, Callie, and I believe in vibes."

I allow myself to imagine working here. Rearranging the pillows into kinder words, making the sections more user-friendly, and playing music that isn't quite so—loud. I can picture girls like Kat lounging on the couch, drinking coffee and talking. Or girls like me, tucked in the corner with a book. "I will."

"Take your time." Ariel walks back over to her stepladder and the pile of books perched on top, waiting to be shelved. "I've scared off everyone else who has applied because they're just not right for the job. When you're ready, it'll be here."

After setting my new computer to my preferences, I spend the next couple of hours choosing a small stack of books. A couple I've read, but have always wanted to own. A couple more are books I've never read. And one is a book on architecture for Greg for Christmas. Ariel raises a judgmental eyebrow at Hiaasen.

"My, um, this guy I'm—" I trip over my tongue describing Alex as my boyfriend. I mean, he is. I think. But it feels strange talking to someone else about him. "He reads these and—you shouldn't judge."

She laughs as she enters the price of the paperback novel into the cash register. "I didn't say anything."

"He likes other stuff, too." I don't know why I feel the need to defend him—or myself—to her, but I do. "He mostly reads Thoreau."

"Sweet baby Jesus, you're not talking about the *Walden* tattoo guy, are you?" Ariel slides her hand down her forearm from elbow to wrist—the exact location of Alex's tattoo. "He buys books here all the time and, yeah, *that* guy can read anything he wants. Are you and him . . . ?" The words taper off into empty space as my cheeks catch fire.

"Well, it's still kind of new and he's gone most of the time, but, um—I guess we are."

She grins. "Not gonna lie. I've been secretly hoping he'll use a credit card so I can find out his name, but he always pays in cash."

"His name is Alexandros. Alex."

"Of course it is." She begins bagging up my purchases. "I mean, what other kind of name would a Greek god have? And you, *Callista* . . . the two of you should just get married and have beautiful demigod babies and—"

"Demigods have one human parent."

Ariel reaches across the checkout counter and pushes her fingers against my forehead. "Shut up, egghead. You're spoiling my story."

I can't help but laugh. "What are you? Twelve?"

"We don't get many guys in this store, let alone hot ones," she says. "So this is a big deal for me. Anyway, he looks like the kind of guy who could be a total dick, but he's always really polite. And quiet. And please tell me he's a good kisser."

I nod. "So good."

"I hate you." She hands over the bag of books and my receipt. "Get out of here and don't come back until you're ready to take the job. Got it?"

"See you later, Dogberry."

There's a short stick of white chalk lying on the top of the sign outside the store, so I use it to write on the empty sandwich board a Zen quote I remember from a book: *Leap and the net will appear.*

I mean it for Ariel, but I hope—I so hope—that it's true.

The moon—which was full and bright on the night of my sponge lessons in the gas-station parking lot—is absent, and the dark seems so much darker than usual as I ride to the house on Chesapeake. The breeze seeps through my sweatshirt, making me shiver. It bothers me that I'm sneaking out in the middle of the night again—that all I ever seem to do is sneak—but if Mom is at the house I can talk to her. Make sure she won't be there when Greg and I arrive.

I leave my bike by the street and go the rest of the way on foot, crossing the scrubby grass and sand lot to the house. The differences are marked from the last time I was here. The windows have been installed, and as I climb the steps to the new front door, I wonder if Mom could even get inside. Of course, this is my mother. She's developed a knack for getting inside locked places.

The front door is secure, but one of the sliding glass doors facing the bayou is not.

"Mom?" My voice bounces through the empty house and I slide off my flip-flops to silence the echo of my steps. I switch on the flashlight I found in Phoebe's kitchen junk drawer and slide the beam around the room. The skeleton frame of walls has been covered with drywall and the concrete floor covered with a rich brown wood. An *L*-shaped counter marks the boundary of the new kitchen and I can picture Phoebe preparing dinner there, looking up from time to time to admire the water or check on the boys.

The stairs to the second floor are finished with a handrail in the same wood, but with modern-looking stainless-steel balustrades. Like downstairs, the walls are hung, and the dormer overlooking the front of the lot is finished and wide enough for Greg's drawing table. I enter my room—*my room*—and the big hole in the outside wall is gone. In its place is a window seat with a set of French doors leading out onto the balcony. And around the window seat is the built-in bookcase he promised. Lying on one of the shelves is a hardcover copy of *Mandy*. I pin the flashlight beneath my chin, pick up the book, and open the cover. Inside is a note from Greg:

Callie,

I can't give you a shell cottage of your own, but I hope this will do.

Love,
Dad

My eyes fill with tears as I tuck the note back into the book and place it on the shelf, hopefully in the same spot he left it. Clearly I was not meant to see this until tomorrow. Sadness and joy tangle in my heart as I make my way back downstairs. I want this house. This room. This family. But the price is my mom, and I'm not sure I'm prepared to pay it.

When I reach the bottom of the steps, the orange glow of a lit cigarette cuts through the dark house, and I catch my mother in the beam of the flashlight. "Mom, you can't smoke in here."

"Look at you," she says, as I swipe cooled ashes into my hand from where she's tapped them onto the kitchen counter, and carry them out to the back deck. "Just a regular little daddy's girl now, aren't you?" The amusement in her voice follows me and I hate it.

"No one is supposed to know you've been here." My hands are dusty with ash when I come back inside. I wipe the residue on my jeans. "Why do you have to trash it?"

"You know, I find it interesting that you care so much about a place that's not your home." She sends a deliberate breath of smoke into the air and I can hardly stand the smell of it anymore. "Or, maybe you'd rather stay here with him. Is that what you're saying?"

"No, of course not." I answer too quickly and I worry that it's a lie. That she's seen the book upstairs. "Greg has been kind, Mom, and it's just—he's excited about showing me the house. So stay away tomorrow until we're gone, okay? Please?"

She doesn't even acknowledge the request. She leaves me standing in the dark uncomfortable silence until the only thing that feels right is to leave. And I'm no more certain about what will happen tomorrow than I was when I arrived.

Chapter 17

"You doing okay, Cal?"

Greg catches me picking at the pepperoni on my slice of pizza, my stomach so knotted by worry that we'll arrive at the house and find Mom there that I can barely eat. I want to enjoy this father-daughter moment, but instead I tell him a half-truth to cover the reality. "Just really excited."

I *am* looking forward to seeing the renovations with him, and I can't wait for him to give me the book he thinks will be a surprise. But . . . there's always a chance of "but" when my mother is involved.

Greg's enthusiasm is almost too big for his body to contain. At this moment, I can see heredity in play. He's just like Tucker. "We can go now," he says. "If you want."

We bike from the pizza place to the house on Chesapeake and enter through the front door. In daylight it's even prettier than in the dark, and the weathered gray shingles, even though they're new, keep the house looking like the one that's been standing in the same spot for decades. As we kick off our shoes in the front hall, there's no evidence my mom's even been here.

"So the choice is yours," Greg says, as we make our way toward the great room and the stairs to the second floor. "We can do the whole house tour first and save your room for last. Or start with your room."

I'm on the lookout for stubbed-out cigarettes or crumpled fast-food bags—classic signs of Mom—but relax when there's not even a sign of leftover ash on the kitchen counter. "My bedroom, definitely."

Following him up the stairs, I feel my own excitement build inside me like the fizz in a soda can, even though I've already seen his surprise.

"Ready?" He opens the door—

—and I see it.

The hardcover shell of the book is lying open in the middle of the floor with all the pages torn out and scattered around the room. Along the spine of the book, nothing but ragged little page stumps remain, and the thought of Mom, here in this room, deliberately destroying a book that was meant for me, hurts as badly as anything I can remember.

"What the hell—?" Greg goes into the room and squats down to pick up the pages as I stand rooted in the doorway, my hand clamped over my mouth, fighting to hold in the secrets clawing their way up my throat.

He looks over his shoulder at me, his dark eyes so sad. He knows. Of course he knows. Who else would do such a thing? "What, um—" He clears his throat. "Do you know anything about this, Callie?"

Anger throbs under my skin like a pulse. I could tell him the truth. We could find her. Turn her over to the police. But it's just a book. She could have broken all the windows or damaged something that might have hurt Tucker or Joe instead of just me. I shake my head and swallow all the words but one. "No."

A tear tracks down my face. I pretend it's not there as he asks again. "Are you sure?"

I nod. "I'm sure."

"This was supposed to be for you." He tucks all the torn pages back into the cover and stands. "So you would know—the only thing I've ever wanted is for you to feel at home."

"I do." He doesn't know I've seen his note.

His face shows everything as he looks at me for a long time. The uneasy shift of his jaw, the lingering sadness in his eyes, the confusion of his eyebrows as they pull together . . . there's so much more he wants to say as we stand here in deadlock. The tear seeps into the corner of my mouth and I swear I can taste the sorrow.

"Do you?" Greg places the ruined book on the window seat and crosses the room.

He wraps his arms around me, and as I hear the steady, reassuring thump of his heartbeat beneath his T-shirt, I feel as if my own chest still might crack open and pour the truth at his feet.

"I wish—" The words come out as a sigh as Greg releases me. There's one small damp spot on his shirt and I can't look at it. "You can trust me with anything, Callie. I wish I could make you believe that."

Even in the earliest of my memories, he's been there. I *do* trust him.

Just not where my mother is concerned.

"So, do you, um—do you like your room?" There's a snuffed-candle feeling between us and I can hear it in Greg's voice.

The window seat doubles as a doorway to the balcony outside and I can picture myself here on a rainy day with a book in my hands. The skylights overhead drench the room in sunshine. And the wall-length bookcase will hold more books than I can even imagine owning. "It's perfect."

His smile lacks the deep creases that usually bracket his mouth like happy parentheses. "We'll have to go pick out furniture soon. If you're interested."

"I am."

I mean it, but I see the doubt in Greg's eyes as he turns to lead me downstairs for the rest of the tour.

My cell phone vibrates in my jeans pocket as I ring up a wool sponge, a pair of sunglasses, and a pair of tickets for the nearly full two o'clock tour boat.

"Thanks," I say, bagging up the purchases for a lady wearing a Wisconsin Badgers sweatshirt. As Theo predicted, the stream of tourists has grown as the holidays approach. Schools are out, so families are arriving, as well as the snowbirds, who will stay until spring. "And enjoy the tour."

When she's gone, I dig out my phone and find a text message from Alex.

On my way home. Even though we have plans for tomorrow, I'd really like to see you tonight.

I catch myself smiling and glance around the shop to make sure Kat isn't looking, but she's busy talking a group of teenage girls into buying matching hemp bracelets so I type my reply.

Sounds good.

Business is steady for the rest of the afternoon, and Kat and I take turns behind the register. It's not my idea. If I had my way, I'd let her do all the selling, but Theo has us on a rotation schedule that forces me to interact with the customers. Talking to them hasn't gotten any less difficult, but selling is easier now that it's the holiday shopping season. And Kat's suggestion of pairing a wool sponge with a bar of soap and calling it a "Greek bath set"—which earned her the Theo Seal of Approval—is the most popular seller of the day.

"So, are we still on for shopping?" She comes up beside me at the checkout counter and gives me a little hip check as I'm ringing the final sale. Theo has locked the side doors and is waiting at the front to let the last customers out. "I've been trying to come up with something really good for Nick, you know? Like maybe Devil Rays tickets or a Kennedy Space Center tour for his big present, but I was thinking tonight we could look for stocking-stuffer-type gifts. A DVD or a nice shirt or something."

I hesitate as I slide the till closed, trying to come up with a good reason why I can't go tonight.

"What?" Kat asks. "Do you not want to go now?"

It occurs to me that I could just tell her no, but she's been talking about shopping all week and I don't want to disappoint her.

"No, I mean—I do, but Greg decided we should do a family dinner and then go see the progress on the new house. It was kind of a last-minute thing."

All I've been doing lately is lying, and I'm sick of myself for doing it, but it doesn't stop me. I hold my breath, watching her face as she removes the contents of the till. Hoping she doesn't know that Greg and I went to the house last night.

"Oh, that will be cool." She stuffs the cash and credit-card receipts in a zipper bag. "Give the boys a hug from me, and take pictures of your new room, okay? I'm dying to see it."

Her blessing only makes me feel worse.

Someone is speaking Greek in a low, hard voice as I approach Alex's boat that night. I stop, hanging back beside a nearby tree, watching the two dark shapes standing on deck. The taller of them is Alex, the other barrel-chested and short. His father. I can't understand the words Nikos is saying, but the anger is clear in the way he alternates between shaking his finger in Alex's face and smacking the side of his son's head with the flat of his hand. Alex's voice is absent in the conversation. He doesn't argue. Doesn't deflect the blows. He just stands there—his shoulders folded forward and his head lowered in defeat—absorbing the abuse. My fists curl into themselves and I stop myself from rushing to his defense, because this is Alex's story—one he hasn't told me—and I've come uninvited into the middle of it. I wonder if I should look away, give him his privacy, but I don't. I watch, my heart aching for him.

It's over when Nikos stalks off into the night. In his anger, he doesn't see me, but Alex does. He steps off the boat and we sit together on the bench.

"So, how much of that did you see?" He looks at the boat, at the river beyond it, but not at me.

"Too much."

"My mother never wanted me to work the boat." He plays with one of my stray curls. "She wanted Phoebe and me to get college educations and not have to work so hard for so little. Then she got sick and what little college money there was—it's gone and my pops had to take out a loan against the boat."

He moves his hand to the back of my head, burrowing his fingers into my hair, sending shivers down the back of my neck as we sit in silence. I steal a glance at him. His eyes are closed, and there's a ghost of a smile on his face.

"So," Alex says finally. "I dropped out of high school to work the boat because Pops couldn't stand the idea of putting Mom in a nursing home. No one forced me to do it. I volunteered."

My eyebrows pull together. "But Phoebe thinks—"

"My sister believes what she's meant to believe," he says. "Trust me, I hate getting the shit beat out of me every week because I didn't bring home enough sponges or because Orfanos down the dock got a better price than I did. But Pops has his pride, you know? He's doesn't want anyone to know there's nothing left, or that the boat's at stake. And if Phoebe found out, Greg would probably offer our pops money, which would embarrass him even more."

I touch the fading bruise on his cheek from the last time his dad punched him. The one he claimed he got in a bar fight. His face carries a powdery trace of salt from sweat and the ocean. Alex reaches up and pulls my hand away, lacing his fingers through mine.

"And the most fucked-up thing is that when my mom dies, I'll be free," he says. "I can't even look at her because I feel so guilty. I don't *want* her to die, but I'm so damn tired."

"It's too much for one person to carry alone," I say.

"Yeah, well . . ." Alex shrugs. "That's just the way life works out sometimes."

The words "your secret is safe with me" are on my tongue, but I feel as if saying them will take away their power. Instead, I lean in and brush the softest of kisses against his lips. *Of course, your secret is safe with me.* He wraps his arms around my waist and shifts me onto his lap, kissing me until the world is a faraway place and the only reality is the two of us here on this bench.

"I missed you," Alex whispers, his forehead touching mine, his fingers curled around the back of my neck beneath my hair, tracing tiny circles on my skin. "All week I've wanted just three things: hot wings, cold beer, and you."

"That's so weird. I've been wanting the same three things."

"Yeah?"

"No, but I missed you, too."

"You know, secrets don't really stay secret if you make out on benches in the middle of the docks."

I don't have to turn around to recognize Kat's voice. But I do. And she's standing just a few feet behind the bench.

"What, um—what are you doing here?"

"I left my wallet at the shop." She starts toward the store, her intended pace faster than her wedge-heeled sandals can carry her. "But don't let me interrupt. I mean, it's not like I'm anyone who matters."

I stand. "I need to go talk to her."

Alex nods and squeezes my hand. "I'll be here."

"Kat," I say, hurrying to catch up with her. "Kat, please . . . I'm sorry."

"It's not really even that it's Alex." She doesn't stop and she doesn't look at me. "I mean, I get that. You're gorgeous and clearly he doesn't think of *you* as a little sister." Kat fights with the lock on the front door. "But you could have at least *told* me. First Connor, now this. It's like you have no idea how friendship works."

She kicks the door with a cry of frustration and her hands to her sides, the key still sticking out.

"Kat, I've never had a friend before. Ever." I give the key a gentle turn and the lock slides back. "It's just been me and my mom for my whole life, and I've never stayed anywhere long enough to have one. Or, *be* one. I guess I've always known that I should have told you about Alex, but I didn't want to upset you. Except—"

She sniffles. "Yeah, I was going to be upset either way, which is just stupid because Nick is so much better. No offense."

"None taken."

"I guess it's just that I'd built Alex up in my imagination to be—I don't even know. Like I had this dumb fantasy that one day he would realize how perfect I was for him." There's a note of embarrassment in her soft laugh. "And even though I know he's so not right for me, the rejection still kind of hurts a little, you know?"

"I'm sorry I didn't tell you."

The shop is lit only by the crustacean Christmas tree

as we step inside and Kat goes to the back room for her wallet. She's back in only a few moments. "So I was thinking that maybe I've been a little pushy. I mean, I just plopped down on your bench and made myself your best friend without thinking that maybe you didn't want one."

"I do."

"Thanks." She smiles. "So do you think now that it's Christmas break and I don't have school we could go shopping on Monday after work? And, you know, maybe talk?"

"Definitely."

"No blowing me off for Alex?" Kat asks, as she relocks the front door.

I hold up three fingers, a holdout gesture from the days I pretended I was a Girl Scout and made badges for myself out of construction paper. Before I realized homeless girls aren't scouts. "I promise."

Chapter 18

Greg is hunched over a bowl of cereal with a computer magazine when I come into the kitchen for breakfast the next morning. My hair is still damp from the shower and under my jeans and green plaid shirt I'm wearing the bikini Kat picked out for me. I could see my breath on my short trek across the yard, so I'm skeptical it's going to be warm enough for the beach, but Alex insists the winter-morning chill will burn off by the afternoon. I take a bowl from the cupboard. "Where is everyone?"

"Phoebe is painting at the new house." Greg slides the cereal box across the table. It's his favorite, a healthy variety that tastes okay but feels like you're eating a bowl of twigs. "And the boys are with my mom for the day."

"I'm, um—going to the beach today with friends."

The air between us feels overstuffed with the unspoken. I add to the thickness by omitting the part in which Alex is the friend, the beach is down in Bradenton, and I'm finally having my real first date. Greg nods. "What time will you be home?"

"Not sure, but don't count on me for dinner," I reply. "And I'll have my phone."

The crunch of cereal fills my head, blocking out the uncomfortable silence, and I focus on each bite so I don't have to look him in the eye. Pretending Thursday never happened is harder than it seems, especially when the image of Greg holding the ruined book is burned painfully into my memory.

He's still eating as I rinse my bowl and put it in the dishwasher.

"I guess I'm going to go now."

"Have fun." Greg glances up at me, flashes a quick smile, and then returns his attention to the magazine. I feel as if I've been dismissed and it stings a little.

"Thanks, um—I'll see you tonight."

I go back to the Airstream for my beach bag before walking over to Grand, where Alex is waiting in his truck. He's sitting sideways on the bench seat, facing out through the open driver's-side door. The sun hits him just right, catching the sun-bleached gold in his curls. He looks like living summer.

“Hi.” I step between his knees and he leans forward to kiss me. His lips are cool as I touch the ragged hem of his faded red board shorts. “Aren’t you freezing?”

“Nope. I’m amphibious.” He steps down from the cab, walks around with me to the passenger side, and yanks open the sticky door. It creaks in protest.

“Amphibious, huh? Born with gills and lay your eggs in water?”

“Well, I was going to say I’m cold-blooded.” He runs his fingers up through his curls and my stomach does a crazy little happy dance. “But now . . .”

I laugh. “Sorry.”

“It’s okay,” he says, as I get in the truck. “I like smart girls.”

He slams the door shut and I lean through the window. Our faces are so close I can see the way his eyelashes go from dark at the base to pale at the tips. “This door isn’t ever really going to fly open without warning, is it?” I ask.

Alex shakes his head. “I only said that so you’d sit closer to me that first time.”

“I would have anyway.”

He kisses me again, then touches the tip of my nose. “So smart.”

The hula girl dangling from the rearview mirror does a wild wind dance as we head south on US 19 with the windows down, past car dealerships, strip malls, fast-food joints, and shabby little pink motels that look as if they haven't been touched in half a century. Reggae spills from a pair of small speakers wedged between the windshield and sun-faded dashboard, attached to a portable cassette player. Alex sings along with the warped song. I like his voice, scratchy and off-key, and how he's not self-conscious about it. I like the way he sticks his arm out the open window and pushes against the wind. And when he looks in my direction, I like knowing that even though they're shaded by dark sunglasses, his eyes are smiling at me, too.

"Is it scary?" I kick my flip-flops off and prop my bare feet on the open window frame. I can see the dirt on my soles in the side mirror. "Snorkeling, I mean."

"Nah." Alex's nose crinkles a little as he shakes his head. "Well, it might be a little at first because you've never done it before, but once you're in the water—it's better than sex."

"Better?"

His laugh is the slightly wicked one that does warm things to my stomach. "Okay, maybe not, but it's better than everything else."

"Will there be sharks?"

"It's possible." He shrugs. "We're more likely to see a ton of fish, and maybe some rays and seahorses. It's a good reef for this part of the state, but the Keys are so much better. I'll have to take you there sometime."

Happiness gives my heart a little squeeze. My life feels so tentative that I like that he's thinking of a future with me in it. Even if it never happens, it feels good right now. "I've never done anything like this before," I say. "Then again, I really haven't done much of anything."

"Nothing?"

"When you live a transient life in a lot of little nowheres . . . it's not really an adventure," I say. "My mom always pretended it was, or—I don't know, maybe she believed it, but all we've ever done is existed. She worked one crappy job after another, and I didn't have time to make new friends and I couldn't go to school, so I just marked time from one move to the next. I taught myself guitar and—"

"You didn't go to school?"

"Just kindergarten."

"No wonder Greg thinks I'm too old for you."

I push his shoulder, laughing. "Shut up."

Alex's hand wraps around my upper arm and pulls me across the bench seat, until my feet are in the cab and I'm against him. With his eyes still on the road, he kisses me.

"Didn't Einstein say something about driving and kissing?" I ask.

The tires squeal as he turns into the parking lot of a mostly vacant strip mall, puts the truck in park, and shifts me onto his lap. "To paraphrase, he said if you can do both at the same time . . ." His lips find a spot on my neck, below my ear, and send heat rushing . . . everywhere, making me wonder if it's possible to be addicted to a person, like drugs, or cigarettes, or sadness. ". . . you're doing it wrong."

His mouth tastes faintly of the sea, as if he's so steeped in it that it's permeated his blood. Flooded his cells. And even if I'm imagining it—which I think I am—I want it. Want *him* so much.

My shirt is completely unbuttoned when I open my eyes and my brain reenters the atmosphere. We're in a parking lot. The highway is only yards away and the whoosh of passing cars is unrelenting.

"We shouldn't do this," I say. His lips touch mine again. "Not here."

"Why?"

"Greg doesn't know I'm with you." I refasten the bottom button, suddenly sober. "Can you imagine his reaction if he finds out not only that we're together, but that we got arrested for having sex in a parking lot in *Pinellas Park*?"

Alex blows out a breath laced with frustration. "Mentioning your dad has exactly the same effect as a cold shower."

From my own side of the cab, I button up my shirt as he merges back into traffic. I watch him from the corner of my eye. I've never turned down anyone for sex, so I'm not sure how this works. His sunglasses are back on and I can't see his eyes, but his mouth is set in a smile and his thumbs tap the steering wheel in time with the music. He seems unbothered.

Alex catches me looking. "What?"

"Are, you, um—is it okay that we didn't—?"

He presses the tip of his finger to the middle of my forehead. "Only one of us was thinking and it was not me."

"So, we're all good?"

Alex grins. "You are here, right now, with me, so yeah . . . all good."

Relieved, I return to my pre-parking-lot position with my feet out the window. Except this time I lie back on the seat, looking at him from upside down, and wonder if this is how my mom felt when she first met Greg. About how quickly someone can go from being a stranger to someone you feel as if you can't do without.

But mostly how, when I'm with Alex, I feel like a normal girl. Like my whole world is right here in the cab of this pickup truck and that's enough.

I stay in this position—with my head against his thigh and his fingertips on my cheek—until we reach the Sunshine Skyway bridge over Tampa Bay. Bright-yellow cables angle down to the deck from two huge support pillars, making it seem like rays of sunshine are beaming down on the bridge. I scramble for my phone and Alex laughs. "Tourist."

I reach back to give him the finger as I stick my head out the window like a happy dog and tilt my phone up to capture a picture of the bridge. The result on the screen is a series of slanted yellow bars with the vivid blue of the sea and sky in contrast.

"Can't tell it's a bridge," Alex says.

"I know." I press the button to put the phone to sleep. "But I'll always know what it's meant to be."

The tops of my feet are splotched pink from the sun by the time we reach the next bridge, the one crossing over onto Anna Maria Island. Traffic slows to a stop as a pair of red-and-white gates block the road.

"Is that a drawbridge?" I climb back out the window, sitting on the door frame, to watch as the deck slowly tilts up to allow a tall white-masted sailboat to pass through. The driver of the car behind us revs the engine impatiently, as if it will somehow speed the boat's progress. The sea breeze carries the scent of the tide and exhaust, and seagulls glide on invisible currents overhead. I take pictures of the drawbridge, a waterfront oyster bar at the side of the road, and Alex, laughing at me through the windshield.

"That was so cool," I say, when the bridge is back in place and we're bumper-to-bumpering our way forward with the rest of the tourists.

"You kill me," Alex says.

The wheels of the truck rumble over the mesh grating of the drawbridge deck as we cross. I take a picture of the little blue bridge-tender building. "I've never seen a drawbridge before."

"It's just—you're making me see through different eyes today," he says. "It's like everything is interesting to you."

"Everything *is* interesting to me."

"Then you"—he slides his arm along the bench seat behind me—"you're going to love snorkeling."

Alex parks in front of a dive shop just off Gulf Drive, the road that runs the length of the island. The glass front door is pasted with flyers for dive trips and upcoming certification courses, and a bumper sticker tells us that "a bad day diving beats a good day at work." This is the kind of life I think my mom always meant for us to have, and even though my stomach flutters with excitement, I feel a little sad that I'm living it without her. Alex threads his fingers through mine as we go inside, and I push the sadness away.

A guy wearing a faded red T-shirt with the shop logo printed on the back is hanging dive masks on a display in the middle of the shop. He looks up as we come in.

"Hey, Alex!" He tucks a stray lock of long dark hair behind his ear as they shake hands and flashes me a grin. "Long time, bro. Good to see you."

"You, too." Alex introduces us. "Callie, this is Dave. He's one of my dive buddies. Dave, this is Callie. She's the girl I eat Drumsticks with in the middle of the night."

"Never heard it called that before." Dave laughs, making me blush. "Doing the wreck today, or the rocks?"

"Rocks," Alex says.

"Nice choice. Viz has been about fifteen to twenty feet the last couple days. Should be lots to see. Maybe even some dolphins. Need gear?"

"I brought mine," Alex says. "But Callie could use some, and maybe a suit if you have a spare."

Dave sizes me up. "I think my sister's stuff would probably fit. Hang on." He crosses to a wooden door covered with white oval-shaped decals from different dive sites around the world. As he disappears behind the door, I wonder if he's been to all of those places. He emerges with a mesh dive bag. "I've got a snorkel, a mask, fins, boots, and a shortie. Need anything else? Got water? Sunscreen?"

Alex nods as he takes the bag. "This'll do it. Thanks."

Dave grabs a disposable underwater camera from a counter display and hands it to me. "Take a camera, too. On me."

"Thanks."

"Anytime. Listen, man, we're doing a trip to Roatan in February. You in?"

Disappointment washes over Alex's face, as if it's seeping right out of his pores. He shakes his head. "Still working the boat."

"No worries, bro. There will always be more trips." Dave slaps his shoulder and turns to shake my hand. "It was great to meet you, Callie."

"You, too."

Alex is quiet as he throws the gear in the back of the truck beside his own dive bag and a small red cooler, and we turn back out onto Gulf Drive, heading toward the north end of the island. I wonder if he's thinking about missed opportunities, too.

"What are the rocks?" I ask.

"The Spanish Rocks," he says. "It's a reef made from some limestone ledges along the bottom. Not sure why they call it Spanish Rocks, because it's neither, but it's been called that as long as I can remember. Anyway, it's a good place to learn."

Alex turns left into a tiny beachfront parking lot where a couple of divers in full wet suits are unloading tanks and fins from the back of their SUV. Something that resembles envy flickers across his face as they carry their gear to the beach, and I worry that he'll be bored snorkeling on the surface with me when he could be underwater like them. He leans over and kisses me. "Ready?"

"I think so."

We get out of the truck. While Alex takes the bags and cooler from the bed, I unbutton my shirt. He pauses, watching.

"Do you have to do that?" I ask. "You've seen me in my underwear before."

He laughs. "I've seen you out of your underwear, too, but I haven't seen you in a bikini yet. Consider me curious."

The bikini is pretty basic—blue-and-white gingham checked with pale-green ties—but Kat declared it The One. The way Alex is looking at me now makes me wonder if she wasn't right. "Happy now?"

"Absolutely." His curls bobble as he nods. He leans forward to kiss me again and I come away with a rash of goose bumps, and I'm not sure if they're from the cool breeze sweeping in from the gulf or his hands on my bare hips.

"The water temperature is about seventy-five, which is fine for splashing around in shallow water at the beach, but it gets cold when you're in the water for an extended period of time, so this will help keep you warm." He hands me a wet suit, but instead of being the full-body style the divers are wearing, it has short sleeves and thigh-length legs. "You do know how to swim, right?"

Mom taught me one summer at a lake in Indiana, and there was a lifeguard at the community pool in Michigan who let me in free so he could stare at my chest. Not that Alex needs to know about that. "Yep."

We put on the suits at the truck and carry the rest of our gear down to the water. We leave the dive bags, beach towels, and cooler far enough up in the sand to keep them from being washed away. The borrowed boots are the right size for me, and once I have them on, we move out into waist-deep water to put on our fins. Tiny streams of cold trickle up my thighs, taking my breath away, and I have to stop to let the water in my suit warm up.

"Oh my God, how do you do this every day?"

"This is a picnic compared to what I do." He puts on his fins, and I watch and do the same. "There are a lot of mornings I'd rather stay in my warm bunk than jump into water this cold and then spend hours walking along the bottom of the gulf, most of the time against the current, cutting sponges off the sea floor. It's hard work, but more than that, it's boring and lonely. But calling in sick doesn't pay the bills, and you've seen what happens when the harvest isn't enough."

"I'm sorry."

The tilt at the corner of his mouth absorbs my apology. "Warm enough yet?"

"I think so."

"Good. Now take your mask and spit in it."

"Seriously? That's a real thing?"

"It helps keep it from fogging up." Alex spits in his own mask, smears the saliva around the lens, and then rinses it in the water. "And before you ask, I have no idea why it works. It just does."

I do the spit-smear-rinse technique, then peer at him through the lens. He looks exactly the same. "How will I know if it worked?"

"If your mask starts fogging up, it didn't work," he says. "Then surface and do it again."

"Now what?"

Alex positions his mask on his face. The strap mats down his curls where it circles around his head. He shrugs. "Swim."

"But—"

He takes my mask and eases it down over my head, being careful not to tug my hair. When it's centered on my face, he moves his hands away. "Does it feel okay?"

"How would I know?"

"It would feel loose here"—he gestures toward the sides near his temples—"or the strap might feel too tight around your head."

"I think it's good."

He holds the U-shaped end of the snorkel out where I can see it. "So now all you do is put this end in your mouth and use it to breathe while you swim."

I lift my legs and put my face in the water. The world goes green and quiet, except for the sound of my own breathing. At first I breathe too fast, as if I'm somehow going to run out of air, even though the snorkel connects me to the world's supply. In shallower water, the sand is dotted with puffy brown sand dollars that look nothing like the bleached white ones we sell in the shop. Tiny minnows hover and dart just above the bottom, and prehistoric-looking horseshoe crabs bulldoze tracks in the sand. For yards, the only change to the landscape is the addition of larger fish and coral fans that look like lone trees in an underwater desert.

Then we reach the Spanish Rocks.

The reef is covered in green and red algae, and corals of white and yellow and even orange. The water around the reef is teeming with silver-striped fish, flashing in the muted sunlight and moving together as if they're dancing to their own silent song. It feels as if the world has gotten so much bigger and I start to understand—if even just a little—why Alex doesn't want to be confined to one small part of it.

"Oh my God," I say into my mouthpiece, but the words funnel up through the snorkel and are lost to the sky above me. I stretch my arm out toward the fish, but the water is deceptively deep and I'm disappointed they're not close enough to touch.

I lift my head out of the water and pull the snorkel away to catch my breath. Alex surfaces beside me as I push the mask up onto my forehead.

"Everything okay?"

I nod. "It's just—this is the most exciting thing I've ever done. It's—there are so many fish and it looks like they're right *there*—" I know I'm babbling, but I'm so overwhelmed that I can't stop. "—and I could touch them, but they're too far away. And it's so beautiful. I want to get closer. I want to see it all."

His smile is so wide and through his mask his eyes are half-moons of happiness. "Diving is even better."

"I want to do that."

"I don't think I've ever converted anyone that fast before." Alex laughs as he slides his mask up and kisses me with saltwater lips. And this time it's not my imagination, because mine are saltwatery, too. "Lucky for you, I happen to know a guy who can teach you."

"Thank you for bringing me."

"Don't thank me yet." He positions his mask over his eyes again. "We're just getting started."

I move my own mask back into place and lower my face into the water again. We swim together over the colorful reef, silently pointing out brown stingrays as they ruffle along the bottom, wings dancing like a dress on a clothesline. Alex dives down and brings back a crab that tucks itself up into the shell on its back, refusing to come out until it's returned to its home beneath one of the ledges. On his next trip to the bottom, he returns with a sand dollar.

"Do you want to keep it?" he asks, when we break the surface.

I shake my head as I hand it back. I don't tell him that I won't need any souvenirs to remember this trip. "It might have a family that would miss it."

He laughs. "You might be right."

The sand dollar tumbles end over end through the water until it lands on the sand, and we continue along the reef.

Alex catches my arm and points at a brown shark moving at a lazy pace near the bottom. He submerges and swims toward the fish and I feel my heart slide up into my throat. Although the fact that Alex is swimming after it should be reassuring, I've never seen a shark anywhere but on television. It jets away, and when Alex comes up from the bottom, we surface again.

"How do you do that?" I ask.

"Do what?"

"Swim down like that."

"You just hold your breath as if you're in a swimming pool," he says. "It's exactly the same."

"I'm afraid I'll accidentally take a breath through the snorkel and drown myself."

"It's pretty unlikely," he says. "When you've already got lungs full of air, there's not really room for more."

"I never thought about it like that."

"Maybe start slow," he suggests. "Draw in a breath, hold it, and just swim down until your snorkel is completely submerged."

I try it once, then again, and it is exactly like holding your breath in a swimming pool. On my third attempt, Alex takes a picture of me underwater, my hair fanning out around me like sea grass.

"See?" he says. "Easy. Next time try to go a little

deeper, until you're able to gauge how long you can stay down. And with practice you'll be able to stay down longer."

We snorkel until the sun is high and warms my back through the neoprene skin, and I ache in places I never knew I had muscles. The swim back to the shore is easier with the waves pushing us from behind, but by the time we reach water shallow enough to stand, I'm trembling from exertion. Alex removes his mask and fins and walks the rest of the way to shore, shaking his head like a wet dog. Water sprays out in every direction as his curls spring back to life. I swim until my belly scrapes the sand, then flop on my back, letting the waves lap at my legs.

Alex laughs as he brings me a bottle of water from the cooler. "You look like a mermaid."

"A tired mermaid." The first sip is brackish from the salt on my lips, but the next is cold and clear, and I can almost feel it moving through my veins. "How do you say 'mermaid' in Greek?"

"*Gorgóna*. Or maybe, for you, *seirína* would be better." I've never heard him speak the language before. "*Deleázontas tous naftikoús stin katadíki tous.*" The words flow easily, warmly. I love how it sounds.

"What does that mean?"

"Luring sailors to their doom." He sits down on the

sand beside me. "And then, in Greek mythology, there are *nýmfes*."

"Nymphs."

"Right." He nods. "But they are more like sea goddesses."

"I think I like the idea of being a sea goddess rather than someone who lures sailors to their doom," I say.

"I can see that about you." He shoulder-bumps me. His skin is warm against mine. "You don't strike me as a vengeful mermaid."

"Could I lure you into taking me to lunch?"

Alex laughs. "*Den tha íthela na apogoitéfso tin theá.*"

"And what does *that* mean?"

"Wouldn't want to disappoint the goddess." He ignores the sand on my skin as he kisses my temple, then moves into the water at my feet and removes my fins. "One of your more wrathful family members might try to smite me." Alex lifts my leg and kisses the inside of my knee. Heat flashes through me like summer lightning. Remembering. He grins and I know we're remembering the same thing.

"I'd never let anyone smite you," I say.

He winks at me as he peels off my boots and helps me to my feet. "If I had a dollar for every time I've heard *that*."

"And here I thought I was your first mermaid."

"Goddess," he says. "You are my first goddess."

As I follow him up the sand to the truck, warmth rises up in my chest. It's silly, I know. Just a joke. But I kind of like the idea of being someone's goddess.

Chapter 19

My shirt doubles as a cover-up, and my hair is knotted and thick with salt, but I'm not out of place among the sandy feet and dripping swimsuits on the patio of the beachfront snack bar. We order baskets of fried clams and shrimp at a pass-through window, and eat them at a plastic picnic table beside a group of tourists speaking a language neither of us can identify. Alex squirts ketchup on his french fries, oblivious to the trio of teenage girls who stare at him as they walk past. His bare foot rests lightly on top of mine beneath the table and he offers me a fried shrimp in exchange for one of my bigger clam strips. When we finish lunch, we return the borrowed gear to Dave at the dive shop and head back toward Tarpon Springs.

The combination of fried food, fresh air, and

snorkeling takes its toll on me before we're even through Bradenton, and I curl up on the bench seat to sleep, my head against Alex's thigh.

I dream I'm a mermaid, my lower half a tail made of iridescent blue and pale-green scales, washed up on a Florida beach. Around me, people are basking in the sunshine, playing Frisbee, and applying piña colada–scented sunscreen. I close my eyes, enjoying the kiss of the air and the warm sand beneath my back, until a shadow blots the sun. I open my eyes and Alex is standing over me with my old, familiar Hello Kitty nightgown in his hands. It's only then that I'm aware that my top half is naked, so I pull the too-small nightgown over my head and squeeze my arms into the sleeves. Alex kneels down on the sand beside me and leans in to kiss me. His face morphs into Frank's as the whiskers under his lower lip brush against my cheek, making me scream.

I wake as the truck swings wildly off the road and skids to a halt on the shoulder. My heartbeat is wild, and although I'm almost certain it's Alex behind the wheel, I don't trust my own eyes. I'm pressed against the passenger door, as far away from him as I can be.

"Jesus Christ, Callie." It's Alex's voice I hear as he throws the truck in park. "You just scared the shit out of me."

My fingers scrabble for the door handle. "What did you do?"

"I didn't do anything," he says. "I just put my hand on your cheek and you freaked out."

I grab his hand and examine his palm. There's a frayed callus at the base of one of his fingers, one that could easily feel like whiskers against a sleeping cheek. "I'm so sorry."

"You don't have to apologize for having a nightmare." He twists his wrist to hold my hand. The callus feels normal now. Familiar. Like Alex. "But you screamed as if you were terrified. What the hell was that about?"

"I need some water."

I get out of the cab and take a bottle of water from the cooler. The label, wet from soaking in melting ice all day, disintegrates into tiny blue-and-white bits in my hand. Alex lowers the tailgate and sits, waiting patiently as I take a long drink. The steel of the tailgate is warm against the backs of my thighs as I slide up next to him—and tell him all about Frank.

Tears stream down my face as I talk, but it feels as if some of the poison inside me has been released. I don't feel clean, exactly, but cleaner. Lighter. Alex has left the tailgate and is pacing a path in the gravel on the side of the road, his fist clenching and unclenching, as if he wants to hit something. Or someone.

"That bastard is so goddamn lucky I don't know where he lives," he says. "I'd slit his fucking throat with my dive knife and laugh all the way to prison."

A tear-soaked laugh escapes me.

"That's not meant to be funny," Alex says.

"It's not." I wipe my face on my sleeve. "It's just—I don't know. In a weird way that makes me happy, because he said no one would believe me if I told." Fresh tears fill my eyes. "And for so long I thought it was true."

"I believe you," he says. "And even though he has issues with me, I think Greg—"

"You can't tell him."

"He needs to know, Callie. Your mom should be held accountable for this, and if they can find this Frank asshole, he should be arrested, too."

"No."

He runs his fingers up through his curls, then drops his hands to his hips. "Cal—"

"She's my mother, Alex. I can't do that to her."

"She doesn't deserve this kind of devotion."

I meet his eyes. "Neither does your dad."

"No." He regards me silently for a moment. "But my mom does."

"And so does Greg," I say. "This truth isn't going to make his life any better than it is right now. Please. Don't tell him."

"Fine," he says, as a black-and-tan Florida Highway Patrol car rolls off the road behind him.

A female officer gets out and walks over to us. "Is everything all right here?"

"Yes, ma'am," I say. "I think I had a little too much sun today at the beach. I felt like I was going to throw up, so we pulled over so I could get some water and . . ." I gesture toward the brush along the side of the road, inferring that I'd vomited in them. My eyes, swollen from crying, seem to solidify the lie.

"There's a Walgreens at the next exit," the trooper offers, her official tone a little softer now. She smiles. "I'd recommend some Pepto and maybe a few minutes in their air conditioning, instead of hanging out here on the shoulder."

I hop down from the tailgate. "We'll do that. Thank you."

We pull back onto the highway as she returns to her patrol car. She follows us for a couple tenths of a mile, before U-turning southbound. Even though I'm in no danger of actually throwing up, we take the next exit to Walgreens, where we buy a couple of Drumsticks and eat them in the magazine aisle.

I fall asleep again when we're back on US 19, but this time my dreams are untroubled and I wake when Alex pulls alongside the curb on Grand. He laughs when I sit up. I tilt in the rearview mirror in my direction as he gets out of the truck, and discover seat marks embossed on my cheek. Also, my hair is pushed up on one side in a righteous case of bed head.

"Wow. Not so much the goddess at the moment," I say, as Alex opens the passenger door for me.

"Not so much," he agrees, wrapping his arms around my waist.

"Thanks for teaching me how to snorkel. And, you know . . ."

He presses his forehead to mine. "Let's not talk about that, because I spent the rest of the drive coming up with new and interesting ways to kill someone. I'd rather just kiss you."

I circle my arms around his neck. "That sounds like a much better use of your time." My lips meet his and he shifts me tighter against him. I haven't had many days worth remembering so I'm reluctant for this one to end. "Maybe you could come over. You know, later."

"Already planned on that."

"Good," I say, kissing him once more. "I should probably go. I told Greg not to count on me for dinner, but he'd probably like it if I showed up. Thanks, um—thanks for understanding why I don't want to tell him about—"

"I don't really understand," Alex interrupts. "I still

think you should tell him, but . . . it's your decision and I can respect that."

My stomach knots as I think about Yiayoúla's scheme to reunite him with his mother. And I realize I have the chance to warn him about what's going to happen tomorrow.

"Alex—"

"Oh, shit," he says, his voice low. "We are so busted."

I turn around to see Tucker come sailing down the block on training wheels, his head covered in a huge white bike helmet that makes him look like a miniature alien. Behind him is Phoebe, pushing Joe in his stroller, her eyes wide with surprise.

"Hey, Phoebs." Alex greets his sister as if she didn't just see us making out. I wish I could be so nonchalant, but I can see the questions in her eyes and I don't want to have to answer them. I look at the ground and say hello.

"Uncle Alex!" Tucker slides off his bicycle and launches himself into Alex's arms. "You were kissing Callie *on her mouth*."

I wish I could melt right into the cracks between the sidewalk, and when I glance at Phoebe, her face seems to suggest she's wishing the same for herself.

Alex laughs. "Yeah, buddy, I was."

"Are you gonna have a wedding?"

"No, but when I do, you'll be the first to know, okay?"

"But—" Tucker looks confused as Alex lowers him to his feet. He's about to ask another question when Phoebe interrupts him. "Tuck, we need to get home to start dinner for Daddy. Remember I said you could snap the beans?"

"Bean snapping!" he cheers, forgetting about the kissing. Tucker climbs back on his bike and pedals away.

"You can help with dinner, too." Phoebe looks first at me, then turns to Alex as she starts after Tucker, who has already disappeared around the corner. "Go home. We *will* talk later."

As I hurry after her, my phone vibrates in my beach bag. I dig it out to find a message from Alex.

Kali tihi, theoula mou.

I text back, asking him what it means, but from around the corner I hear the rumble of the engine as he starts the truck. Phoebe doesn't say anything as we walk to the house. When she unbuckles Joe from the stroller, he wriggles out and toddles over to me, grabbing my hand. "Up, Peach." I carry him into the house.

"We should probably start with the bread because it needs time to rise," Phoebe says, as I follow her into the kitchen with Joe still in my arms. She sets Tucker up at the table with a bag of green beans and a colander. He snaps off the ends of the beans, pretending they are puny humans and he is the Incredible Hulk.

"Do you always make everything from scratch?" I ask, as Phoebe takes a large container of bread dough from the refrigerator and pulls off a generous lump.

"Not everything," she says. "But I love to cook, so I try."

"Down." Joe squirms and I lower him to the floor. "Cook."

He opens a drawer filled with plastic food and throws a cucumber, a waffle, and a can of grape soda into a toy pot. Phoebe chuckles. "He has his father's skill in the kitchen."

"What, um—what do you want me to do?" I ask.

"Grab five potatoes from the pantry," she instructs. "The peeler is in the drawer beside the sink."

"I don't know how to peel potatoes."

Phoebe places the blob of bread dough on a wooden pizza paddle and takes a moment to show me how to scrape the peeler along the potato skin.

"My mother taught me how to do this when I was just a couple years older than Tucker," she says, and I bristle, thinking she's making some sort of judgment against my mom. I can pack a suitcase in less than five minutes, I can wash my hair in a rest-stop sink, and I know all the words to all the songs on Pearl Jam's first album, but my mother has never taught me any practical life skills. “I loved peeling apples the best,” Phoebe continues. “I would challenge myself to do it in one continuous strip. Got pretty good at it, too.”

She hands the potato and peeler back to me, and I continue on my own. It’s not as effortless as she makes it seem.

“I was not one of the popular girls,” she says, as she kneads her fingers in the dough. Her braided silver ring and sparkling diamond wedding band are lying on the counter beside her. “I was raised traditionally, so I was the girl who cared about getting good grades, willingly went to church on Sunday mornings, and played clarinet in the marching band. Your mom, though—”

“You knew my mom?”

“Not personally, but Veronica Quinn was the coolest girl in school, so everyone knew who she was,” she says. “If Veronica got her hair cut, the next week you’d see half a dozen girls with the same style. And no one in Tarpon Springs had ever heard of Doc Martens until your mom started wearing them, usually with ripped tights and baby-doll dresses. And her name . . . well, I was going through a phase when I hated my name, and Veronica seemed so *normal* and cool. My friends and I would pretend to be scandalized by her, but then spend hours at the drugstore arguing over which shade of red lipstick was the one she wore.”

“Revlon Certainly Red,” I say. “She likes it because

it's one of the only colors that's never been discontinued."

"Yes!" Phoebe pumps her fist, making me laugh. "Nailed it." She sets aside the bread and takes a whole chicken from the refrigerator. "Anyway, I thought if I was more like her that maybe Greg would think of me as a girl, instead of part of his extended family. But Revlon Certainly Red looked ridiculous on me and I threw it away after applying it just that one time."

"It looks ridiculous on me, too," I offer. "If it makes you feel any better."

Phoebe smiles, as she lifts the bird into a roasting pan. "Actually, it does. Thanks."

"So, you liked Greg in high school?"

"Always," she says. "Even when he was with your mom and afterward, when she broke his heart. I dated a couple of guys in college, but . . . okay, I have to admit it feels a little strange talking about this with you because you're Veronica's daughter."

"It's okay that he loves you more than her." I pick up the next potato and scrape the peeler down the length. "He deserves that."

"Thank you." She slides the roasting pan into the oven. "Greg is, was, and always will be the love of my life. And our family might seem boring to you—"

"It doesn't," I say. "It's not."

"Anyway, I don't keep things from him, so I just want you to know that I'm going to tell him about this . . . *thing* between you and Alex."

"I figured."

"Ever since our mom got sick, Alex has changed. And not in a good way," Phoebe says. "He was on the college-prep track in high school, but then he dropped out. I mean, the thing with Mom sent all of us into kind of a tailspin, but she wanted him to go to college. If I were in his shoes, I'd do everything I could to honor her wishes, not throw away the life she wanted for me."

I understand now how she could miss the truth. She's not even looking for it.

"The point is, you just came home and the last thing you need is to get involved with someone whose own life is a mess," she says. "My brother is not a good influence."

I take a vicious swipe with the peeler. "Everyone seems to think they know exactly what I need, but no one has ever asked me what I think. Alex and I aren't running off to elope or anything. We're just hanging out."

"I think your dad is afraid you'll get your heart broken."

"But isn't that my risk to take?"

"You're only seventeen—"

"My mom and Greg were sixteen," I point out.

"Exactly."

"It's not the same."

"After what I witnessed today," Phoebe says, "I'm not so sure I'd agree."

The front screen door slaps shut and Greg calls out a hello. Saving me once again from an answer I don't have. He comes into the kitchen.

"So, everything's— Hey, Cal." Greg kisses me on the cheek as if this morning's frostiness was from another lifetime, then kisses Phoebe. "I didn't expect you home from the beach yet, but it looks like you brought half of it with you."

I look down to find a dusting of sand—and a few bits of potato peel—around my bare feet, and that I forgot I was still wearing my bathing suit and shirt when I followed Phoebe home. "Oh, um, I'll sweep it up when I'm done making a bigger mess."

"It's okay." Greg steals a green bean from Tucker's colander and crunches it raw. "Anyway, I was about to say . . . they installed the appliances in the kitchen today and the painting is just about finished, so we should be able to have Christmas in our new house."

Phoebe's face practically glows. "I can't wait to fit everyone around the dining-room table."

I'm momentarily forgotten—along with the potatoes—as they debate renting a do-it-yourself truck versus hiring professional movers, and discuss where to put the Christmas tree in the new house. When I'm done peeling, I leave the skinless spuds in an empty pan and head for the back door.

"We'll finish up when you get back," Phoebe says, and I wonder if she's talking about mashed potatoes or Alex. Either way, I don't really want to come back because I know that while I'm taking a shower, she'll probably be telling Greg everything.

Chapter 20

The trouble with living in an Airstream is that I can't stand in the shower until the water goes cold, because that means having to buy a whole new tank of propane. I have to find other ways to delay the inevitable. My bed gets made for the first time in days. I water the plants. Look up the translation for *Kali tihi, theoula mou* and, despite everything, grin stupidly to myself when I learn it means "Good luck, my little goddess." Search local dive shops on the Internet. And for the first time since I arrived in Tarpon Springs, I take out my guitar.

The calluses that come with years of playing are gone now, so the strings bite into the soft skin of my fingertips as I form the notes, and my nails—the pale-pink polish chipped after my day in the ocean—feel too long to play comfortably. But the steadfast consistency of the sound is reassuring. I play the intro to "All Apologies" until my hands remember and I sing along, even though my voice was not made for singing. The screen door tells me when Greg comes into the trailer, and my fingers miss the next chord.

"I was never much of a Nirvana fan," he says. "Except that song. I loved that one."

"Yeah. Me, too."

"So, I came out here with a speech all prepared and now . . . this threw me off." He gestures at the guitar as I put it away. "I wasn't comfortable with the idea of you seeing some mystery guy, but I'm even less comfortable knowing that it's Alex."

"Why?"

"He's not what you need right now." Greg's not saying anything different from what Phoebe said in the kitchen, but his words are gasoline and a match.

"How do you know what I need?" I ask. "You don't even know me."

"Whose fault is that?" Frustration drives his hands to his hips, his posture defensive. "You haven't shared anything about your life. You ignore the rules. You keep secrets. And we both know who was responsible for the mess at the house the other night. You lied to protect her, and I suspect you're the one who told her about the house in the first place. I've given you a home, Callie. Stability. A *future*. How could you do that?"

"Do you expect me to forget she exists?" I'm shouting and it occurs to me that the neighbors might hear, but I don't care. "Like I'm just supposed to swap her out for another parent. Right or wrong, she was my everything, Greg. Not *you*. And now you act as if you're some kind of savior, but you know what? I've been saving myself my whole goddamn life."

"What does that mean?"

"Nothing," I lie. "It doesn't mean anything at all."

He looks at me for a long moment and I know he doesn't believe me.

"So maybe I'm not the savior, but I'm sure as hell not the villain. Obviously I'm not keeping you and your mother apart. When I brought you home, we made a deal that if you wanted to leave, I'd let you go." He gestures at the trailer door, his voice low. Controlled. More awful than yelling. "If life is so much better out there with her, don't let me stop you."

Through the screen I can hear the incessant cricket song that's become a lullaby over the past couple of months. I don't know why I tell the lies I tell, especially when I don't mean them. What I mean to say is *Greg, I love you. Please don't let me go.* But I'm afraid to say it, so I just watch as he walks out of the trailer.

"Dinner is at seven." There's acid in his tone, and I wonder if it burns his mouth as much as it does my heart. "If you feel like joining us."

"I don't."

Greg and Phoebe are setting up folding tables end-to-end in the backyard to accommodate what quickly becomes a celebration. Cheers erupt like fireworks each time someone new arrives. People laugh. Glasses clink. And somehow the food—including the mashed potatoes I never finished learning to make—seems to multiply in an almost biblical way. When Kat comes around the corner with her parents and little sister, I want to go out and see her, but shame binds me in place.

These people love me. I know this. They loved me when there wasn't even a me around to love, but I wonder if I'll ever really belong to them. Or if they'll ever feel as if they belong to me.

Maybe it's time to go.

I take my guitar from its case and unstring the low E so I can remove the rubber-banded bundle of money that is my life's savings. It's not much—a couple hundred dollars—but it's more than I've ever had.

Greg's laugh drifts across the yard and I feel empty inside, as if my heart has been scooped out. I read somewhere that heartache triggers the same part of the brain that responds to physical pain, creating the same sensations. It hurts to think about leaving my dad. Alex. All of them. And I'm so confused.

"Callie?"

Kat's on her tiptoes at my window with her nose, lips, and palms flattened against the screen. I can't hold back a smile and my heart shifts back into place. "Permission to come aboard?" she asks.

"Yeah, sure."

I hide the money in my pillowcase and set aside the guitar as she enters the Airstream. Kat flops down on the bed beside me, threading her fingers between mine, and the scent of her flowery perfume wraps around me like a comfortable blanket. When her head rests against my shoulder, her personal space invasion is complete. It doesn't bother me so much anymore. Not at all, really.

"I bet you're going to miss this old trailer." Her words rattle me, making me feel as if she can see straight through to my intentions.

"What?"

"Well, knowing Greg, your room at the new house is probably amazing," she says. "But you have to admit that living in an Airstream has been pretty damn cool."

I blow out a silent breath of relief. "Definitely."

"So, um, how was your date?"

"Are you sure you want to know?"

Kat squeezes my hand. "Completely."

I edit out the nightmare about Frank, but tell her everything else, including my fight with Greg. Including the fact that my mom is still somewhere in town. "She's waiting for me, so we can leave."

"But you're staying, right?" Tears fill her eyes and my resolve crumbles.

"I don't know. Maybe."

"Please, don't go."

"I don't belong here, Kat."

"You're wrong. Just look." She grabs my hand and pulls me into the main part of the trailer, gesturing at nothing and everything all at once.

My laptop is propped open on the table with the GED book beside it, the orange-slashed pages held open by the highlighter that did the slashing. My growing collection of books is lined up alphabetically on the shelf above the refrigerator, and taped to the fridge door is a drawing Tucker made of a stick-figure girl—you can tell she's a girl by her triangle skirt—with tons of squiggles radiating from her head. Me, and my hair. Hanging on the wall at the foot of my bed is a snapshot of Kat and me, wearing our Tarpon Sponge Supply Co. T-shirts on my first day of work. And the last thing I see every night before I go to bed, pointing down at me with its gnarly fingers, is the sponge from Alex.

"Before you got here, the Airstream was a storage

shed for Christmas decorations, but you've made it your *home*. You're trying to convince yourself you don't belong so you don't hurt your mom," she says. "But if you leave . . . Callie, you're going to break Greg's heart again."

"No matter what I do, one of them gets hurt."

"So maybe you need to stop thinking about *their* feelings and decide what's best for *you*," Kat says. "What do *you* want, Callie?"

She hugs me as if this is good-bye, and I cling to her, wishing I didn't have to make a decision at all.

Kat and I are selling dive-tour tickets out in front of the shop the next morning when my grandma's car pulls up alongside the curb with Alex's mother in the passenger seat. Kat lights up and runs into the street to hug Yiayoúla, who gives me a pointed look from over Kat's shoulder. As if she knows I don't want to take up my role in this performance. I step forward to open Evgenia's door.

"I didn't know you were coming today," Kat chatters as Yiayoúla pops the trunk. "Let me help you with that wheelchair."

Alex's mom babbles something at me as I help her from the car. She pats my hand, which makes me think she's saying something nice, and I smile at her vacant face. It must be terrible to be trapped inside her uncooperative body, knowing what she wants but unable to vocalize it. Evgenia shuffles forward just enough for my grandma to position the chair behind her. The disease has progressed since I last saw her, and it makes me think maybe Yiayoúla is right. Alex needs to see his mom.

He comes through the side door of the shop wearing his traditional Greek costume and it steals my breath away. Until the smile I know is meant for me slips away, replaced by a flash of anger in his eyes as they meet mine. His smile returns as he crouches in front of the wheelchair to Evgenia's level.

"Hey, Ma." His voice is low and tender, and he's so good that I almost believe him when he tells her it's nice to see her. Her hands tremble as she reaches out to touch his face, and her words are nothing more than a tangle of sounds. The whiteboard is on her lap, but he seems to understand without her writing it down. "*S'agapó, ki ego, mamá.*"

I love you, too, Mom.

Yiayoúla gives my elbow a squeeze that telegraphs her hope. I should feel happy about this, but I don't. Alex is hurting, and it's my fault. I try to catch his eye as he stands, desperate for him to know how sorry I am for my part in this, but he doesn't even look at me.

"It's not every day I have such a special guest," he

says, leading the way up the ramp to the boat. At the top, he scoops Evgenia into his arms. She looks so small and fragile as he gently places her on a bench in the shadiest part of the boat. "You get the seat of honor."

Yiayoúla takes her place beside her friend as I wheel the chair back down the ramp, where Kat is waiting.

"What the hell is going on?" she whispers.

I fill her in quickly as the rest of the passengers board the boat.

"God, Callie, this is a train wreck," she says. "Alex looks miserable, but Mrs. Kosta's condition is going downhill so fast. Yiayoúla Georgia has a point. He might be pissed now, but not as much as he'll be with himself if he doesn't get a chance to say good-bye."

"I don't want to do this."

"I'll do it," Kat says.

"What?"

"I don't have anything to lose," she says. "I'll take the blame. I'll tell him I was in on it instead of you."

She runs up the ramp before I can protest and slides onto the bench beside Yiayoúla as the boat swings away from the dock. Kat's willingness to sacrifice herself is probably more than I deserve, but when Alex looks back at me there's no relief, only hardness, in his eyes—and I know letting her take the blame has made a bad thing worse.

Waiting in the gift shop is torture, and when I fail to ask a customer if she wants to try on the T-shirt she holds indecisively against her chest, Theo shoos me out like a stray dock cat. "Go. Take your break."

The lump in my throat makes eating impossible. Instead, I keep watch from my favorite bench until the tour boat returns to the dock. Kat disembarks first, running down the ramp to fetch the wheelchair. Once Evgenia is back on solid ground, Alex heads in my direction. His eyebrows are storm clouds. He stops just a few feet away from where I sit, but the space between us feels immeasurable.

"I know you did this." His voice is quiet, but his finger spears the air in angry jabs. "You had no business, Callie. Of all people, *you*—I trusted *you*."

He gave me his secret and I gave him mine in return, yet he's the only one of us who kept it safe. There is no excuse that will fix this. "I'm sorry."

The same mouth that kissed me and helped erase the pain Frank inflicted twists into a sneer and he shakes his head. "Save it. I'm done."

"Alex, please—" My vision blurs as he walks away. Kat rushes past him, but he doesn't acknowledge her, either.

"I tried." She rummages through the pocket of her shorts and produces a balled-up tissue, dabbing my face. I watch as Alex lifts his mother into the passenger seat of his truck, and my whole body aches for him. "I swear, Callie. I told him it was all my idea, but he didn't believe me."

I brush her hand aside, the attention too much. I can't breathe and Yiayoúla is bearing down fast, and I don't want to talk to her at all. "I have to go."

Threading my way through tourists and cars, I take off down Dodecanese, waiting for my feet to settle into the familiar rhythm of running away. Instead, I'm winded by the time I reach Hope Street and I have to slow to a walk to catch my breath. Tarpon Springs has changed me.

Once on Hope, I see something I've never noticed before. Tucked between two houses is a tiny white brick church. Beside the driveway, a sign written in both English and Greek says it's the Saint Michael Shrine. Unprepared to go home and unwilling to go back to the docks, I make my way up the walk. Up the steps. Inside.

The walls are hung with gold-trimmed icons of saints I don't recognize, and the scent of incense clings to the air. From a table beside the door I pick up a pamphlet, which explains that the shrine was built in thanksgiving by a woman whose son was healed of a mysterious illness after praying to Saint Michael Taxiarchis. Michael the Archangel. People have made pilgrimages over the years to pray for healing. For miracles. Keeping the pamphlet will cost me a dollar, so I put it back with the others and take a seat in a little wooden pew.

"I don't know how to pray." I feel stupid talking to a room of flickering red votive candles and stained-glass windows. "But everything's a mess and I don't know how to set it right. I need some kind of sign. Or a miracle. Whatever you've got, I'll take it."

I sit there, wondering if I'd recognize a sign if I saw one, but nothing changes. No one comes in. None of the statues move, or weep, or tell me what to do. My pocket vibrates with each new incoming text, but they're not from Saint Michael and I don't feel like talking to anyone else. I give the archangel one more minute to conjure up a miracle before I leave, stuffing my unspent lunch money in the donation box hanging on the wall beside the door.

The driveway is empty when I reach Ada Street, and there's no one inside the house as I rummage through the hall closet, looking for a suitcase. I find a red one—larger and nicer than my old tweed bag—that belongs to Phoebe. It bothers me to steal it, but I do, filling it with the things I can't bear to leave behind: the computer, my favorite books, the picture of me and Kat, Tucker's drawing, the finger sponge. I can almost hear my mom laughing at me for not packing clothes. It feels just like before. Packing for another town. Another thrift store. Another me.

Except now I'm not sure I know how to leave *this* me behind.

I pull the wad of money from the bottom of my pillowcase and use a bungee cord from the storage shed to strap my guitar to the suitcase. It's heavy and the little wheels aren't as smooth as I've always imagined them to be, but I manage to wobble my way to the bookstore downtown.

"Hey!" Ariel greets me as I walk in the door. Then she takes in my puffy-from-crying eyes and the rolling monstrosity behind me. "What's going on? Are you leaving?"

"I, um—yeah," I say. "I was wondering—if you were going to go to the worst bar in town, where would you go?"

Her eyebrows hitch up. "Okay, *not* what I was expecting you to ask, but there's this place on the river that's—hang on, let me get my keys. I'll drive you."

She grabs her purse from behind the checkout counter and flips the open sign to closed. I'm kind of relieved she's just willing to agree to this and not ask a lot of questions.

"You're just going to leave the shop?" I ask, as Ariel locks the front door.

She shrugs. "It's too far to walk, especially with that albatross of crap you're dragging around, and besides, the store's dead. And you might need backup."

"Is it that bad?"

"I went there once on a dare." Ariel unlocks the doors of an ancient Porsche that's faded to near pink, with gray primer spots dotting the hood. "It's kind of like the Pirates of the Caribbean ride at Disney World. Only not fun. The people who hang out there are the undesirables. Drug dealers. Criminals. Shrimpers in town for the day while their boats are being off-loaded."

Ten minutes later, she pulls into the parking lot of a place called the Boat House. The name seems jaunty and nautical, but the bar is built on a pier that looks as if it's one wrong footstep away from toppling into the river. Ariel's car is surrounded by motorcycles and I feel fairly certain the two grubby guys hunched beside a dented pickup aren't exchanging phone numbers. This bar kicks up an unidentifiable dread in my stomach and I don't want to go inside. I don't want my mother to be in there, but there's a better-than-average chance she is. This is her kind of place.

"Remind me again why we're doing this," Ariel says, as we approach the front door. I can already smell the stale cigarette smoke and soaked-in beer.

"I think my mom is here."

She grabs the door handle. “Couldn't you just call her and ask?”

I shake my head as Ariel pulls open the door. Sun-blinded, I blink until my vision returns to normal. Nearly everyone in the bar is staring at us, and none of them seem particularly friendly. Except my mother, who smiles at me from behind the bar as if she's been expecting me all along. “Look what the cat dragged in.” She closes the tap on the pitcher of beer she's pouring. “Guys, this is my baby girl.”

Chapter 21

Some of the men are missing teeth, and their eyes are hungry. I am a drop of honey in a room of ants. An eight-year-old girl in a room of Franks. The undercurrent of menace pushes me backward against Ariel. I wonder if it's just my imagination until I realize that she's trembling, too.

Mom comes out from behind the bar. "Surprised to see you," she says, smoothing my hair away from my face as if it's just us. Over her shoulder a man with a dirty-blond ponytail shot through with gray leers at us as he talks to the guy at the bar beside him. "But nice. I've missed you."

"Can we, um—can we go outside?" I ask.

Her dark eyebrows lift—maybe because I don't tell her I've missed her, too—but she calls out to the giant of a man behind the bar that she's going out for a smoke break. Back outside, the Florida sunshine floods my dark corners, making me feel more at ease.

"In the car if you need me." The parking-lot gravel crunches beneath Ariel's sneakers as she leaves us to talk.

"So my court date is coming up." Mom props herself against an older red Hyundai and taps a cigarette from the pack in her hip pocket. "I'm going to be honest, Callie. I don't want to go to jail. I've been laying low, but once I miss my date—" She takes a drag off her Marlboro.

"I'm ready," I say. "We can go now."

"Really?" Her face is luminous and in it I catch a glimpse of the Veronica Quinn she used to be. Her excitement bubbles out of her in a happy laugh and I feel lighter than I have in days. "Okay, we've got a car." She pats the Elantra. "Got a good deal on it from Tony, but it's left me cash-strapped."

I show her the roll of bills. "I've got my savings from the gift shop."

"That's my girl. Think it's enough to get us to Oregon?"

A knot creeps into my throat. "Oregon?"

"Yeah." She paces and smokes. "I was thinking about how beautiful it was there, remember? And there are so many little hideaway towns tucked along the coastline."

I only have one outstanding memory of Oregon. "What about Colorado?"

"Well, you're never going to believe it, but I caught up with Frank," she says. "Remember him? I found him on the Internet and gave him a call. So I was thinking if we were in Oregon maybe—"

"No." The word comes out more forcefully than I anticipated and her eyes reduce to slits. Except for my stray complaint the last time, when we were packing to leave Illinois, I've never offered an opinion. Never disagreed. But no matter how messed up things are here in Tarpon Springs, they're infinitely better than going back to Frank.

"We're going to Oregon," she says with a familiar note of finality. "We had it good there, Callie. You loved Frank."

"No, Mom, I didn't."

"Of course you did. You were young, so maybe you don't remember—"

"I remember everything." I press the rubber-banded roll of money into her hand. "You can have it all, but I'm not going."

"What the hell is wrong with you?"

"Frank molested me."

Her laugh is short, sharp, and dismissive. I can hear the echo of his voice in my head, reminding me that she won't believe. "Now you're just talking crazy. I get it.

You don't want to go to Oregon, but you don't have to make up—"

"I'm not."

The smile slips from her lips. "Callie—"

"It's true, Mom. Sometimes when you were asleep or at work, he would come to my room—"

"No." She shakes her head and I hear Frank whisper *I told you so*. "That can't be right."

"He would take off my nightgown." My voice is shaking. My hands are shaking. I close my eyes and think of Alex, pacing angrily at the side of the highway as I told him this truth. It gives me the courage I need to keep talking. Tears stream down my cheeks and curl under the edge of my chin, trickling down my neck. "You remember the one with Hello Kitty on the front? And he would put his fingers—"

"Callie, stop it!" She clamps her hands over her ears, as if silencing me will block out the truth. Frank is laughing his phlegmy laugh. *I told you so.*

I wipe my face on the bottom of my T-shirt. "You know what? You're never going to change. You'll spend the rest of your life running away from reality and making one bad decision after another. Believe me or don't, but Frank hurt me, Mom, in a way no little girl should ever be hurt. And you let him."

"I didn't know." Her eyes are glazed with tears, her

voice husky with remorse. "Callie, you have to believe me. I didn't know."

"Yeah, but you should have."

I look over at the primer-freckled Porsche where Ariel is waiting and watching. Even from a distance I can see the concern on her face. For me. Someone she barely knows. This is what good people do for each other. Unless she gets help, my mother will never be that kind of good.

"We won't go to Oregon." There's desperation in the way she clutches at my hands. As if a change in destination will solve everything. "You can pick the place this time."

"I love you, Mom." I give her hands a gentle squeeze and then I let go. "But I'm going home."

I don't look back as I walk to Ariel's car because I'm afraid if I do, the guilt will send me running back to my mother. Or, worse, I'll turn around and she'll already be gone. I don't look back because if I never see her again, I want to remember her with tears in her eyes. Feeling something for me.

Sadness spreads inside me, organ to organ, cell to cell, until it feels as if I'm made of pain. It hurts to think. It hurts to breathe. Ariel asks only where I want her to take me and even giving her Greg's address—my address—is painful. But I don't cry anymore. I'm finished.

The driveway is still empty when she drops me off, and at first I wonder why Greg and Phoebe have been away so long, but then I realize I've only been gone a little more than an hour. Not long enough for anyone to notice I was missing. Not long enough to even *be* missing.

Ariel lifts my baggage from the truck. "Are you going to be okay?"

"I don't know." I was so certain I'd be leaving Tarpon Springs today that I have no backup plan. "I'd have been lost without you today. Thank you."

"No problem." She gets in the Porsche and rolls down the window. "Hey, have you thought anymore about the job?"

Only now do I realize that I walked away from the gift shop in the middle of my shift. Even though I'm pretty sure Theo secretly wants to fire me, he'll probably take me back if I show up for work tomorrow morning. I think it's time to let us both off the hook. "I'll take it."

"Yes!" Ariel's grin is huge as she reaches up for a high five. "Stop by after the holidays and I'll teach you everything you need to know about selling books, okay?"

When she's gone, I return everything to where it belongs—Phoebe's suitcase included—until there's no evidence that I ever left, and get in my bed. A second later, I nearly jump out of my skin when the screen door slams.

"Oh, thank God." Kat is standing beside me. The grit in my eyes and the alarm clock on the dresser behind her tell me I've been in bed longer than a second. She crawls in beside me. "I've texted you eleven billion times and you didn't answer. I've been crazy worried."

"I'm sorry. I just—there was something I needed to do."

"Do you want to talk about it?"

"Not really." Right away I feel bad because I know Kat wants me to be the kind of friend who confides in her. "I mean, I *do*, but right now it's too hard. Give me some time?"

She rests her head on my shoulder, her hair tickling my nose. "Sure."

"You're a space invader, you know that?" There's no unkindness when I say it. Kat might not be the person I imagined having as my best friend, but now I can't imagine anyone else.

"Does it bother you?" she asks.

"Not at all."

We lie quietly for a minute or two, the afternoon sun sending a shaft of gold across the comforter, making it sparkle. I find my thoughts drifting to Alex. Wondering what he's doing right now.

"Stop thinking about him." Kat breaks the silence.

"I'm not."

"Liar." She props herself up on her elbows. "It's

classic breakup behavior to think about him, but Callie, he's an idiot. I mean, he's pissed off because you made him do something he didn't want to do? *So what?*"

"Isn't he an idiot for not liking you back?"

"Please." She rolls her eyes. "I've always known it was just a stupid crush, but you—you mean something to him. And if he can't get over this, then he doesn't deserve you."

"I've never thought of myself like that."

"What? Someone to be deserved? Of course you are," Kat says. "And *any* guy who can't see that is an idiot."

"Hey, Kat?"

"Yeah?"

"Would you hate me if I quit the shop to go work at the bookstore downtown?"

"Can I still come over and invade your space?"

I nod. "Absolutely."

A devious smile dimples her face. "Do I get a discount on books?"

I laugh. "I don't know. Maybe?"

"Good enough."

There's a knock on the door. "Callie, may I come in?"

It's Phoebe.

"Sure."

Kat stands and hauls me into a hug. "I'm going to take off, but I'll call you tomorrow, okay?"

"Do I have a choice?"

"Nope." She laughs as she passes Phoebe in the doorway. "You're stuck with me now."

My stepmother and I share an awkward pause until she clears her throat. "So, um—I stopped by my parents' house this evening to check in on Mom and found her sitting at the kitchen table with my brother."

I look at the floor. I want Alex to make peace with his family, but hearing about it feels like salt in the wound.

"She was—" Phoebe's voice cracks. "He'd been there most of the day, and she was just so happy." She wipes a tear away with the back of her hand. "Thank you."

"I really didn't do anything," I say. "I just had a stupid idea. Yiayoúla did all the work and I chickened out at the last minute."

"For the first time in years, our family feels whole again," she says. "Georgia didn't make it happen, Callie. You did. I'd call that a miracle."

A miracle?

Saint Michael Taxiarchis must have misunderstood.

This was not the miracle I wanted.

Chapter 22

On Christmas Eve, the house looks as if it was torn from the pages of a decorating magazine, with fresh wreaths on every window and a Christmas tree that stretches toward the high living-room ceiling. There's no indication of the sweat we put into getting everything moved. Everything decorated. There's no evidence that the only words that Greg and I have had time to say to each other were things like: Grab an end? Or, have you seen the screwdriver? We haven't said anything meaningful. We haven't apologized.

The house fills quickly as Greg's brothers arrive with their wives, then Yiayoúla with a towel-wrapped casserole dish of cranberry-apple stuffing, and finally the Kosta family.

Kat declared my cream-colored Christmas dress to

be "smoking hot" when she helped me pick it out, but there's little consolation in that when Alex comes in the front door with his tanned face shaved clean and his tattoo peeking out from the pale-blue cuff of his shirt. He is beautiful and there's nothing Kat could have done to prepare me for it. He hands Phoebe a bottle of wine and Greg takes a shopping bag filled with gifts, nestling it among the mounds of brightly wrapped presents surrounding the Christmas tree.

"Merry Christmas." Alex's voice is low as he greets me, but there's no trace of his usual warmth. We are strangers, even though my body wants to lean into him. By the time I say "Merry Christmas" back, he's walking away.

I retreat to the kitchen to pour a glass of sparkling cider, but the kitchen is part of the great room, so there's nowhere to hide. My grandma comes up alongside me and ruffles one of the tiers on the hem of my dress. "You look like the Christmas angel," she says.

I hand her my glass and pour a second. "Maybe they should build me a shrine."

"Save feeling sorry for yourself for some other day," Yiayoúla scolds. "He's been living at home ever since we took Evgenia on the tour. Look at them, Callista. Really look. She is finally at peace."

I watch Alex laughing as his mother writes

something on her whiteboard and I can almost see the love between them, gold and shimmering, and I know she needs him more than I do.

Greg taps his glass with the edge of a knife, calling for everyone to take their places at the table. There are cards lettered with all our names. My seat is beside Alex. The soft fabric of his shirt brushes my bare arm, and a shiver runs down my spine. We don't speak to each other at all during dinner, and afterward he goes outside to the deck with the men, while the women clear the table and do the dishes. Tucker is underfoot, asking over and over when we're going to open presents, and in the post-dinner chaos, we almost miss the doorbell.

"Callie, will you get that, please?" Phoebe asks.

I open the front door, and Kat barges through with two shopping bags like the ones Alex brought in earlier.

"I come bearing gifts," she announces. "Phoebe, this bag is from our family to yours. It's cookies and all kinds of other Christmas treats. And, Callie hid all her presents at my house so none of you would peek, and then forgot to bring them home."

She hands me the second bag, then pulls me up the steps to my bedroom, our heels tapping on the wooden risers.

"Oh my God, Callie, this dress looks even more

amazing tonight than it did at the store," she says. "Alex is probably outside right now plotting a way to get you under the mistletoe."

"Why did you do all this?"

"I told you," she says. "I love Christmas. And I hated the idea of you sitting here feeling bad that you didn't have any presents to give. Besides, someday I'm going to need you and you're going to come through for me in a big way. Because that's what friends do, right?" But before I can answer, Kat just keeps talking. "Oh, I almost forgot." She rummages through the shopping bag and produces a tiny Christmas-colored envelope. "This is for you."

Inside is an evil eye bead knotted on a black cord, just like the one she's wearing.

"I can't guarantee it will keep away evil," she says, as she loops it around my wrist and tightens the knots until it's a perfect fit. "But maybe it will remind you that you're not alone. You have me. You have Greg. You have this whole big, crazy, annoying Greek family and we all love you."

This time it's me who hugs her. "You're the best."

"And I will *never* let you forget it." She looks at her watch. "But now, I gotta jet. My mom's waiting and she'll kill me if I linger too long."

"Merry Christmas, Kat."

She kisses my cheek, then wipes the gloss off my face with her thumb. "You, too, Callie. Love you."

Her heels clomp on the stairs and she calls out "Merry Christmas!" as she dashes out the door. From the office dormer I watch as she runs down the walk to her mom's car. After they've driven off, I find my phone and send her a text.

Love you, too.

The Christmas Eve presents are unwrapped and Tucker is thrashing around in the discarded papers as if they're autumn leaves—his new toys already forgotten—when Phoebe suggests pie. In the dessert rush that follows, I go upstairs and trade my Christmas dress for a pair of jeans and the red cashmere sweater that Yiayoúla gave me as a gift. No one notices when I slip out the front door.

Outside the air is crisp, the night silent, and only one car passes me in the time it takes me to ride my bike to Ada Street. I can't help wondering where my mother is tonight. Did she leave Tarpon Springs? Is she safe? I imagine her out West somewhere, maybe in the desert where the Christmas lights are real, scattered across the night sky, and I imagine her missing me as much as I miss her.

The old house looks sad in its emptiness as I prop the bike against the porch. Old Mrs. Kennedy next door spies me through her kitchen window and waves as I pass, and somewhere in the neighborhood someone is listening to "O Holy Night." The sound is thin, diluted by distance, but it walks with me as I cross the yard to the Airstream.

The first thing I see when I open the trailer door is the worn-away velveteen of my mother's black ballerina flats, and my brain just cannot process this because they're on her feet. And she's lying on the floor.

"Mom?"

I rush inside and switch on the overhead light. Her skin is waxy white and as I drop to my knees beside her, I notice that the edges of her lips are tinged blue and she's barely breathing.

"Mom!" This time I shout, but she doesn't respond. She doesn't move. "Oh, God. Mom. What did you do?" I give her shoulders a violent shake, but she remains limp and she won't wake up. Hysteria bubbles up from my chest and out of my mouth as I shake her again and scream. "*What did you do?*"

My hands are trembling so badly it takes me two attempts to get to the keypad screen on my phone.

"Why would you do this?" I talk to my mom as if she was conscious, as if she can hear me. "If I call for an ambulance, everyone will know where you are. You'll go to jail. But if I don't—" I look at her again and this time she doesn't appear to be breathing at all. "No. You can't do this to me. No, no, no, no . . ." I say the words over and over as I dial 911.

The female voice on the other end of the line is calm as she asks about my emergency, but I am running on pure panic.

"It's my mom. She's unconscious and I can't tell if she's breathing." The words fall as fast as my tears. "I don't know CPR and her lips are blue and—please help me. I don't want her to die."

"Calm down, sweetie. Can you tell me where you are?"

I give her the address and explain that we're in an Airstream behind the house.

"Is your mother taking any medications?" she asks.

"I don't think—" I look around. Beneath the table is a crumpled plastic bag containing a single green tablet. I crawl under and grab the bag. "I found a pill."

"Can you describe it?"

"It's green," I tell her. "With an 80 on one side and the letters *OC* on the other."

"Do you have any idea how long she's been unconscious?"

"I don't know. I just found her."

"An ambulance will be there shortly," the dispatcher says. "Is there someone nearby who can wait with you?"

My mind goes immediately to Greg. "Yes."

As always, he answers on the first ring.

"Dad?"

"Callie, what's wrong? Where are you?"

"At the Airstream," I say. "Mom is here and she's not—I need you."

"I'll be right there."

I sit down on the floor and lift my mother's head onto my thigh. Her skin is damp and cold, and her hair feels coarse under my hand as I stroke her head. "I'm here, Mom." Tears and snot mix on my face and I wipe the mess on the sleeve of my sweater. "I'm so sorry I left you, but I'm here now and I'm not going to leave you again. We can go to Oregon, if that will make you happy. I promise. Just stay with me, Mom. Don't go."

The ambulance arrives first, and the world grows fuzzy around the edges as the trailer fills with people using medical terms I can't understand. They feel my mom's neck for a pulse and speak in numbers. They pull back her eyelids to shine a light into her vacant eyes, and their voices are replaced by the hum of bees in my ears. One of the paramedics says something to me, but the buzzing is too loud and all I can do is blink in reply. They take Mom away from me, lifting her onto a gurney and sliding a needle into her vein that attaches her to a bag of clear fluid. And then they leave. I scramble to my feet to go after them as Greg comes into the Airstream and catches me up in his arms.

"I have to go with her." Even my own words sound as if they've been dredged through maple syrup, and I'm shivering. I don't know what's wrong with me. "I told her I wouldn't leave."

"I'll drive you." Greg says, taking a blanket from the backseat of the SUV and wrapping it around me. Beyond him, the paramedics are closing the doors of the ambulance and the flashing red lights blend in with the Christmas decorations on the house across the street.

"But—"

"We'll be right behind them," Greg says, opening the passenger door. "I promise."

My eyelids are thick and sticky as I open them, and the only familiar sight is Greg, sitting in a chair beside me. I'm not sure where I am, but his presence is comforting. The worry lines on his forehead relax and he smiles. "Hey, hi," he says softly. "You're awake."

"Hi." My throat is dry and it takes almost too much effort to speak. "Where—?"

"We're at the emergency room."

Everything rushes back in bright flashes of memory. Airstream. Mom. Paramedics. Overdose. I try to sit up, but my body is heavy with a weariness that feels as if I've lived too many lifetimes. "Mom? Is she okay?"

Greg nods. "She's in recovery right now. Stable condition."

"I promised I would stay with her."

"You wouldn't have been allowed, Cal. They had to, um—pump her stomach. And you were in shock, so I had one of the nurses administer a sedative to help you relax until they let us see her."

"Can we?"

He nods. "Soon."

There are dark circles under his eyes and I wonder if he's slept, or if he kept vigil beside my bed all night.

"I'm sorry," I say. "For everything."

"We don't have to talk about this now."

"I want talk about it," I say. "I love it here with you, and Phoebe, and the boys, and—I love you, Dad. I don't want to leave."

He brushes my hair back from my forehead the way Mom does and I allow myself to take comfort from the gesture, instead of feeling as if I'm betraying her. I'm doing what Kat suggested. This is what I want. He smiles. "I don't want you to leave, either."

The privacy curtain around us slides open, and a

doctor comes in. His name, Dr. Labasilier, is embroidered in blue on his white lab coat. “How are you feeling this morning?”

“Better.”

“I like the sound of that.” His accent is French Caribbean, and it reminds me of the vending-company guy who used to collect the money from the machines at the Super Wash. He was one of those people who could whistle high notes without losing the tone, and his smile made me feel as if my insides were made of bubbles.

“Also, I’ve got good news for you.” Dr. Labasilier straps a blood-pressure cuff around my arm and begins pumping the bulb. “Your mother is awake and you may see her in thirty minutes. You’re welcome to wait, but I might suggest you’ll feel more refreshed if you go home, wash up, and have a bite to eat.”

The cuff releases with a whoosh.

“You’re free to go,” he says. “Merry Christmas.”

Chapter 23

"I've never missed church on Christmas before," Greg says as we ride the elevator up to the hospital's third floor, after a quick trip home for showers and breakfast. A note on the kitchen counter from Phoebe explained that she's taken the boys to Christmas services with her family and that she'll meet us at the hospital later. I feel bad that all the Christmas Day presents from Santa are still waiting, unwrapped, under the tree, and I don't know when Tucker and Joe will have the chance to open them.

"I'll be okay," I tell my dad. "If you want to join them."

He shakes his head. "I think God will understand that my daughter needs me more than he does."

My mom's room is the first on the left, and a nurse is

checking her chart. My dad hangs in the doorway as I enter the room. Mom's eyes are closed, but I can see the rise and fall of regular breathing, and a monitor beside her beeps softly along with her heartbeat.

"Mom?" I say it softly so I won't startle her, and touch my fingers to hers. They're warmer now and a tube stretches up from her hand to a bag of clear fluid. Her eyes open, and a tear escapes from the corner, trickling down toward her ear.

"I'm sorry," she whispers. "I'm so, so sorry."

I reach for a tissue and wipe away the trail the tear left behind. Another follows and I erase that one, too. There's no strength in her grip as her fingers curl around mine, but I can feel the plea in them. I can see it in her eyes.

"*Forgive me.*"

Forgiveness has never been something I've had to consider. Never an option. I've always granted it because she is my mother, but the price I've paid for her choices has been high and I have a right to be angry. Except choosing anger, choosing blame, won't bring back all that was lost. The only thing I can do is hold on to what I have right now, so that it can't ever be lost again.

My fingers answer first, squeezing back gently, and I lean over to whisper in her ear.

Just one word.

"*Always.*"

She gives me a tiny, weary smile. "I need to talk to your dad for a minute, okay?"

Greg and I swap places. I'm leaning against the wall outside the room when Phoebe comes around the corner from the elevator. She's wearing her dark-green Christmas dress and heels—and she's crying. "Where's Greg?"

"Phoebe?" His voice comes from Mom's room and they reach each other just outside her door. "What happened?"

"My mom—" She crumples against him and his arms go around her, sheltering her. "She didn't wake up this morning. She's gone."

Greg says soft words of comfort, words just for her, as she sobs into his chest. Watching makes me feel like an outsider, but I don't know what to do. I want to be with my mom, but that feels selfish when Phoebe's just lost hers.

"Where are the boys?" I ask.

"Alex dropped me off here, then took them home so they wouldn't see her like that," she says, her tissue fighting a losing battle against her tears. "It's a blessing that she died peacefully in her sleep, instead of suffering the agony of being starved to death by her disease, but—I can't believe she's gone."

"I'll go home and stay with the boys so Alex can be

with you and your dad," I say. "Let me just say good-bye to my—" I stop abruptly, not wanting to remind her that my mom is alive.

"Oh, God, Callie." Phoebe starts sobbing again. "I can't take you away from your mother."

"No, it's okay," I say. "She needs the rest. I can come back later."

Mom lifts a tired hand as I enter her room, waving me off. "Your family needs you," she says. I listen for sarcasm, for anger, but it's not there. She just sounds drowsy, and she blinks slowly, fighting off sleep.

"I'll be back as soon as I can," I say. "I promise."

Alex is sitting on the top step of the back deck while Tucker and Joe wallow happily in the detritus of Christmas. They've unwrapped every gift, including the presents from Kat and the architecture book I bought for Greg. A blue *Sesame Street* monster chatters on the television as Tucker cracks open a black velvet jewelry box. Inside a pair of sapphire earrings sparkle blue. "Look, Joe! It's pirate treasure!"

Taking the box from Tucker earns me a cry of protest. "Santa did not bring those for you." I stash the earrings on the mantel above the fireplace, then gather all the unwrapped presents not intended for toddlers and discard the wrapping paper. Leaving the boys to play with proper Christmas toys, I go outside to Alex.

"I can stay with the boys if you need to go," I say, lowering myself to the same step. My hands tremble with wanting to touch him.

"Not yet." He shakes his head. "How's your mom?"

"She, um—she'll be all right. I mean, she'll probably go to jail but . . ." *But my mother is still alive.* "I'm sorry. I'm so, so sorry."

"Thanks." His voice is hollow. Sad. And he leans forward, resting his folded arms on his knees. The gesture stings a little, as if I'm too close and he needs to get away, until I feel his fingertips whisper-soft on the back of my calf. I should offer words of consolation, but I don't know what to say. Instead, we sit a long time without speaking. The rich blue of the bayou sparkles in the sunshine, and behind us, Tucker and Joe are oblivious to how much the world has changed overnight.

"There's a job waiting for me at a dive shop in the Keys." Alex breaks the silence first. "Now that my mom's gone, there's nothing keeping me here anymore."

It hurts to be lumped together with the father who smacks him around and a sponging job he never wanted. To be considered nothing.

"Now you can take that dive trip to Roatan in February." I hope the words sound light and excited, even though my heart is shattered and sharp. He turns to look at me, and those hazel eyes tell me I failed.

"Oh, shit. Callie, no." He touches my face with both hands, his thumb catching a tear I never meant to cry, and my breath hitches in my throat. "I didn't mean you. You're not nothing. You're the best kind of something."

"Don't go." It's selfish of me to ask this of him when he's already sacrificed so much, but he's mine and I want to keep him.

"Come with me." His kiss is so gentle, so perfect, that it takes everything I have to keep from saying yes. I've never been in love before, but this moment is bittersweet and tender and terrible and perfect. Surely this must be it.

I want to go with him, but then I think about my dad and Phoebe. About my little brothers. Yiayoúla and Kat. My new job. My mom. I have so many more reasons to stay. I'm not ready to leave yet. "My family is here."

"I know." He touches his forehead to mine and sighs. "This sucks."

A laugh escapes me. "Yeah."

"So, what do we do?"

"I don't know," I admit. "But we can't just let go. I won't do that."

Alex's mouth relaxes into his easy grin and he kisses me again. "Then I guess we figure something out."

Hope blooms on the surface of my sadness. It's improbable that our relationship will survive the time and distance. Except improbable is not impossible. There are so many maybes in life, but sometimes you just have to put your faith in possibility.

We hold hands as we go back into the house, where Joe is crashed out on the floor and Tucker has used a chair to pull the "pirate treasure" down from the mantel. Alex and I exchange guilty smiles before he kisses my cheek and tells me he needs to go home. It feels like good-bye. I mean, I know I'll see him again at Evgenia's funeral, but this is it.

The end of us.

For now.

Chapter 24

Mom comes into the visitation area wearing a loose-fitting blue uniform that looks more like emergency-room scrubs than prison garb. Her hair is shorter than she's ever worn it before and a shade of dark auburn I've only seen at the roots. Without her signature red lips, the bottom of her face seems unfinished. Un-her. She smiles when she sees me and I'm surprised by how much younger she looks. Rested. Maybe even a little bit . . . happy.

"There's my girl," she whispers into my hair as she wraps me in the fiercest of hugs. She's more substantial now. Softer. She kisses my temple and presses her forehead to mine. "I was afraid you wouldn't come."

It took a whole month before Greg's and my applications to visit were approved by the Florida Department of Corrections. "Of course I'd come."

Mom pulls back and smooths the hair away from my face in her familiar way. Her hand pauses against my cheek. "Look at you. So damn beautiful." She smiles again and glances over my shoulder at my dad. "Greg, thank you for bringing her."

"You doing okay?" he asks.

She tilts her head and crinkles her nose. "As well as can be expected, I guess."

Dad touches my elbow. "I'm going to grab a sandwich and maybe do some reading. Let me know when you're ready to go, okay? No rush."

I nod. "Thanks."

The tables around us are filled with reunited families, and the air is festive and chattery. Some of the visitors recognize each other from their weekly treks to the prison and call out greetings to each other. Others argue over what they perceive to be the best tables.

"Let's go outside," Mom suggests. "It's quieter."

We push through a set of double doors to a covered pavilion, stopping at a vending machine for bottles of water before finding empty spaces at one end of a picnic table. At the other end, a couple sit opposite each other, their brown-skinned fingers entwined as they talk in voices only they can hear. I feel a pang of sadness when they lean across the table to kiss, but I push it away, reminding myself that I will see Alex again.

"I like your hair," I tell my mother.

She touches the pixie fringe at the back of her neck. "Do you? The roots were growing out so I figured—it's hard to keep your color up in here."

"How are you, Mom? Really."

"It's not like in the movies, you know?" She picks at the label on her water bottle, her fingers fidgety. I realize she hasn't lit up a cigarette yet. That's usually the first thing. "I'm safe and I know where I'm going to sleep at night. I mean, we've lived in places worse than this, and the food isn't bad."

"Mom." I reach across the table and still her busy hands, looking at her until she looks at me. "I don't want to hear about the jail conditions."

"I'm sick, Callie, and I know that without medication I do impulsive and stupid things, like leaving you alone with Frank. Like leaving your dad. But I don't feel like myself anymore. It's as if part of me is missing, and I hate it."

Her jail sentence was shortened to just six months, contingent on her staying on medication and getting counseling. I worry that when she gets out on probation she'll backslide and run away again. I worry that she'll resent me for sending her here. "I'm sorry," I say.

"Don't." She holds up a warning finger, and for a moment I see a glimpse of fire.

"If it wasn't for me, you wouldn't be here," I say. "You'd be—"

"If it wasn't for you, I'd be *dead*," she interrupts. "God, Callie, if I could go back and do it all over again—"

"Don't do that to yourself."

"I deserve it."

"I love you, Mom."

There are tears in her eyes when she smiles at me. "There are so many ways you could have turned out. You could be like me, with feelings my body just can't contain. The life we've lived could have made you hard and unforgiving. But you're so strong and your heart is so good . . . you're just like Greg, you know? And that's how I know you'll always be okay."

"Are *you* going to be okay?"

She lifts one shoulder in a half shrug. "I hope so."

I wish she had a better answer, but right now it's the best she can offer. "Me, too."

"Let's talk about something else." She takes a sip of water and grins. "What's the capital of Nebraska?"

I laugh. "I'm not six anymore. I know my state capitals."

"Prove it. Capital of Nebraska."

"Lincoln, Mom—"

"No, it's Omaha."

"It's *Lincoln*."

Mom laughs and reaches across the table, brushing the backs of her fingers against my cheek. They're soft and for a moment I am six again, with the future stretched out like a highway before us. "A girl as smart as you can do anything she wants," she says.

This time . . . I believe.

Author's Note

* Tarpon Springs is an actual Florida town, and the Greek-themed sponge docks area really exists. While Kat is only joking about Connor being a token non-Greek friend, there is a very active Greek-American population in Tarpon Springs, and names like Ekaterina, Callista, and Alexandros are not unusual.

* The Shrine of St. Michael Taxiarchis is a real thing, too. It was built in the 1940s by Marie Tsalichis after her son fell ill with—and miraculously recovered from—a mysterious disease (possibly meningitis), and there are accounts of people being cured of their ailments after visiting the shrine.

* Sponges—which are primitive animals, not plants—are a renewable resource because they grow back after

they've been cut. Divers in Tarpon Springs have been harvesting the same beds for more than a hundred years.

* Pastitsio (pah-STEE-tsee-oh) is a dish made with pasta, meat, tomato-based sauce, and a custard-like cheese sauce. As Greg mentions, pastitsio resembles lasagna, but the addition of cinnamon and nutmeg gives it a distinctively different flavor.

* Galaktoboureko (gah-lahk-toh-BOO-reh-koh) is a dessert of custard baked in a flaky pastry called phyllo and served with honey poured on top. It's one of my favorite Greek foods.

* Another Greek dish is dolmades (dol-MAH-thes), which is made from grape leaves stuffed with a rice filling that contains herbs and sometimes meat. Like Callie, I'm not a fan, but it's a popular dish in Greece and most of the surrounding countries. It's also called dolmas.

* Learn some Greek:

korítsi mou (ko-REE-tsee-MOO): my girl

yiayoúla (yah-YOU-lah): grandma (the actual word is yiayiá, but the addition of -oula makes it a little more affectionate)

matákia mou (mah-TAH-kyah-MOO): my little eyes, the apple of my eye

latría mou (lah-TREE-ah-MOO): my beloved, my adored

gorgóna (gor-GOH-nah): mermaid

seirína (see-REE-nah): siren, mermaid

yia sou (YAH SOO): hello

efharistó (EF-hah-ree-STOH): thanks

s'agapó (sah-gah-POH): I love you

Acknowledgments

I owe a world of gratitude to . . .

The city of Tarpon Springs for being such a cool place. Please forgive any added businesses, park benches, and trees that might not otherwise exist. Also, any inaccuracies in the world of sponges and sponge diving are solely mine.

Tumblr. Yes, *tumblr*, for being my happy place when I need it. And efharistó to Georgia for helping a total stranger with Greek translation.

Carla Black, Kelly Jensen, Ginger Phillips, Grace Radford, and Gail Yates for reading and cheering me along while I wrote this book. Couldn't have done it without you. And Carla, you brainstorming star, thanks for the brilliant title.

Josh Berk, Cristin Bishara, Tara Kelly, Miranda

Kenneally, Amy Spalding, and the crew of Barnes & Noble 2711 in Fort Myers, Florida, for the exact same reasons as last time. I love you guys.

Suzanne Young is the best writing partner in the world. Thanks for sticking with me all these years, Suz.

The late Charles Singler, who answered my questions about law enforcement and extradition. Uncle Charlie, you will be missed.

Kate Schafer Testerman, Victoria Wells Arms, and the team at Bloomsbury for falling in love with Callie and Alex the way I did. Special thanks to Regina Flath for a cover that makes my heart beat a little faster every time I look at it.

My family . . . Mom, Jack and Marilyn, Caroline, Scott, and especially, *always*, Phil. Because I love you best of all.